James Darmesteter, Helen Bachman Jastrow

Selected Essays of James Darmesteter

James Darmesteter, Helen Bachman Jastrow

Selected Essays of James Darmesteter

ISBN/EAN: 9783337277178

Printed in Europe, USA, Canada, Australia, Japan

Cover: Foto ©Andreas Hilbeck / pixelio.de

More available books at **www.hansebooks.com**

SELECTED ESSAYS OF
JAMES DARMESTETER

THE TRANSLATIONS FROM THE FRENCH
By HELEN B. JASTROW

EDITED, WITH AN INTRODUCTORY MEMOIR
By MORRIS JASTROW, Jr.
PROFESSOR IN THE UNIVERSITY OF PENNSYLVANIA

BOSTON AND NEW YORK
HOUGHTON, MIFFLIN AND COMPANY
The Riverside Press, Cambridge
1895

To

ANNIS LEE WISTER

EDITOR'S PREFACE.

ALAS, that this volume, which was to introduce James Darmesteter to a larger public on this side of the Atlantic, appears as a memorial to his career, — now forever closed. At the time that the translator was putting the final touches to her work, the sad news came from Paris that James Darmesteter was no more, — dead at the early age of forty-five. Rarely has the death of a scholar aroused such general grief, the echoes of which reach to distant Persia. It is hard indeed to bear the thought that one who had so much to live for, one from whom so much was still to be hoped for, should now be lying in the embrace of the silent grave; the voice that spoke so eloquently forever hushed, the mind so full of plans for science and humanity at rest. Death came to him suddenly, though not without warning, and those who knew the slight frame which held the gigantic intellect hardly dared to hope that it could long endure the strain of ceaseless labor, of ever-increasing toil. The end, as described by one of his colleagues,[1] was pathetic in its simplicity as well as significant. On the afternoon of October 19, 1894, " James Darmesteter, seated at his writing-table, drooped the head, heavy with knowledge and thought, on his frail chest, and vanished from among us."

With him there passed away one of the most remarkable personages in the world of contemporary science and letters. By general consent he was regarded, after Renan's death, as the most distinguished scholar of France. He shared with Renan — whom he affectionately spoke of as his " master " — marvelous breadth of learning, profound originality of thought, splendid literary ability, and keen sympathy with the problems and movements of the day. Like Renan, too, he was reared in humble surroundings, and at a tender age learned to face the struggles of life ; and with more obstacles to overcome than Renan, his ascent on the ladder of fame bears witness to his strength of character as well as to his talent. In the touching memoir that he wrote, a few years ago, of his elder brother Arsène, he gives an account of his childhood.[2] James, the younger, was born on the 28th of March, 1849, at Château-Salins in

---

[1] Gaston Paris, *Contemporary Review*, January, 1895.

[2] Preface to Arsène Darmesteter's *Reliques Scientifiques*, Paris, 1890.

Lorraine. His father was a poor Jewish book-binder. In 1852 the family moved to Paris. It was the ambition of the parents to educate their sons for one of the learned professions, and amid many struggles and hardships, the foundation for their later distinction as scholars was laid. Reared in orthodox tradition and surroundings, they were initiated into Jewish lore almost prior to their acquiring secular knowledge. When, finally, James was enabled to enter a *Lycée*, his extraordinary ability began to display itself. Graduating in 1867, he passed several years in various studies and in laying plans for the future, before he finally turned his attention to Oriental philology. No doubt the knowledge of Hebrew and of Talmudic literature, acquired in boyhood, had much to do with the attraction that the literature and languages of the East exercised upon him, but it was the distinguished philologist, Michel Bréal, who first suggested to young Darmesteter the thought of taking up the study of Zoroastrianism as his life-work. The ease with which he acquired the mastery of languages and of philological method was astonishing, — an ease that led his professors to compare it to the manner in which children learn a game. The very first fruits of his studies assured him a high rank among Persian scholars; before he died he

was universally acknowledged to be the greatest
authority in his special domain, even by those
who were not prepared to accept all of his theories. Besides various volumes and numerous
essays, embodying the results of researches that
have greatly aided the interpretation of Zoroastrianism, his French translation of the Zend-
Avesta, with a commentary (completed a little
over a year ago), — three large quarto volumes,
— remains as the most enduring monument of
his vast erudition. This production, enriched by
a series of essays, in which are summed up Darmesteter's views of the late origin and gradual
growth of the sacred collection, forms a new
point of departure for the further studies of
other scholars. The French Academy honored
itself by crowning this great production with its
prize of 20,000 francs, granted biennially, for the
most noteworthy achievement of French scholarship.

What might have been for others a task of
a lifetime was for Darmesteter but an incident
in his career, and, unsurpassed as he is in his
specialty, one does not think of him as a specialist. He entered into numerous other fields
of investigation, and his activity passed beyond
the confines of technical scholarship into the
domain of modern literature, and even into politics. His Persian studies led him necessarily

to Sanskrit literature. His excellent classical knowledge enabled him to make a valuable contribution to Latin philology. To his knowledge of Aryan languages he added the study of Semitic tongues. The work on "the Mahdi" (published also in English translation) gives evidence of the mastery he had obtained in the vast realm of Arabic literature.

Even when dealing with abstruse subjects, his rare powers as a writer were shown. Whatever issued from his pen bore the mark of the literary artist, and so it is not remarkable that modern literature exercised a strong fascination upon him. Besides a masterly study of Macbeth, he published a volume of essays on English literature, and edited various English classics. A poet by nature, he enriched his own literature with a volume of poems, in which he unfolds an exalted conception of Christ. Deeply impressed by the poems of Mary Robinson, he translated them into French in 1888. The work laid the foundations of a friendship between two kindred souls, and led to the perfect union which illumined the closing years of his life.

Darmesteter was an ardent patriot, and the sad condition of France at the close of the Franco-Prussian war afflicted him profoundly. He gave expression to his burning sentiments in a volume of " patriotic selections," published under the pseudonym of J. D. Le Français. Nothing that touched the thought or life of the people among whom he was thrown seemed foreign to his spirit, and he found time while on a visit to Persia and India, for the purpose of gathering further fragments of the Zend-Avesta and of studying Zoroastrianism at its source, to collect the popular songs of Afghanistan. In an extensive work upon the subject, published on his return, he demonstrated the historical value of these songs, and showed that the language in which they are couched follows in direct succession to that of the Zend-Avesta. With all these labors, and with his duties as professor of Persian at the Collège de France, in addition to a professorship at the Ecole des Hautes Etudes, he found time to perform the exacting services demanded of him as secretary of the Société Asiatique, in which capacity he published yearly a masterly review of all contributions made to Oriental science, by French, and, in part, by other scholars. Even this did not exhaust his boundless capacity for work, and great was the astonishment of his friends to learn a few years ago that he had accepted the editorship of a leading political and literary review, "La Revue de Paris," to which he made several noteworthy contributions.

Endeared to his soul were the studies of his

childhood, — Hebrew and the subsequent Rabbinical literature. In an essay on the history of the Jews, he outlined the great epochs in the fortunes of this people in such a manner as was possible only to one who possessed a complete mastery of the sources for this subject. But it was the Old Testament rather than the later literature that appealed strongest to him, and within the Old Testament it was the Prophets that answered to the needs of his own religious nature. In the course of years he moved far away from the lines of orthodox tradition, but the echoes of the faith of his childhood never ceased to stir his soul. It is a significant phase of his career that in proportion as the philosophy of his life grew deeper and clearer, the hold the Hebrew Prophets took upon him grew stronger. In his search for the solution of the problems confronting the present age, he turned to them, and found in their stirring utterances, when freed from all dogmatic incumbrances, the key to salvation which others like himself had sought elsewhere in vain. His essay on the Hebrew Prophets gives us an insight into Darmesteter's own nature which no biography could furnish. No one has penetrated deeper than he into their spirit, and his ability to do so is the outcome of his intense sympathy with the moral struggles and the moral ideals of humanity.

The essays included in this volume have been chosen with a view of illustrating at once the many-sidedness of Darmesteter's activity and the man himself. That a single volume could not exhaust this illustration will be evident from the sketch given of his achievements in the short space of life granted him. With a view, therefore, of preserving in a measure the uniform character of the volume, the selection has been confined on the one hand to Darmesteter's work in Oriental literatures, and on the other to such of his general essays as are more particularly of present interest.

From his Iranian studies, an essay on Afghan life as illustrated by Afghan songs has been selected, which the author himself regarded as one of his most satisfactory productions. The essay on the supreme God of the Aryans may be taken as representative of Darmesteter's mastery in the wide range of the Aryan literatures. Passing to his Semitic studies, the essay on the history of the Jews has been chosen mainly because of the novelty the subject will presumably have for most readers, for whom the history of the Jews terminates with the capture of Jerusalem by the Romans. As an example of Darmesteter's marvelous power of condensation in literary composition, this essay, too, is a noteworthy achievement. In a compass of less than

forty pages he passes in review a history covering almost as many centuries. His study of the
Hebrew Prophets has a permanent value quite
independent of the possible results of future
researches in this field. Of his popular productions this essay is likely to be the most enduring. Alas for the day when his conception of
the part played by the prophets in the drama
of history ceases to be impressive! Of the
more general topics treated by him, the essay
on " Race and Tradition " is a valuable study of
a pressing problem of modern science, while his
memoir on Renan, originally prepared for the
Société Asiatique (of which Renan, at the time
of his death, was president), may be expected
to aid in bringing about a clearer and worthier
conception than is popularly current of one of
the master minds of the century. Most interesting of all, perhaps, as affording again a picture of a character as rare as the mind of the
man, is the beautiful essay on the " Religions of
the Future," in which he unfolds his conception
of the part to be played in the coming age by the
two forces, — science and the prophetic ideals,
— upon which, in his judgment, the salvation of
humanity hinges.

Of these seven essays, two — "Afghan Life
in Afghan Song " and the " Supreme God in
the Indo-European Mythology " — were written

by Darmesteter in English, which he handled
with the same ease as his native tongue. The
editor wishes to express his acknowledgment to
the editor of the " Contemporary Review " for
his kind permission to republish these articles.
The essay on Renan appeared by special arrangement in the " New World," translated by
Mr. N. P. Gilman, who courteously granted the
use of it for this volume. It is, perhaps, proper
to state, however, that the translation as here
published is somewhat modified in form. The
remaining essays, forming the bulk of the work,
were translated by Helen B. Jastrow, who desires to express her acknowledgment to Mr.
Simon A. Stern for having kindly examined the
manuscript prior to its being sent to press, and
to Mrs. Caspar Wister for her most careful re-
vision of the proofs. It has been the aim of
the translator, while clinging as closely as possible to the original, to convey to the English
reader, at least in some degree, the impression
of Darmesteter's charm of style.

It is perhaps needless to add that when Darmesteter touches upon questions dealing with the
religious life, his views are not such as may be
acceptable in the nature of things to many of
his readers. It is possible, too, that in some of
his earlier productions he unwittingly wounds

by a certain severity of expression; but such is his earnestness and sincerity, such his love for humanity, though at times concealed beneath a self-assumed mask of irony, such his undying faith in the ultimate victory of what is good and noble, that what is best in his work must find an echo in every heart.

Such a man becomes our master even though we do not follow him in every particular. Perhaps, too, we should remember that Darmesteter lived in France, and that at times he is influenced by the special conditions prevailing there. But how trite this limitation appears in the presence of his message to mankind; how it vanishes at the sound of the voice lifted to give hope and to cheer the dying century. Ours is the irreparable loss that this voice ceased to speak so soon!

MORRIS JASTROW, JR.

PHILADELPHIA, April, 1895.

CONTENTS.

THE RELIGIONS OF THE FUTURE.

I.

For almost a century, France and indeed all Europe have been in quest of a new God — seeking everywhere for an echo of a coming gospel. And they need this gospel, not only because humanity needs faith, but, above all, because it needs a rule of life. Every religion that is engulfed, though it be for the ultimate gain of a better faith, drags down morality with it for awhile; and the modern conscience, in uprooting Christianity, uproots itself.

Hence the wail that fills our age, — the wail of the orphan, who no longer has a heavenly father to advise and to guide him. It is heard throughout the century, above the crash of wars and revolutions, above the triumphant shouts of science, above the sarcasms of egotism and skepticism, above the incessant bustle of life pursuing its course. René hears it at the dawn of the century in the forests of the New World; it reaches Rolla on his bed of debauch; it ennobles all the poetry of the first half of the century; it even pierces through the dry literature of the Second Empire and through the filthy literature of the Third Republic. And now the century at its close begins to whisper words of faith, wanders in quest of a revelation from Ibsen to Tolstoi, from Buddha Gaya to Fiésole, hails in grandiloquent tones a god without substance who comes not, and attempts to fold its hands for a *credo* in which it no longer believes.

Twenty-six centuries ago, in a similar crisis which shook the conscience of a small, half-civilized tribe of Judea, a voice cried:[1] —

"Behold, the days are coming, saith the Lord, that I will send a famine in the land, not a famine of bread, nor a thirst for water, but of hearing the words of the Lord.

"They shall wander from sea to sea, and from the north to the east shall they run to seek the word of the Lord, and shall not find it.

"In that day shall the fair virgins and young men faint for thirst."

And to-day, too, the fair virgins and young men gaze in vain from sea to sea; from no rock bursts forth a spring at which the soul's thirst may be quenched. The divine word is not in Ibsen, nor yet in Tolstoi, and neither from the north nor from the east comes the light.

[1] Amos viii. 11–13.

II.

Religion is, or should be, the highest expression of science and of the human conscience. It was this at its origin under the form of mythology, and by its divine symbolism. But since it is the nature of a religion, when once organized through dogma and by means of a priesthood, to become fixed and hardened, a time comes when science and the divine conscience, incarnated and solidified, stand opposed to science and the ever-changing and progressing human conscience. This is precisely what has happened to Catholicism in the course of the last centuries, and consequently it is at present a resisting force, instead of an active and progressive one.

Upon the awakening of scientific thought at the time of the Renaissance, the incompatibility of Catholic dogmas with the new force soon became apparent. One may well believe, however, that, had the church been less afraid of the new force, had she accepted it boldly, and not treated it from the very first as an enemy, the divorce would have remained for centuries in the domain of logic, without passing over into reality. The church might have allowed the earth to revolve as it chose around the sun, without endangering either the Bible or the confessional. Logic, all-powerful in the

realm of pure reason, is indolent in the realm
of practical reason. Man never knows exactly
what he believes: he becomes conscious of his
belief only under pressure. But from the moment that the church threw down the gauntlet
to scientific thought, and endeavored to stifle it
under the weight of its unjustifiable assertions,
the outcome of the imposed conflict was no
longer doubtful, and the mystery of dogma,
forced out of its obscurity, could not long endure the strong light of the enemy.

Sooner or later were doomed to disappear,
not only all biblical cosmogony, to which the
church gratuitously attached so much value,
but also the essential dogmas of Christianity,
the Incarnation, the Resurrection, the Mystery
of the Mass, — in short, all the "ecstacy of the
cross."

In France the victory of the Catholic Church
over Protestantism hastened the downfall of
Christianity by permitting only the extreme
parties to survive, and by suppressing the tran-
sitional stage between Christian tradition and
the modern conception which the happy inconsistency of the reformers had brought about.
Louis XIV., in revoking the Edict of Nantes,
revoked Christianity also.

When Catholicism began the conflict with
science, it also entered upon the more dangerous conflict with conscience. To its former fear

of truth was now added the fear of justice.
After having for centuries elevated the ideals
of the West, protected the feeble and suffering,
introduced a modicum of peace, order, and even
of justice amid the barbarity of the Middle
Ages, and incited individuals to marvelous
deeds of devotion and charity, it remembered
only one of all Christ's precepts, — "Render
therefore unto Cæsar the things which are Cæsar's." And it allowed Cæsar to define the
rights of Cæsar, and instead of strengthening
justice, believed itself called upon to justify
force. And when the dreams of human equality
and fraternity carried to the Occident by primitive Christianity were about to be realized, there
stood opposed to them a church with anathemas
ready on her lips. Thus it happened that the
church, driven from the domain of science,
was also expelled from the domain of conscience. Not having known how to direct man
into the way of right thinking, she no longer
knew how to keep him in the path of right
doing.

III.

As long as the ardor of the struggle lasted,
science — free thought, philosophy, untram-
meled investigation, or whatever name one
chooses — triumphantly presumed to take the
place of its rival. The disillusion has come,
even before the completion of the victory.

Science equips man, but does not guide him. It illumines the world for him to the region of the most distant stars, but it leaves night in his heart. It is invincible, but indifferent, neutral, unmoral.

Let us leave aside practical science, which is clearly nothing more than an instrument, and, like every instrument, capable of good or bad, according to him who handles it. It works for the devil as for God, discovers melinite as it does vaccine, provokes war as it does peace, destroys as well as creates; changes the amount of good and of evil, but not their proportion. The other science, — the true, the great one, that which labors not for recompense, but is an end in itself, that which enlarges the soul to the measure of God, which dignifies it with all the beauty of the universe, calms it with the silence of infinitudes, — what has it to say to the man who comes to it in search of guidance through life? Science believed herself queen of the world, and when the dechristianized Christian comes and says, " Thou hast blown upon my Christ and reduced him to dust, thou hast closed the avenues of heaven to me, thou hast made life for me a thing without object and without issue: well then, give me something in place of what thou hast taken from me; tell me what I shall make of my life; I will obey thee blindly: command," she grows disturbed, stam-

mers, and recognizes with confusion and terror
that all she has to tell him is, that her great
discovery, her last word upon human destiny,
expresses the same thought that had been hovering over the religion she has condemned, —
"Life is not worth living." Command humanity! She does not know how, she cannot,
she dare not, — she would lie. What orders,
indeed, could she give him? In the name
of what power? By what incoercible need?
Her kingdom is not of this world. Her kingdom is that of raptures, where the realms of the
infinity of space and of time meet, where the
eternal panorama of the fleeting forms of life
rolls by. It is the glare of great nature which
science adores for the moment, before it falls
into everlasting destruction. And when humanity falls at the feet of the scholar and cries
out, "Thou art the oracle of God, the priest of
the new times! Speak, what shall I do?" he
has only floods of bitterness and renunciation
for a humanity which nevertheless does not wish
to die; or, indeed, he answers the distressful cry
of the simple-minded, who are better than he,
with irony and the contempt born of voluptuous counsels; or, feeling the impotency and
frailty of all unaided science, he beats his breast
and is silent.

Because of this omnipotence and impotence
of science, the whole moral order falls to pieces.

All the principles by which man and society
live are called upon to justify their validity by
convincing proofs, and, since they do not rest
upon such proofs, they are condemned and
wrecked. To science in the hands of the
thoughtless, everything that can be explained
is justified, and man, emanating from the brute,
is pardoned when he returns to that state. In
consequence, the idea of law is obliterated.
Among men, among all classes of the people,
desire regulates the measure of right. Everywhere is seen the expansion of self, bestial or
sanctimonious ; literature is given up to these
ruts, and the extreme refinement of intelligence
leads through every channel to the unbridling
of the human beast.

IV.

It is clear, however, that this unbridling cannot last. The modern soul is better than its
doctrines, and beneath the scum on the surface
the fount of the ideal flows on as deep as ever.
The soul well knows that this cannot be the
final expression of the emancipation of thought;
but that there must lurk somewhere a dishonor-
ing and deadly sophism. The impulse which
drives a part of the young generation to mysticism is nought but the first reaction of conscience seeking an outlet towards the pure air,

— a sterile reaction, — for mysticism is death to the soul, but the forerunner of a fruitful revolt. In endeavoring to retrace its steps and bend again under the yoke which it had broken, the modern soul attempts the impossible. It knows that it cannot abjure science, and it knows, too, that it can only be saved by an assertion of conscience which science cannot dictate, and which should control science.

The truths that would save us are not far to seek. They are current in the streets, but anæmic and bloodless. In order to become again living and triumphant realities, they require only to be conveyed to us by a voice speaking with authority. The one heard eighteen hundred years ago is hushed, because some of its words are repealed, words that were spoken to help men to die, and not to help them to live, and impotent in a world eager for justice, for life, for light. And now, behold humanity unwittingly ascending towards the higher source, towards the misunderstood masters of Christianity, "whose disciples we are, we all who seek a God without priests, a revelation without prophets, a covenant written in the heart." [1]

In turning towards these men, humanity is not retrograding twenty - six centuries; it is they who were twenty - six centuries in advance. Humanity was too young to read them.

---

[1] Renan's *Histoire du Peuple d'Israel*, vol. iii. p. 340.

But they could wait without fear, sure of the eternity of their creed, and sure that humanity, in its march towards the future, would be forced to retrace its steps to the mountain, and pass back from Golgotha to Zion.

V.

The purpose of prophecy is not to found a new religion, nor to convert the world to Judaism. How could a movement intended to teach man to dispense with altars, rituals, and myths be supposed to build up new altars, new rituals, new myths? As for Judaism, if its right to exist is due to its being the depositary and guardian of the Bible,[1] it is a positive religion, enriched by ritual, and cannot endure if it renounces its ritual, nor spread if it retains it.

The rôle and the mission of prophecy is not, then, to add to the number of religions and priesthoods, but to vivify the two actual religions which to-day are struggling for the mastery in France, and to-morrow will be content peacefully to share her between them, — the religion of science and that of Christ. Unity of form is of little import for the future. This unity exists only in the vision of imbecile advocates of outward conformity, the Torquemadas or

---

[1] Pascal, *Pensées*, xv. 15.

the Pobiedonosefs. But for the peace and the work of the world, there must be a communion of spirit beneath the free and graphic opposition to forms, so that the churches may no longer be separated by the "anathema," but march on under various flags to the conquest of misery, of vice, and of sadness.

Of all the forces bequeathed to us by the past, prophecy is the only one that can appeal to both religions, and make of them two sects of the same religion of progress. It alone can restore to the church the breath of the future by investing with a meaning the formulas with which it started out. And it alone can give to science the power of moral expression that the latter lacks. For the letter of the prophets is in the church, and their spirit in science.

VI.

The spirit of the prophets is in the modern soul. It matters little that they spoke in the name of a God, — Jehovah, — and that the modern age speaks in the name of human thought. For their Jehovah was only the apotheosis of the human soul, their own conscience projected heavenward. They loved everything that we love, and neither reason nor conscience has lost anything through their ideal. They have installed in the heavens a God who wishes neither altars, nor holocausts, nor canticles, "but that right shall gush forth as water, and justice as a never-failing stream." Righteousness was to them an active force; the idea was converted into a fact before which all other facts pale. By virtue of believing in justice, they advanced it to the rank of a factor in history. They had a cry of pity for the unhappy, of vengeance for the oppressor, of peace and of union for all mankind. They did not say to man, "This world is worthless." They said to him, "This world is good, and thou, too, be good, be just, be pure." They said to the wealthy, "Thou shalt not withhold the laborer's hire;" to the judge, "Thou shalt strike without humiliating;" to the wise man, "Thou art responsible for the soul of the people." And they taught many to live and to die for the right, without the hope of Elysian fields. They taught the people that without ideals "the future hangs before them in tatters;" that the ideal alone is the aim of life, and that it consists not in the glory of the conqueror, nor in riches, nor in power, but in holding up, as a torch to the nations, the example of better laws and of a higher soul. And lastly, they spread over the future, above the storms of the present, the rainbow of a vast hope, — a radiant vision of a better humanity, more exempt from evil and death, which shall no longer know war nor unrighteous judges;

where divine science will fill the earth, as the waters cover the bed of the ocean, and where mothers shall no longer in bearing children suffer a sudden death. Dreams of seers, to-day the dreams of scholars.

The spirit of prophecy is in science, but concealed and voiceless. For this reason anarchy reigned during the interregnum of the "Word," for the spirit exists and operates only through the magic of the words that give expression to it. In the beginning there is always the "Word." But the utterances of these old prophets, though most ancient, remain young, and the new age has not yet found, either among its philosophers, its moralists, its poets, nor even in its manuals of municipal ethics, words with a magic power equal to theirs; in their speech is concentrated all the tyranny of conscience and of the ideal.

VII.

On the day when the pulpit of the Catholic Church will place in the mouth of Christ the words of the prophets, — a bold stroke, but possible without a renunciation, since it involves only a mounting to the source, — on that day will the church take a new lease of life, and be able to assume once more the supreme direction of human society. Although its life appears to be ebbing, the church is still the sole organized force of the Occident, the heart whose throbs, if vivified by young blood, could make themselves felt to the ends of the earth. Even to-day, in a disabused and hostile society, the moment a word of goodwill emanates from this central seat of authority, a thrill of filial expectation passes through the whole of Europe, — Catholic, Protestant, and Infidel. Since there is no longer a pope-king, the papacy, stripped and become in a more striking degree the ideal and immaterial centre, the intangible Rome of the great Catholic empire, — the only intangible Rome, since it is the impalpable Rome, — seems to feel that humanity expects an arbiter in the struggle of nations and classes. Already the church timidly tries to raise its voice in this conflict, but the fatality of its traditions, stronger than its instinct, shuts it up in a circle of impotent and superficial formulas. The necessary revolution which would change the spirit of Christianity without changing a dogma, a rite, a priestly gesture, would also restore to Europe a centre, an arbiter, a guide ; would make of the church — now an obstacle — a living force. It may be that a disastrous schism is necessary to bring this about; perhaps the genius of a Monk Hildebrand will suffice.

Christianity has received its formulas from the prophets, but it has dissipated them into metaphors. Will it be able to recover their meaning? Thou art come to fulfill the prophets: fulfill them!

If the church misses its opportunity; if, in the name of an immutability which is simply a fiction of dogma contradicted by its history from the very beginning, it opposes the summons of the future with a *Non possumus,* — the necessary work will be done otherwise, and with greater difficulty. The gain which the spirit of the future could extract from this admirable instrument of unity and of propaganda will be lost for the work, and the scientific sect will be called upon to assume sole charge of the world.

THE PROPHETS OF ISRAEL.

THE Bible is a book more generally respected than known in France, and biblical criticism, though cradled there, is a new thing. Without going as far back as to Richard Simon,[1] the ingenious Oratorian who caught a glimpse of the problem and of the proper method, but whose attempt, stifled by the too cautious orthodoxy of Bossuet, bore no fruit, it is to a Frenchman to whom is due the initial discovery from which modern exegesis has been developed. In 1753 the physician Jean Astruc, professor in the Collège de France, noting in Genesis the alternate use of two different names for God, *Jehovah* and *Elohim*, drew the conclusion that our Book of Genesis is the result of a fusion of two prior and independent Geneses.[2] Thus theological and edifying exegesis, which is in reality a form of preaching sufficient only to a faith without curiosity and without intellectual disquiet, gave way to historical exegesis, which, through teaching us how the texts

---

[1] *Histoire Critique du Vieux Testament*, 1678.

[2] *Conjectures sur les Mémoires originaux dont il paraît que Moïse s'est servi pour composer le livre de la Genèse*, 1753.

are constructed, gives us a clearer conception of
how the ideas themselves are formed.

Astruc was a believer, with the mind of a
scholar. It is a long stretch from Astruc to
Voltaire, and from the "Conjectures sur la
Genèse" to the "Bible enfin expliquée." For
all that, this little pamphlet in some respects deserves a place of honor in the history of modern
criticism. Voltaire's good sense was too profound ever entirely to fail him, and, amidst the
mass of puerilities with which he thought suc-
cessfully to crush the Bible together with Christianity, he struck, without suspecting it, the very
keynote of historical exegesis. Whether the
honor of the discovery be due to him or to his
master Bolingbroke, the fact remains, as M.
Renan declared, that Voltaire, a century before
Reuss and the German school, discovered the
exact date of the first religious code of Israel.
In "L'Examen de Bolingbroke" may already
be found the theory attributing a portion of the
Pentateuch to the prophet Jeremiah, — an hypothesis which, so far from being one of the
boldest, is one of the most probable of the modern school. A whole century of German disser-
tations, and interminable discussions upon the
"Grundschrift" and the "Fragments" have
resulted in establishing the proposition that this
dangerous buffoon casually advanced, and Gavroche proved to be a century in advance of all the

German universities. Science has shown Voltaire no recognition, and Reuss, in his review of the history of exegesis, does not even mention his name. Justly so, for his unintelligent genius perceived the truth without grasping it; besides which, he enveloped it in so much impurity that no one thought nor cared to pick it out. Science has recruited herself .without him and against him.

What biblical criticism has come to be, after the patient labor of nearly a century, is almost exclusively the work of Germany. It is the result of the unfettered efforts of theologians, especially of Protestant theologians, for they only can permit themselves the happy inconsistency of reconciling belief in the historical development of religion with a past faith in the authority of revelation. This purely German, theological, and Protestant origin of biblical criticism has imparted to it its triple imprint, and is perhaps one of the principal causes of its slow progress. In a general way, it has lacked suppleness and proportion: it wished to know all, to explain all, to define all; it claimed to reach the primitive elements of formations ten times modified, and of which we possess only the residuum; it applied to synthesis, which demands a sacrifice of unimportant facts without historical value, the niceties of analysis, in which nothing must be ignored or neglected. The result is a series

of complicated and obscure structures, with queer
corners that hide detail, and with but little light
and space for the free play of facts and the cur-
rents of history. Added to this, theological and
Protestant fastidiousness superimposed many a
burden that a lay science would have ignored;
and biblical criticism has thus often been
dragged into the beaten path of rationalism, —
that weak compromise between free thought and
the belief in the verbal inspiration.

But on the other hand, and in spite of, or
rather by virtue of, this slow method, the German scholars brought to their task an amount
of patience, conscientiousness, and religious
reverence worthy of admiration. Every word
of the Book was considered in all its aspects,
no resource was left untried; and those who
now come upon the scene find the ground
cleared, the material gathered, and the problem of biblical origins nearer a definite solution than the problem of the Homeric poems.
Edouard Reuss[1] and Graf,[2] his pupil, are the
two men who within the last forty years have
given the science a definite shape. Although
these two scholars both belong to the German
tradition, there is some satisfaction in remem-

---

[1] *La Bible, traduction nouvelle avec introduction et commen-
taires,* 13 vols. 8vo, Paris, Sandoz et Fischbacher, 1874–1878.
[2] *Die Geschichtlichen Bücher des Alten Testaments,* Leipzig,
1865.

bering that they are both of Alsatian origin, and that Reuss, who at the time of his death [1] was the head and master of biblical studies, was born at Strasburg, and was professor there for fifty years. Reared in the German school, and having written nearly all his works in German, Reuss, after the disasters to France, remembered that he was by birth a Frenchman; and when he came to sum up the work of his life, and of three generations of scholars, he chose French as the medium for his admirable translation of the Bible, — a touching legacy from Alsatia to France, doubly precious as a mark of recognition for the past, and as a means of scientific regeneration for the future.

The work of Reuss and of his school paved the way towards freeing biblical criticism from the thraldom of theological and scholastic hierology. It is fortunate, both for biblical criticism and for France, that the latter after a century of neglect should have taken it up again. The science apprehended by Voltaire, and killed by him, has been restored to us by the man who bears the closest resemblance to Voltaire, and yet differs from him most widely. [2]

[1] In 1890.

[2] E. Renan, *Histoire du Peuple d'Israel*, 5 vols. 8vo, Paris, Calmann Lévy, 1887–1893 [English translation published by Roberts Bros., Boston].

Renan's "Histoire du Peuple d'Israel," while
leaving its impress upon the scientific evolution
of France, will also form an epoch in its religious evolution.   Force of circumstances gives
to this work of science the character of a philosophical achievement.   In this case, as in "Les
Origines du Christianisme," and even more so
perhaps, the work of M. Renan, in spite of the
commonplace and superficial criticism that pre-
tends to see in it merely the irony of a disillusioned mind, is the great constructive work of
the century.   Through his intellectual grasp,
embracing as it did all forms of thought and of
human sympathy, as well as by his antecedents
and his early education, M. Renan was predes-
tined to show to France and to the Voltairean
party of Europe the permanent element in the
gods of humanity.   Fully to understand religions, a little skepticism is necessary; but what
is also needed, and to an even greater degree,
is the imagination of a believer.   For the first
time, religious criticism was approached in a
spirit of sympathetic freedom, in a spirit of intelligence and love.   The scientific weakness of
Voltaire and his French followers was due to
the fact that they were not fortunate enough to
have had in their childhood those hours of naïve
faith, those souvenirs which, as years go on,
suddenly loom up amidst the tumult of reasoning sense, and illumine with a supernatural light

the obscure paths of the primitive mind, where science can but blindly grope, — an alien. Woe to the scholar who approaches things divine without having in the depth of his conscience, in the hidden indestructible recess of his being where the souls of ancestors sleep, an unknown sanctuary, whence at times rises a breath of incense, a line of the psalms, a pitiful or triumphant cry that as a child he may have sent forth to Heaven, as his fathers did before him, and which brings him into instant communion with the prophets of old.

I.

One of the masters of modern philosophy has remarked that the admirable translations scattered by Renan throughout his book had impressed him for the first time with the true spirit of the Bible. It may be said of the entire work, that it is the first which has ever enabled one to grasp the development of the spirit of Israel. I have no intention of giving a summary of M. Renan's book; one does not summarize Herodotus. I desire merely, so far as I am able, to set forth the consummate originality of the work, the thought that pervades it from beginning to end, constituting its novelty as well as its attractiveness.

Its novelty consists in having made prophecy the centre of interest of the history of Israel,

its power of attraction, in the unlooked - for
kinship existing between the heart of the prophets and the heart of the twentieth century.
It is due neither to the historical interest of the
subject, nor even to the genius of the writer,
that this purely scientific work, which does not
recoil upon occasion from the driest exegetical
discussions, should have fascinated and impressed even the *critics of the boulevard*, and
given them a momentary glimpse of the grave
and vital problems involved: it is due to the
touch of the magic wand with which the historian has struck the old stony text and caused
the entire modern soul to gush forth.

The great change in perspective, which the
new criticism introduces into sacred history,
consists in making the central figure of this history not Moses on Mount Sinai, but the company
of prophets, the men who spoke to Israel during the last two centuries of the Jewish kingdom, and during the Babylonian captivity, from
about 800 to 536 before Christ. The prophets,
who according to the traditional conceptions
appear in times of defection to recall to Israel
forgotten truths, are in reality the creators of
these truths, and prophecy, in place of being
the flower of Judaism, is its very root.

Prophecy is not a phenomenon peculiar to
Israel; all the ancient nations had prophets,
that is, men who spoke in the name of God or

of supernatural powers. The prophet differs
from the priest. The latter is a personage without great originality, the guardian of an established ritual, the potency of which is not at all
dependent upon the personality of the priest.
The prophet is the man possessed of God, and
through whom the will of God is revealed to
men. But among the other nations, and even
in Israel in ancient times, the prophet, seer,
diviner, sorcerer, hypnotizer, vacillates between
the charlatan, the fool, and the inspired one.
What is unique in Jewish prophecy is that it
became the all-powerful weapon, not of charlatans and of fools, but of those inspired, in whom
the mind and the conscience of modern humanity found their first successful and lasting expression. The work of these prophets survives
in a hundred pages of the Bible and — in three
religions.

The material weapon of· the victory of prophecy was *Jehovah*, the national God of the
Jews. It is possible that the prophetic movement had commenced before the definite evolution of Jehovah, but it was through him that it
conquered; and, in order to comprehend the
evolution of prophecy, it is necessary to trace
the development of the idea of God. Let us
sketch it rapidly, first according to the Bible
and then according to history.

According to the Bible, Jehovah, after having revealed himself to the patriarchs, made definite choice of the descendants of Jacob as his people; to them will he make known his law, and through them to the world. He delivers them from Egypt by the hand of Moses, and on Mount Sinai reveals and offers to them his law. Israel accepts this law, enters into an alliance with Jehovah, becomes his people. As long as she observes the compact and follows Jehovah's law, Jehovah protects her and causes her to prosper; when she fails to do so, he delivers her into the hands of her enemies.

Israel conquers the land which Jehovah promised her ancestors; but she forgets her vow, adopts the idolatry of Canaan, and Jehovah abandons her to her oppressors. Hearing her cry of distress and repentance, Jehovah sends judges to save her. The kingdom is established under the auspices of Jehovah, but David alone keeps it within the path of the Lord. The national unity is destroyed under the second successor of the royal psalmist. Both the kingdom of Judah, which to the end clings to the house of David, and the kingdom of Israel, torn asunder by military revolutions, are unfaithful to Jehovah; Israel continuously so, and Judah, with occasional reversions to faith. The prophets that Jehovah sends to Israel — Elijah, Elisha, Micah, Amos, Hosea — announce in

vain the punishment that is imminent, until the
day that Assyria comes to wreak upon Samaria
the vengeance of the Lord.

Judah survives her sister a century and a
half.   The glowing utterances of the prophets
accentuate the return of Judah to Jehovah.
But neither the piety of Hezekiah nor that of
Josiah can expiate the sacrileges of those who
preceded them and of those who followed. Jerusalem is condemned in turn; Judah goes in exile
to Babylon.   But trial has purified the outlaws.
Jehovah will restore to them liberty, glory,
the moral control of humanity.   A scion of
David shall cause justice and the name of the
God of Israel to reign throughout the world.
Babylon succumbs, Cyrus restores the promised
land to the exiles, and, lo! under Zerubbabel,
Ezra, and Nehemiah, Israel is committed to the
single worship of Jehovah and the single law
of Moses.

All through Renan's "Histoire du Peuple
d'Israel" one may observe how the application
of the scientific method has shattered the framework of a narrative infantile, — or divine in its
simplicity, and how it has brought to the surface the infinite complexity of human affairs.
The miracle of a uniform, continuous revelation,
ever present and complete from the moment
when it descended from heaven, is supplanted
by the no less miraculous history of a progres-

sive revelation proceeding from the heart of
man, and from the fervent meditations of certain seers, slowly evolved, transformed, adapted
to the stature of humanity; and Israel, in place
of being the elect of God, has herself created
God in the sweat of her brow.

Israel, once in possession of a doctrine which
she believed to be a revelation from above, and
which consequently appealed to her as eternal,
removed her recent conquest into the farthest
limits of her past, and rewrote her history under
the spell of an ideal. Hence the successive
revelations of Jehovah to the legendary ancestors of the race, — to Noah, to Abraham, to
Jacob; hence the revelation from Sinai, and
the colossal figure of Moses transformed from the
leader of the exodus to the legislator; and hence
all this drama of national history, which takes
on the form of a continuous struggle between
God and man, in which God finally triumphs in
order to save man.

All this is merely a sublime fiction. The
historical texts, considered by themselves and
freed from edifying glosses which a triumphant
doctrine added with a view of showing the actual accomplishment of the divine word in the
progress of the world, make it perfectly evident
that all these heroes of prehistoric times, these
patriarchs, — first symbol of Jewish sanctity, —
Moses, the supreme legislator, the man of God;

the liberating judges sent by divine pity to the rescue of a repentant people, — even David himself, the prototype of the Messiah, ignored with perfect security the majority of the principles that constitute the heart of organized Judaism.   It was a time when Rachel piously carried the Teraphim with her from her father's house;[1] it was a time when Gideon, sent by Jehovah to save his people, profited by the victory through the erection of an *ephod* that all Israel came to adore;[2] a time when the tribes, eager for conquest, dispute for the possession of the most popular idols.[3]   It was a time when angels walked through the streets and in the fields; when Jehovah comes to dine with Abraham, like a mere Jupiter coming down to Philemon;[4] when each stone recalls a divine apparition,[5] every old oak and every terebinth has its divine souvenir; when the two worlds are still as intermingled as in the time of Homer; and when the race of Elohim still commingles with the daughters of men.[6]   It was a time of idolatry and of religious ignorance, of which the Book of Judges has left us an admirable and naïve picture; a time of religious as well as of political anarchy, when there was no genuine master either in heaven or on earth; when there

---

[1] Gen. xxxi. 19.

[2] Judges viii. 24 *sq.*

[3] Judges xviii.

[4] Gen. xviii. 1 *sq.*; Judges xiii.

[5] Gen. xxviii. 19.

[6] Gen. vi. 1 *sq.*

was no recognized rule either for souls or for men; and when the utterance was doubly true, "In those days there was no king in Israel: every man did that which was right in his own eyes." [1]

Nevertheless, in this period of idolatry, Jehovah already existed; the proper names of the time of the Judges prove this.[2] He was already a distinct figure; he was a national god, or, to speak more exactly, a tribal god, the god of *the children of Israel;* but as yet he was only a figure among many others in the crowd of *Elohim*, those which Israel inherited from the most ancient traditions of the Semitic race, as well as those that she had since acquired, and was constantly acquiring through the various nations with whom chance brought her into contact. The theory has been propounded that Jehovah was brought from Chaldea by Israel, amidst the mass of myths and ideas which she owed to the old civilization of Babylon. Was Jehovah, as M. Halevy would have us believe, the special god of Moses and the Levites? Or, indeed, did Moses take him from his father-in-law Jethro, the priest of Midian,[3]

---

[1] Judges xxi. 25.

[2] *Joshua*, that is to say, *Jeho-shûa*, "Jehovah is a help;" *Jotham*, "Jehovah is perfect," etc.

[3] Exodus iii. 1 *sq.*

whose flocks he tended at Sinai and by the
bush of Horeb? Renan, with his subtle conception of *hasards décisifs*, has in fact advanced
the seductive theory that Jehovah was the local
god of Sinai, the flaming mountain, and that it
was there that Israel, flying from Egypt, encountered him. He was the first god that Israel
met with after her departure from the house of
slavery, and the first to whom she could offer a
grateful sacrifice. "Did there really take place
in the sight of Serbal a religious act, a sort of
consecration of the people to the god of the
mountain, so effective that from that day the
god of Sinai was the special god of Israel?
Did Moses, the chief of the people, take advantage of one of those frightful storms that are
frequent in that country to make them believe
in a revelation of the thunder-god who dwelt on
high? Had the manner in which the ninth century before Christ pictures the connection of
the law with Sinai, any points of contact with
the real facts? or did this sublime legend arise
in the course of four or five centuries, growing
like the soap-bubble, which becomes more brilliant and highly colored as it becomes emp-
tier?" [1]

Renan leaves the question undecided; skillful
indeed he, who would venture to solve it in the
present state of the documents. And, after all,

---

[1] Renan, *Histoire du Peuple d'Israel*, i. 191, 192.

the real interest of the question lies rather in the date of the birth of the ·god, than in the process of conception. It would doubtless be interesting to know whether the flash that transfigured the world were struck from the flint of Sinai; but the great fact to be kept in mind, and which remains, is that Jehovah, god of the nation, whether created or adopted by Israel, could only have been born the day that Israel began her career as a nation. The moment that Israel stepped on free ground after crossing the Red Sea, a new god was conceived in the hidden recesses of Jewish thought. The tradition that shows us Jehovah revealing himself to Israel by the mouth of Moses rests upon an historical basis; for the departure from Egypt, the first event in the national existence of Israel, marks the first pulsation of the national god. This new god differed little essentially from the other gods that Israel had encountered, and might still encounter, in the course of her religious vicissitudes; he was neither more moral, nor more gracious, nor greater; he differed from them in one point only, but that an essential one: it was he who saved Israel.

Jehovah then lay dormant during four or five centuries. He was there, but he was not the sole figure, either in Israel or outside of Israel. He had priests, he had an invisible image which floated in a sacred ark, the palladium of the tribe of Ephraim. But his universal and constant presence was not felt. Other Elohim and other images were still worshiped, and it was quite customary to consult the gods of the neighboring nations, — the Phœnicians, Philistines, Moabites. Meanwhile the anarchy of the tribes, rendering them defenseless against their neighbors, began to weigh upon them. Attempts at unity were made from various sides; the Israelitish nationality began to take shape. It took definite shape upon the establishment of a kingdom; and it is not purely accidental that its first king is consecrated by Samuel. With the forbidding and august figure of this seer, the jealous god makes his first appearance in history. When the people demand a king of Samuel, they say to him, "Give us a king who may judge us, like all the other nations." It was not only a king they wanted, but a god after the fashion of other nations. Israel need no longer submit to the reproaches and insults of the nations round about, that ask, "Which is thy god?" Moab has Chemosh, Tyre has Baal, the Philistines have Dagon, Israel has Jehovah. With the victories of David, with the glory of Solomon, with the construction of the temple that gave to Jehovah a permanent abode and a constantly absorbing centre for his cult, Jehovah definitely becomes the particular god of Israel. And the triumphs

of David prove that he is more powerful than
the neighboring gods. "Who is like unto thee
among the Elohim, O Jehovah?"

It is a long stretch from this Jehovah, the
protecting god of the tribe, to the one god, the
universal god, the god of justice. As yet he is
not even the jealous god, except according to
the theory of a small party that tries in vain to
establish officially the principles that it elabo-
rates, and which will be obliged to protest for
a long time and without success against the
tolerance, the contradictions, and the religious
torpor of official Jehovism. While erecting a
splendid temple to Jehovah at Jerusalem, Solomon neither considers himself unfaithful to
him, nor likely to provoke his wrath, by offer-
ing sacrifices to the gods of all his foreign mis-
tresses. A national god is not for that reason
a unique god, and one good for all purposes.
He devotes himself to the great interests of the
nation, assures it peace, victory, good harvests;
but why need he occupy himself with details
and petty interests? *De minimis non curat.*
Every god has his special province, and when
King Ahaziah falls sick he undoubtedly possesses the right to consult the Baal-zebub of the
Philistines.[1] Idolatry does not frighten the

[1] 2 Kings i. 2. "And Ahaziah fell down through a lattice
in his upper chamber that was in Samaria, and was sick: and
he sent messengers, and said unto them, Go, inquire of Baal-

worshiper of Jehovah; and when Israel separates from Judah, Jeroboam's people are not
shocked by the erection of the golden calf as
a symbol of Jehovah at Dan and Beer-sheba.[1]
Even in the temple of Jerusalem, the brazen
serpent receives the prayers of the believer
down to the days of Hezekiah.[2]

The jealous god does not actually triumph
until about 622, scarcely half a century before
the fall of Jerusalem.   But about 875, the god,
weak and uncertain at the outset, becomes conscious of himself and of his ambitions with
striking clearness.   This takes place during the
crisis provoked by the invasion of the Phœnician gods in Israel under King Ahab.   At
Jerusalem, the city of the temple, Jehovah met
with little opposition; he was a god like those
of other nations, and the regular transmission
of power in the family of David favored a

zebub the god of Ekron, whether I shall recover of this dis-
ease.

"But the angel of Jehovah said to Elijah the Tishbite,
Arise and go up before the messengers of the King of Samaria, and say unto them: Is there no god, then, in Israel, that
ye go to inquire of Baal-zebub, the god of Ekron?

"Now therefore thus saith Jehovah: Thou shalt not come
down from that bed on which thou art gone up; but shalt
surely die.   And Elijah departed."

[1] 2 Kings xii. 28.

[2] 2 Kings xviii. 4: "He removed the high places and broke
the images, and cut down the Ashera [*i. e.* the sacred pole],
and broke in pieces the brazen serpent that Moses had made,
for unto those days the children of Israel burned incense to it."

tranquil Jehovah of a sacerdotal and serene type. It was otherwise in Israel, agitated as she was by perpetual revolutions.[1] About 900, Omri, who founded Samaria, mounted the throne. Under him Israel, still semi-barbarous, and not wholly emerged from the patriarchal life, was largely exposed to the civilizing influences of her rich and powerful neighbor, Phœnicia. Ahab, son of Omri, marries a Phœnician princess, Jezebel. Through her, or rather through Phœnician influence, the worship of the divinities of Tyre is introduced, and Baal obscures Jehovah. Foreign oppression is needed in order that the gods and their subjects may become cognizant of each other. All the pride of the Israelitish element, deeply wounded by Phœnician insolence, added to the contempt for a more refined and materially superior civilization, whose corruption and scars were alone brought home to her; in short, all the prejudices of the Bedouin, and all his virtues, found a support for their

[1] After the death of Solomon, abont 975, the kingdom is divided in two : Judah and Israel. Judah, with Jerusalem as its capital, remains faithful to the family of David until it is destroyed by Nebuchadnezzar, King of Babylon, in 588, after a duration of four centuries. Israel goes from dynasty to dynasty, through a dozen revolutions, and succumbs in 721 to the blows of Assyria, nearly 130 years before Judah. The prophets often designate Israel as Samaria, from its capital, or as Ephraim, its principal tribe, and sometimes as Joseph, the ancestor of Ephraim.

protest in Jehovah, who came forth from the
ordeal more powerful than ever, more imperious
and moral by contrast. The traits of Samuel
reappear in Elijah the Tishbite. This dark
and powerful figure, whom legend has enveloped
in a veil of flame, took a strong hold upon the
imagination of the generations that followed
him; a human archangel carried to heaven
alive,[1] a divine precursor whose return was
awaited by the first Christians,[2] an eternal wan-
derer for whom the Jews still leave an empty
place each year at the feast of the Passover.
But here the halo of the legend is but the reflection of history, the radiance of a real personality, and it is impossible to doubt the existence
and the achievement of this great "troubler
of Israel."[3] His name is synonymous with a
successful war of the jealous god, a war to the
knife, of Jehovah against Baal, that ends in
the extermination of the Phœnician god. It is
in the school of the prophets, fashioned after
Jehovah's image, that the monotheism of Israel
is forged like a bar of iron. A curious echo of
the semi-Voltairean arguments that were current in these schools is preserved in the sarcasms
hurled by Elijah against the priests of Baal,
calling in vain for the heavenly fire on the sacrifice offered to their god: "Cry a little louder

[1] 2 Kings ii.   [2] John i. 25.
[3] 1 Kings xviii. 17.

then; forsooth, he is a god; perhaps he is talking, or engaged, or he is on a journey, or perhaps he is asleep and must be awakened." [1]

Elijah is separated by about a century from
the prophets, in the proper sense of the word;
or rather from those whose works we possess.
This century, of which nothing remains but
legends, must have been the most fertile in the
moral history of Israel; for the first prophets
already present all the traits of the prophetic
literature. Jehovah is no longer merely the
jealous god, the god who strikes and punishes
those who forget or who scorn him: he is already the god of virtue, the god of justice; he
is already the god of the poor and the oppressed, the god who asks not sacrifices of those
that serve him, but a pure heart. A beautiful
page from the legend of Elijah fleeing before
Jezebel may be regarded as a symbol of this
transformation: —

"And he went a day's journey into the wilderness; he sat down under a juniper-tree, and
prayed for death, saying, It is enough, Jehovah, take away my life, for I am not better
than my fathers. . . . And the voice of Jehovah came to him and said, What dost thou here,
Elijah?

"And he answered: I have been very jealous
for the Lord God of hosts; for the children

[1] 1 Kings xviii. 27.

of Israel have forsaken thy covenant, thrown down thine altars, slain thy prophets with the sword, and I alone am left, and they seek me in order to kill me.

"And Jehovah said, Go forth and stand upon the mount before Jehovah. And behold, the Lord passed by, and a great and strong wind rent the mountain, and broke in pieces the rocks before Jehovah, but Jehovah was not in the wind; and after the wind came an earthquake, but Jehovah was not in the earthquake; and after the earthquake a fire, but Jehovah was not in the fire; and after the fire there came a still small voice."[1]

It is this still small voice that henceforth mingles its note with the thunderbolts of Jehovah, and gives to prophecy that unique blending of passion and tenderness which was destined both to shatter and to melt the stony heart of that ancient world.

II.

In truth, the century following after Elijah gave birth to a new phenomenon; a god became the instrument of morality.

We cannot trace the origin of the movement that culminates in the purification and idealization of Jehovah, placing him beyond the pale and above all other gods, clearing the entire

[1] 1 Kings xix. 11, 12.

heavens to make room for him, and attaching to his name and to his worship all the force implied in conscience. With Amos and Hosea, the first prophets whose writings we possess, this task is already accomplished. Nothing essential was added to it after them; even they did not invent anything, and owe their title of priority merely to the chance which occasioned the loss of the work of predecessors, whose names the Bible has perpetuated, and whose works the author of the Book of Kings and the author of Chronicles still possessed, — Nathan, Gad, Iddo, and others. It is probable that, already in the war that Elijah waged against Baal in the name of Jehovah, politics and theology were not the sole questions at issue, and that the powerful moral impetus of prophetical Jehovism had already become manifest. Elijah is not only the enemy of Baal and his idols, he is the arbiter sent to threaten the murderer of Naboth with the wrath of Jehovah, in order to avenge the poor man who is stripped and slaughtered;[1] and the first evangelical parable was recited ten centuries before Christ, by the prophet Nathan, stigmatizing in David's presence and in the name of Jehovah the royal murderer and adulterer.[2]

---

[1] 1 Kings xxi. 18 *sq.*

[2] " There were two men in the same city, the one rich and the other poor.

The eleventh century, that culminated in this movement, is one of the great epochs in the history of the human soul. It was a century of an intense moral crisis, of painful unrest, comparable to that of the first century of our era, and to that of the century in which we live. Israel sought her god and found him not. She vainly strove to wrest the secret of justice and of truth from the impotent idols erected by her first king in the name of Jehovah, for the purpose of weaning the people from their attachment to Jerusalem. Many, doubtless, in accepting the new gods of Phœnicia, had hoped to find peace of mind in them, and they wandered from one god to another, "halting between Jehovah and Baal," without rest and without hope. It was a century of anguish and of trepidation, whose wail has not reached us, and which none of its children has portrayed. An echo, however, of this anguish remains in a page which ushers in prophetic literature, and

"And the rich man had large cattle and small cattle in great number.

"And the poor man had but one small lamb, which he had bought and nourished, and it grew up together with him and with his children; it ate of his meat, drank from his cup, lay in his bosom, and was to him as a daughter.

"And there came a traveler unto the rich man, and he did not take of his own flock, large or small, to entertain the guest, who had come unto him, but took the poor man's lamb," etc. (2 Samuel xii. 1 *sq.*)

summarizes the moral drama of the century now drawing to its close: [1] —

"Behold, the days are coming, saith the Lord Jehovah, that I will send a famine in this land, not a famine of bread, nor a thirst for water, but of hearing the words of the Lord.

"They shall wander from sea to sea, and from the north to the east they shall run to seek the divine word, and shall not find it.

"In that day shall the fair virgins and young men perish for thirst; and they that swear by the sin of Samaria, saying, Long live the god of Dan! Long live the way of Beer-sheba! shall fall, never to rise again."

When prophetic literature appeared, the moral and political horizon stretching before the eyes of the dreamers of Israel and of Judah consisted of a number of small states, Moab, Edom, Tyre, Philistia, Israel, Judah, all contending with one another with the bitterness characteristic of small states. War and pillage were the order of the day, perpetual razzias supplying captives for the slave trade of Tyre and the Greek islands. Farther off, a powerful state, Damascus, and, still farther, mighty Assyria, with their vast armies, their wars of extermination, their frightful systems of deportation and transportation in mass, already throw the shadow of death upon this

[1] Amos viii. 10–14.

chaos of lawless communities. The gods are as wicked and as bigoted as men; religion is become a school of prostitution in the temple of Astarte, of barbarity on the altars of Moloch; worship vacillating between silly and atrocious practices; divination, sorcery, imposture, are closely bound up with all the cults. And when the prophet of Jehovah extends his gaze to his own people, he beholds political and moral anarchy. Israel is divided against herself, and presents a united front only when opposing Judah. Bloody military revolutions create and overthrow kings, and all the horrors of a pretorian régime exist in a kingdom of several square miles. In the intermittent hours of peace, force remains absolute master, as in the time of war; the poor are oppressed by the rich, and, worst of all, justice is purchased by the powerful. The temples are full of foreign innovations; Jehovah himself affords no succor; his cult is reduced to a system of pure idolatry, a ritual of sacrifices and fasts, without a moral basis; nowhere a voice speaking with authority. It is at such a moment that the moral force resting in the exclusive character of Jehovah reveals itself.

The cruelty, the degradation, the iniquity, characteristic of those times, were certainly no worse than in preceding centuries, both in Israel and in the rest of the Semitic world; nor worse

than those which prevailed later in Greece and
in Rome, in the most flourishing centuries of
literature and art. It was part of the spirit of
prophecy to be dumfounded at human ferocity
as at something against nature and reason. In
the presence of the iniquities of the world, the
heart of the prophets bled as though from a
wound of the divine spirit, and their cry of
indignation reëchoed the wrath of the deity.
Greece and Rome had their rich and poor, just
as Israel had in the days of Jeroboam, and the
various classes continued to slaughter one another for centuries, but no voice of justice and
pity arose from the fierce tumult. Nations were
born and perished, living from day to day at
the mercy of the accidents and the appetites of
the hour, without comprehending that a nation,
in order to live and to deserve to live, needs an
ideal that may determine its destiny. In default of such, it must perish, with no reason for
its existence, "with its future hanging before it
in tatters."[1] Therefore these ancient words,
fierce and violent, have more vitality at the
present time, and answer better to the needs of
modern souls, than all the classic masterpieces
of antiquity. Therefore these stray pages, sent
forth twenty-six centuries ago among two semi-
barbarous tribes, and exposed to the vicissitudes
of chance, constitute a production that will live
forever.

[1] Deuteronomy xxviii. 66.

III.

All the essential doctrines of prophecy appear in the first two prophets remaining to us, Amos and Hosea; the former occupied rather with social justice, the latter more religious, and concerned with morality and with God. Both belong to the Israelitish prophets, if not by their nationality, — for Amos was born in Judah, — at least by their purpose, which is, the regeneration of Israel. Israel, torn by dissensions, had greater need of reformers, and offered them a more favorable field than Judah, who, in default of a very high code of morality, had at least, thanks to the legal prestige of her kingdom, that most important of political advantages, stability. Prophecy does not take root in Judah until after the overthrow of Israel. At Samaria, just as somewhat later at Jerusalem, the dream, or rather the arrested project, of the prophets is to bring about the realization of the model State, the State conformable to the views of Jehovah, and therefore based upon justice.

At the time that Amos appeared, Israel had reached her highest point of temporal power. King Jeroboam II. (825–775 B. C.) had conquered for himself a part of the empire of David. He had crushed Moab, whose god Chemosh had not been able to save it as in the days

of King Mesha, and in the field of Heshbon he
had silenced "the joy of the orchards and the
songs of the vintage." But his victories over
Damascus, Gaza, Tyre, Edom, Moab are to
the prophet merely an omen of the impending
vengeance of the Eternal upon Israel. Damascus, Gaza, Tyre, Moab, Edom expiate their
past atrocities, and Israel, equally guilty, must
suffer in turn. She must expiate her sin "because she sold justice for silver, and the poor
for a pair of shoes;"[1] because her nobles, reclin-
ing upon their ivory couches, pick the lyre, to
play like David, and drink wine from full cups,
without grieving for the affliction of Joseph.[2]
For this reason, in truth, shall they build themselves houses of hewn stone, but shall not dwell
in them; plant pleasant vineyards, but shall not
drink of the wine. Let them go to Calneh,
to great Hamath, to Gath of the Philistines,
and see the fate which awaits them! They
shall pass into exile at the head of the band,
and their exultation shall cease. It is Jehovah,
the Lord of Hosts, who swears: "I abhor the
pride of Jacob, I hate his palaces."[3] And he
will besiege her city, starve it, empty it, pass
the scythe over Israel, destroy her sanctuaries,
and raise the sword over the house of Jeroboam.

It required a brave heart to fling these cries
at the victors, in the height of their triumph:

[1] Amos ii. 6.   [2] Amos vi. 4.   [3] Amos vi. 8 *sq.*

"Therefore the prudent shall keep silent in that time, for the people hate those that rebuke at the gate of the tribunal, and they abhor those that speak uprightly."[1] The priests especially bore malice against those men who, without authority, presumed to put into the mouth of Jehovah things which they, his priests, had never thought of. The priest of the royal sanctuary, Beth-el, denounced the intruder to King Jeroboam. "Get thee away to Judah," he says; "earn thy bread by retailing thy prophecies there!" "I am neither prophet," answers Amos, "nor the son of a prophet. I am but a herdsman, and a gatherer of sycamore fruit; but Jehovah took me away from my flock and said unto me, Go prophesy unto my people in Israel!"[2] For when the Lord commands, the prophet must speak, despite the one who seals his lips. "When the lion roars, who would not tremble? When the Eternal speaks, who would not prophesy?"[3]

Neither priests nor cult could save Israel from the wrath of Jehovah! "Bring your sacrifices every morning, and your tithes every three days, and loudly proclaim your freewill offerings, since you are fond of this, O children of Israel! But Jehovah hates and despises all your festivals. What cares he for your

---

[1] Amos v. 9, 13; ii. 2.   [2] Amos vii. 10 *sq.*
[3] Amos iii. 8.

holocausts, and for your offerings of fatted
calves? He will roll the altar upon the head
of his worshipers, and crush them under the
ruins.[1] Should they seek refuge in Sheol, his
hand would drag them thence; should they ascend to the heavens, he would bring them
down.[2] . . . Away from me with the noise of
your songs, that I may not hear the sound of
your lyres; *but let righteousness gush forth as
water, and justice as a never-failing stream!*"[3]

God, however, can never entirely abandon
his chosen people. The sinners only among
them shall perish. Israel and Judah shall be
reunited. God will raise up the fallen taber-
nacle of David, and by closing up the breaches
and removing the ruins will rebuild it as it was
before.[4]

The same background of ideas is found in
Hosea, but with a more personal Jehovah, more
intimate, closer to Israel, jealous with the jealousy of love and not of pride; whence results
new imagery, which is not without influence on
his successors; and impressive utterances, which
are only equaled by the second Isaiah.

Hosea is several years later than Amos.[5]

---

[1] Amos iv. 5; v. 2; ix. 1 *sq.*

[2] "Quand vous habiteriez la montagne de l'aigle,
Je vous arracherai de là, dit l'Eternel."

— V. Hugo.

[3] Amos v. 23, 24.   [4] Amos ix. 9 *sq.*

[5] Reuss places the period of his preaching from 784 to 700.

Political decomposition was progressing. The transitory and deceptive splendor of Jeroboam was past: *pronunciamentos* made and unmade kings. Assyria appeared on the horizon, destined to engulf everything. And Israel, in place of proceeding in the path that Jehovah opens to her, amuses herself with international intrigues; turns to Egypt, turns to Assyria; puts off moral reform, plunges into the morals and practices of her allies and ephemeral protectors. She consults divining rods, sacrifices upon the high places, burns incense upon the oak and the terebinth, and there is neither truth, nor love, nor knowledge of God; there is only swearing and lying, killing and adultery. Therefore the tempest will carry her off on its wings.[1] In vain do they turn towards Ashur; Ashur has no remedy for their scars. Let them come back to Jehovah, call upon him in their anguish![2]

Why has the daughter of Israel forgotten her betrothal with Jehovah, and why does she debauch herself with the Baals? She knows not that it is Jehovah who has given her the corn, the wine, and the oil that she offers to her false gods, — the gold and the silver of which she makes their idols. Therefore Jehovah will take back his corn and his wine, and the wool and the flax with which she would cover her

---

[1] Hosea iv. 1, 2, 19.   [2] Hosea v. 15.

nakedness. He will ravage her vineyards and
her fig-trees, and change them·into brushwood.
But no, Jehovah can never entirely repudiate
her who gave him the love of her youth. He
will bring her into the wilderness, where they
have loved each other; he will console her; she
shall sing there, as in the days when she came
out of Egypt, and the plain of sadness shall
become the door of hope.[1] How could God
abandon Ephraim, whom he had guided in leading-strings, whom he had taken in his arms,
had attached to himself with all a man's fibre,
with bands of love? The heart of Jehovah is
turned inward, and melts with compassion: "I
will not destroy Ephraim; for I am God, and
not man. I am the holy one in the midst of
you; I will not come to destroy!"[2]

Ah, that Israel would again turn towards
Jehovah! "For he who tore them will heal
them, who wounded them will bind them up.
He will revive them after two days, and on the
third day he will raise them up."[3] For God
loves them, and for that reason he strikes them
through the prophets, and kills them by the
words of his mouth.[4] Let them not come to
him with sacrifices. "For I desired mercy and

[1] Hosea ii. 10, 15.   [2] Hosea xi. 3, 9.

[3] Hosea vi. 1, 2. Text afterwards applied to the resurrection of Christ.

[4] Hosea vi. 5.

not sacrifice."[1] Let them turn again to Jehovah, for it is not the Assyrian who will save
them; it is Jehovah who is their God, their
only God since their sojourn in Egypt, their
only saviour! "That which destroys thee, O
Israel, is that thou art against me, against thy
saviour; turn back to Jehovah, thy God!"[2]
Let them seek the Lord; it is still time; he will
come to teach them justice. They have ploughed
wickedness and reaped iniquity;[3] let them now
sow the seeds of righteousness, and they shall
reap mercy.[4]

The framework created by Amos and Hosea,
or by their lost predecessors, is that which will
be adopted by all the prophets that follow, for
their preaching, their threats, and their hopes.
The uniformity of the foundation is varied only
by the individual genius of each, and by the
advance of history. In each prophet there is
a code of ethics and of politics indissolubly connected, — for to them ethics and politics were
one, — and without the change of an axiom from
first to last. The only thing that changes,
because affected by exterior circumstances that
are of course subject to change, is each one's
conception of the future, or rather the manner
in which the inevitable future will be realized.

[1] Hosea vi. 6. [2] Hosea xiii. 9.
[3] Hosea x. 13. [4] Hosea x. 12.

That which is not based upon justice must perish;

Jehovah has revealed justice to Israel;

Israel should realize justice;

Justice will be realized some day.

These are the four axioms of prophecy, the four invincible certainties that constituted its supernatural power. And the last of these four, in equipping it with hope for all eternity, preserved it from the crushing influence of time. But when and how will justice be realized? Upon this point the prophets differ. Those who came first, beheld the glorious advent near and direct. It is Israel who, obedient to their voice, will of her own accord realize, through the hand of her kings, the divine will in the promised land. In order to open her eyes and her heart completely, many blows from on high will perhaps be needed, many chastisements from the hand of God, and from the hand of man. But the bitter experience of the expiations that follow all iniquity like its shadow, the natural reactions that suppress every outbreak of wickedness, will finally teach her, and make of her the happy servant of God. On two occasions, under Hezekiah and under Josiah,[1] the prophets believe the end attained. Their ideal seems about to become the law of the State, and to pass into reality through the hand of the civil power. The illu-

[1] Hezekiah, 726–697; Josiah, 640–610.

sion was brief, and it was soon seen that under existing circumstances there was no hope for the divine plan. The political world of the day is too corrupt, too deeply sunk in egotism, in narrowness of thought and of heart, to follow the call of the very small minority represented by the prophets. The present nation, such as it has become in the course of centuries, will not carry out the new order: she is, consciously or unconsciously, its inveterate enemy; she is the obstacle and must perish. Israel must be swept away by a tempest that shall engulf the impure element, and then the purified débris, reared and nurtured by the prophetic doctrine, will come back to Palestine to found the ideal state. History thus divides the prophetic drama into three acts: the first is animated by the bold illusion which attempts to construct the future directly from the present; the second is filled with the necessary destruction; the third by the restoration held out as possible.

The first act is dominated by Isaiah, the second by Jeremiah, the third by the great "Anonymous" of the Captivity.

IV.

The cries and the tears of Amos and Hosea were lost upon Israel. Adventurers succeeded one another upon the throne. One of them,

Menahem, ripped up all the women that were
with child, in the cities that resisted![1] Israel is
at the point of death, and recovers her energy
only in attacking Judah: "Every man eats the
flesh of his own arm, Manasseh against Ephraim,
Ephraim against Manasseh, and both together
against Judah."[2] A king of Israel, Pekah,
who reigned longer than the others (758–738),
combines against Judah with the king of Damascus, and Jerusalem is kept at bay by this
fratricidal coalition.[3] When the news that the
Syrians of Damascus were encamped in Ephraim
arrived at the court of Ahaz, king of Judah,
his heart was stirred, and the heart of his people, as the trees of the forest are stirred by
the wind. "Fear nothing," says the prophet
Isaiah, "fear nothing, neither be faint-hearted
in the presence of the two ends of these smok-
ing firebrands!"[4] The two allies did not know
that they were but two dying nations already
doomed. From the other side of the Euphrates,
the Assyrian hordes were already hastening on,
and, in response to Jehovah's beckoning, were
descending upon all the valleys and into all
the byways of Damascus and Ephraim.[5] The
king of Assyria, Tiglath-Pileser, entered Damascus, killed the king of Syria, and carried

---

[1] 2 Kings xv. 16. (771–760). [2] Isaiah ix. 20, 21.
[3] 2 Kings xvi. 5 *sq.* [4] Isaiah vii. 4.
[5] Isaiah v. 26 *sq.*

her people captive. Israel was dismembered
and obliged to pay tribute. Galilee and all the
land of Naphtali were subdued, and their population carried captive to Assyria.[1] And Ephraim,
though humilated and dismembered, raised his
head higher than ever with the words: "In
place of the fallen bricks we will rebuild with
hewn stones; for the sycamores that are cut
down, will we put cedars in their place."[2] The
new king, Hosea, forms compacts with Egypt,
a mere shadow of the old conquering Egypt, a
"frail reed that pierces the hand of him who
leans upon it." "The guides of this people
lead them astray," exclaimed Isaiah, "and those
whom they lead are engulfed. Also, Jehovah
will cut off the head and tail from Israel in one
day."[3] Israel, rebel against Assyria, succumbed after three years' resistance (721), her
last king dying on the shores of the Tigris.

Isaiah had already been prophesying for
many years in Judah when the news arrived of
the downfall of Samaria. For a long time he
had preached in the style of Amos against the
cupidity of the rich, against the iniquity of the
judges, against the hollowness of the worship.
"Woe unto them that join house to house, that
add field to field, till there is no place left, so
that they may be there alone![4] Woe unto

---

[1] 2 Kings xv. 29.   [2] Isaiah ix. 10.
[3] Isaiah ix. 10, 14.   [4] Isaiah v. 8.

them that rise up early in the morning to run after wine, that prolong the night in the heat of drunkenness. The lyre and the harp, the tambourine, the flute and wine, that is their life; but the work of the Lord they do not regard. Therefore my people will go into captivity unexpectedly. Sheol will open its gaping jaws, and all this brilliant pomp, this joyous throng, and all this magnificence shall descend into it.[1]

"Woe unto them that decree unrighteous decrees, and to the clerks that write unjust sentences, turning aside the needy from judgment, taking away the right from the poor of my people. And what will you do in the day of reckoning, and in the desolation which shall come from afar?[2]

"To what purpose is the multitude of your sacrifices to me? saith Jehovah. I am sated with the burnt-offerings of rams, and the fat of fed beasts. Bring no more vain oblations. Incense is an abomination unto me, and your new moons and sabbaths, your solemn assemblies. I hate them, they are a trouble to me, I am weary of them. When you spread your hands towards me, I will hide my eyes from you, for your hands are full of blood. Wash and cleanse yourselves. Put away your evil doings from before my eyes. Cease to do evil! Learn to do good, seek justice!"[3]

---

[1] Isaiah v. 11 *sq.*   [2] Isaiah x.   [3] Isaiah i. 11 *sq.*

Despair often possessed the prophet. In vain had the seraph purified his lips with the live coal from the altar of the Lord. The nation to which he spoke remained impure, and his words fell upon indifferent and insensible ears. Then, like all disillusioned apostles, — like Moses of old, he appealed from the present generation to a generation to come, and with bitter irony declared himself sent by God to steel the heart of his people. "Go and tell this people: hear ye indeed, but understand not! and see without perceiving! Render the heart of this people insensible, make their ears heavy, and shut their eyes; lest they see with their eyes, and hear with their ears, and understand with their heart, and be converted and be healed!

"Then said I, Lord, how long? And he answered, Until the cities are ruined and depopulated, and the country laid entirely waste. And if there remain a tenth of the inhabitants, they shall be decimated in turn. And like the terebinth and the oak, whose trunk remains in the earth when they are cut down, their trunk will become a holy race."[1]

In the mean time, under the lash of these disappointments, the soul and the dream of the prophet continued to broaden. Amos and Hosea dream only of moral salvation for Israel and

[1] Isaiah vi.

the chosen people. The rest of the world is
unknown to them, or is merely the unconscious
instrument of the reform and salvation of Israel. What Isaiah sees, is Israel saved, and
saving the world. In the midst of nations
given over to brutal games, he' dreams for
Israel the ascendency of noble example and of
the ideal. He sees a day coming, at the end
of time, when the mountain of Jehovah's house
shall be exalted above all the mountains, and
all nations shall stream unto it, and throngs of
people shall come saying: "Come ye, and let us
go up to the mountain of Jehovah, to the house
of the God of Israel, that he may teach us of
his ways, and that we may walk in his paths.
*For from Zion shall go forth instruction, and
from Jerusalem the word of the Eternal!*"[1]
The decisive word is launched, a universal religion is founded.

The fall of Samaria, in 721, agitated men's
consciences profoundly. The prophets utter a cry
of mingled triumph and sadness. In the presence of the immensity of the point at issue — the
salvation of the nation and the salvation of souls
— the tame and ungenerous reproach, "Did we
not tell you so?" took on a supernatural meaning. Had not God said so? Judah, half re-
joiced, half terrified by the downfall of her
sister enemy, sees the truth of the prophetic

[1] Isaiah ii. 2 *sq.*

doctrines, bursting forth with a sinister gleam
out of the flame that consumed Samaria. Why
should Judah escape Israel's fate, if she, too,
remain deaf to the divine voice, and show herself still blinder with the example before her
of threats that had been realized? And the
princes and the people ceased their raillery for
an instant when the prophets, lashing them with
the charges that had been brought against Israel,
announced the inevitable punishment following
upon the pride and egotism of the rich, upon
the harshness and impurity of morals, upon the
madness of a policy dragging itself in the
beaten track of duplicity and international violence.

By a fortunate chance, at the time of the
fall of Samaria, the throne of Judah was occupied by Hezekiah, a young man of twenty-
eight, highly gifted, lettered, and open to new
ideas, while independent enough to pursue his
own policy, and to maintain his independence
even in the presence of Isaiah. He placed his
enthusiasm and his power at the service of the
prophet; he became the Constantine, or rather,
the Açoka, of idealistic Jehovism. The reform
was first evident in the cult, — an indication that
the sacerdotal caste, hitherto indifferent or hostile, and with no particular antipathy to idolatry, was taking part in the prophetic movement.
From this compromise between sacerdotal Je-

hovism and prophetic Jehovism resulted, within a century and a half, organized Judaism. Through this compromise the conception of the prophets abandoned its high plane; but this was necessary, in order that the idea should become real. A religion, however lofty, can influence mankind only by external forms that give it a mould capable of resistance, by the necessary mummery without which mankind does not take ideas seriously. If prophecy had remained in the realm of spirit, it would never have been able to penetrate Israel, and through Israel the world.

The transformation of ritual Jehovism to prophetic Jehovism greatly raised the moral standard of the nation and of the government. The reign of Hezekiah was one of literary and political prosperity. Himself a poet, he surrounded himself with poets; perhaps among the latter was the author of the greatest religious poem ever written, the Book of Job, — that tragic conflict of doubt and faith which, through the medium of poetry, balances the protest of conscience against the triumph of wickedness, the misgiving of innocence vainly searching for the crime which it is compelled to expiate, and a mournful, vague confidence in the final justice of God. The ancient kingdom of Israel, devastated and depopulated by the Assyrians, fell into the hands of Hezekiah, by reason of the

disturbances in Assyria that followed the death
of the conqueror of Samaria, so that the ruin
of Samaria had on the whole brought about the
reëstablishment of the national unity.   The
kingdom of David was reëstablished, and the
prophet, hailing Hezekiah as the child of Jehovah, uttered a cry of triumph which seven centuries later gave birth to Christ.

"No more darkness for the one who formerly
dwelt in anguish.   The land of Naphtali [1] has
been afflicted in the past; future days shall
glorify the shores of the lake [2] beyond Jordan,
the district of the Gentiles.   The people that
walked in darkness have seen a great light,
they that dwelt in the land of the shadow of
death.   For unto us a child is born, unto us a
son is given, the empire rests upon his shoulder.
His name shall be Wonderful, Counsellor, Hero
of God, the Everlasting Father, the Prince of
Peace, born to increase the empire and bring
peace without end to the throne of David and
to his kingdom, to reëstablish it and strengthen
it with right and with justice from henceforth
forever." [3]

Hezekiah thus became the prototype of the
Messiah, or rather — since the idea of the far-

[1] Forming the district of the Gentiles, or Galilee, whose
population in the preceding generation was deported to Assyria.

[2] The Lake of Genesareth.

[3] Isaiah ix.   Cf. Matthew iv. 13–16.

distant Messiah, the Messiah of the latter days
was not yet in existence — he was the Messiah himself, the anointed of the Lord. And
when, eight centuries later, in the days of the
Roman persecutions, at a time when the expectation of the avenging Messiah was the sole
vital force remaining to Israel, the proscribed
Jews asked of their leaders, "When forsooth
will the promised Messiah come who is to save
us?" an old rabbi, shaking his head sadly,
answered them: "The time for the Messiah is
past, the Messiah will come no more; for he
has already come: his name was Hezekiah."

The fall of Samaria had strikingly demonstrated the divine character of prophecy. History steadily advanced the cause by facts. Samaria, because of her infidelity and perverseness towards Jehovah, fell before the Assyrian;
the latter did not know that he was merely the
instrument of Supreme Justice, and he descended upon Jerusalem ripe for conversion.[1]
The plague saved Jerusalem, and the prophet,
in the secret of Jehovah, cried aloud: —

"Woe be to Assyria, the rod of mine anger,
the staff to which I have intrusted my vengeance! Does the axe boast to him who handles it? or does the saw raise itself against him
who puts it in motion? Therefore shall the

[1] The invasion of Sennacherib: Isaiah xxxvi., xxxvii.; 2
Kings xviii. 13 fin. xix.

Lord, the Lord of Hosts, send leanness among his fat captains, and upon his glory he shall kindle a burning flame. Be not afraid, oh my people who dwell in Zion, of this Assyrian who smites thee with a rod, and lifts up his staff against thee, after the manner of Egypt. The axe of Jehovah passes over the high branches of Ashur, and the forest of Lebanon is hewn to the earth." [1]

Then, at the sight of the crushed Assyrian, a vision of peace that has ever since haunted the universe passes before the eyes of the prophet. War had come to an end, hatred had ceased, Jehovah became the arbiter of nations. The nations no longer raised the sword against one another, and swords were to be forged into ploughshares. The race of David was to supply the ideal king, the judge upon whom the spirit of Jehovah would rest, the spirit of intelligence and wisdom, the spirit of knowledge and of the fear of Jehovah ; he will not judge from hearsay, but will judge the feeble with justice, and will decide with equity in behalf of the humble. The wolf shall dwell with the lamb; the calf, the lion, and the sheep shall pasture together, and a little child shall lead them all. For there will be no more sin, no more evil over the whole domain of the sacred mountain; and the knowledge of God will fill

[1] Isaiah x. 5.

the earth as the waters cover the bed of the ocean.[1]

V.

The triumph of prophecy did not last. Hezekiah died, and left as his heir Manasseh, a child twelve years old (696). The regency was the signal for a *libertine* reaction which lasted sixty years. The long reign of Manasseh — more than half a century — bore the same relation to Hezekiah's reign as did the restoration of the Stuarts to the reign of Cromwell's saints and of the Puritans. They had had enough of the morality of Isaiah and his school; of these men constantly inveighing against the people of the world, ever talking of an insolent, angry God, these men who insisted upon dwelling on the miseries of one's neighbor, as though it were not quite sufficient to be occupied with one's own pleasures. The reaction carried with it the prophetic Jehovah, his code of morality, and his social doctrines. Jerusalem again became the hospitable rallying point of all the gods of Syria, who erected their altars even in the temple of Jehovah. Manasseh himself, it is said, made his sons pass through the fires of Moloch. Sorcerers, wizards, magicians, were all-powerful at court, and pleasure reigned supreme for an entire half-century.[2] Prophecy

---

[1] Isaiah xi. 1 *sq.*   [2] 2 Kings xxi. 1–9.

was reduced to silence; there was not a single prophet in Manasseh's time.

A child's regency had taken away the power of the prophets; a child's regency gave it back to them (639). A popular reaction of which we can see only the effects without being able to follow its history, and doubtless superinduced by the excesses of the old régime, brought the proscribed doctrines again into favor. This reaction found a powerful exponent in the person of a priest of Benjamin, Jeremiah.

Jeremiah generally figures as the prophet of the Jeremiads. He owes this reputation to a small collection of elegies upon the fall of Jerusalem, of which he is not the author. In the forty years of his prophetic carer he preached, he stirred up, he cursed; he lamented but little. Once he lamented over the death of King Josiah; but this death, that shattered all his dreams of the future, left him no tears for the other events of the century. With Jeremiah, in fact, prophecy becomes conscious of the radical impossibility of realizing, in the present, the reforms capable of saving the nation. He abandons all hope of the nation that is voluntarily and inevitably running its ruinous course, and dreams only of preparing future nations that shall rise out of the ashes of the present one.

Jeremiah was a priest, the first prophet-

priest. I hardly venture to go to the length of
M. Renan, who sees in Jeremiah a new form
of prophecy in which the priest dominates the
prophet. "The religious character," says M.
Renan, "becomes more pronounced; the tribune
leans towards the priest. Amos and Hosea —
and at certain moments Isaiah — astonish us
by their boldness, their love of the people, their
disinterestedness in regard to theological and
liturgical questions. Their anger pleases us.
When they see how unjust the world is, they
would like to shatter it in pieces. They reason
somewhat like the anarchists of our day: if the
world cannot be bettered, it must be destroyed.
Jeremiah is very much less occupied with the
social question, and with the triumph of the
anavim. He is, above all, a pious man, characterized by a rigid morality. He is a fanatic,
it must be confessed, full of hatred towards his
adversaries, stigmatizing all who do not at once
admit his prophetic mission as reprobates, for
whom he wishes and foretells death."[1] I, for
my part, confess that I find it difficult to recognize, in the substance of the utterances of
Jeremiah, any essential characteristic that dis-
tinguishes him from previous prophets. Priest
he undoubtedly was, and from the historical
texts it is evident that he exercised considerable
influence upon the caste to which he belonged.

---

[1] *Histoire du peuple d'Israel*, iii. p. 154.

It is probable that he accomplished its conversion to prophetic Jehovism, and availed himself of it to bring about the triumph of his platform. But the priest in him is merely the servant and the instrument of the prophet; in him, as in Isaiah, the prophet is uppermost, that is to say, the reformer of the moral life, of the social life, of the political life. The only difference lies in the singular personal character of the man, and in the equally singular circumstances that surrounded him. Jeremiah is certainly the natural and legitimate successor of Isaiah, but with a ruggedness of character, an intensity of conviction, an indomitable courage, and a contempt for all conventionalities and popular prejudices, that make of him an unequaled individual in the most individual group of men that ever existed. He did not make his appearance, like Isaiah, at a comparatively happy time: he appeared at an unfortunate moment, at a time of irreparable blunders, in the furnace of final catastrophes. He is the prophet of the *Finis Hierosolymæ!*

Jeremiah commenced his propaganda in his native village of Anathoth. The ground was doubtless not very favorable, nor the authorities very patient; his compatriots drove him away with threats of death. He left Anathoth with Job's sad question on his lips: "Thou art always righteous, O Jehovah, and how can I

argue against thee? Yet must I tell thee that
which I think. Why does the way of the
wicked prosper? Why do those who deal treach-
erously live in peace? Thou hast planted them
and they have taken root, they grow and they
bring forth fruit; and nevertheless thou art
near their lips only, and far from their heart.
And me, Jehovah, thou knowest, me thou hast
seen, thou hast tried my heart." [1] But in spite
of all his trials, he is filled with the absorbing and overwhelming certainty of his mission;
and it saves him from discouragement. "Before I formed thee in thy mother's womb I
knew thee, said the Lord; before thou camest
forth out of her entrails, I had sanctified thee
and had ordained thee prophet to the nations.
Then said I, Alas, Lord Jehovah, I cannot
speak, I am but a child. And Jehovah answered: Say not, I am but a child; to all that
I shall send thee thou shalt go; and whatsoever I command thee, thou shalt speak. Be
not afraid before them, for I am with thee to
protect thee, the word of the Eternal. And
Jehovah put forth his hand, and touched my
lip, and said unto me: Behold, I put my
words on thy lip. Lo, I have this day set thee
over the nations and over the kingdoms, to root
out and to pull down, to destroy and to demol-
ish, to build and to plant." [2]

[1] Jeremiah xi. 21 *sq.*; xii. *sq.*   [2] Jeremiah i. 5 *sq.*

Jeremiah proceeded from Anathoth to Jerusalem, the place where the battle was to be won
or lost. There he found unhoped-for auxilia-
ries in the temple itself. The high priest Hilkiah was won over to the prophetic cause, and
prophecy, stifled under Manasseh, was revived
in the heart of a woman, the prophetess Hul-
dah.[1] The young prophet of Anathoth brought
fresh ardor and energy into this charged atmosphere that was merely awaiting a directing
force. Had he a personal influence upon the
young king scarcely twenty-two years old? Perhaps. In any case, the apostleship of Jeremiah
was a fortunate one, and scarcely four years
had passed when a decisive event occurred.
The news suddenly spread that the high priest
Hilkiah had found in the temple the "Book of
the Law of Jehovah." The king had the book
read to him from beginning to end, and this
reading moved him so deeply that he had it
read publicly before all the assembled people,
and promulgated it as the law of the nation.[2]

Modern criticism has demonstrated, in a
manner leaving little room for doubt, that this
book of the Law, found again, it is said, in the
temple, is no other than the book of Deuteronomy, that fine, systematic summary of Mo-
saic legislation that comes at the close of the
present Pentateuch. Moreover, it is probable

---

[1] 2 Kings xxii. 8 *sq.*   [2] 2 Kings xxiii.

that the book handed to Josiah was in any case
revised, if not composed, by the prophets of
that time, and for some immediate purpose.
This has often been spoken of as a pious fraud.
The term is but half exact, and can only be
applied to the *mise en scène;* for the essence of
the book contained not an idea, not a precept,
not a threat, not a promise, that had not been
in the mouth of the prophets for the last two
centuries. Not a line of it was written for
the purpose of introducing a new idea under
cover of an ancient authority, the peculiar mark
of an Apocrypha. Deuteronomy was, indeed,
the book of the Law of Jehovah, such as the
first prophets already had in mind for Judah.
When the prophets spoke of the law of Jehovah, they were asked: "Where is this famous
law? Tell us, once for all, what it demands of
us." A book was needed to close the mouth of
the scoffers, to settle the disputed points among
men of good intent, to substitute the permanent
authority of the written word for the fleeting
influence of speech. Preaching may create a
religious ferment; to bring this ferment to
an issue a document is needed. What made
the Book of the Law an entirely new thing,
overpowering even to many who had had the
law dinned incessantly into their ears, was the
fact that for the first time it appeared in its
entirety as a systematic and coherent whole.

"This code," says M. Renan, "was one of the
boldest attempts that has ever been made to
shelter the weak;" and, more efficacious than
the intermittent and scattered utterances of the
prophets, it appealed to ready minds with all
its accumulated force.

We do not know how far the new law was
applied and became the code of the State. The
book of Kings is the work of the sacerdotal
caste, and gives us full information only regarding the purification of worship, which especially
interested the clergy, and which was, moreover,
comparatively easy of accomplishment. Ritual
precepts were applied rigorously, strange cults
were proscribed, the idolatrous priests were expelled, those who had sacrificed in the temple
were put to death; and the valley of Gehenna,
where human offerings had taken place, was
defiled.[1]   But it is easier to reform a cult than
the soul, and in the material triumph of Jehovism the old prophetic protest continued:
"When I commanded you the day that I
brought you out of Egypt, was it concerning
burnt-offerings or sacrifices?"[2]

Josiah was only twenty-six years old at the
time of the promulgation of Neo-Jehovism
(637). A long reign, like that of Manasseh,
might perhaps have brought about its realization in the law and customs, as it was realized

---

[1] 2 Kings xxiii. 3–24.   [2] Jeremiah vii. 22.

in the cult. Unfortunately Josiah was caught
in the whirl of foreign politics and perished.

Asia was upturned by a formidable revolution. Assyria had succumbed to the coalition
of nations that she had so long trodden under
foot, and had gone down to rejoin her victims in
Sheol, where she was greeted by the exultation
of the prophets: "Nineveh is laid waste, who
will bemoan her? Where are her comforters?
Thy shepherds slumber, O King of Ashur;
thy captains are in repose. And all those that
hear of thee shall clap their hands; for over
whom has not thy everlasting ferocity passed?"[1]
Babylon and Chaldea had directed the assault
against Nineveh. But Egypt, rejuvenated for
a time under the dynasty of Psammetichus,
attempted to seize the empire of the world,
dropped by Nineveh, before Chaldea had grasped
it. Necho, the king of Egypt, marched towards
the Euphrates. Josiah, vassal of Babylonia,[2]
believed it his duty to bar the way against the
adversary of his suzerain. "I have no quarrel
with thee, king of Judah," Necho said to him.
Despite this proclamation, Josiah marched
against the Egyptian, and met him at Megiddo.

[1] Nahum iii. 7, 18, 19.

[2] The alliance with Babylon, the rival of Nineveh, as the
only means of counterbalancing the formidable advance of
Assyrian conquest, was a part of the political traditions of
Judah since the days of Sennacherib and Hezekiah. 2 Kings
xx.; Isaiah xxxix.

Here Josiah fell, pierced by an arrow, and was brought back to Jerusalem to die; the men and women sang lamentations over him, that for a long time were revived each year on the anniversary of the disaster. Jeremiah composed an elegy, which is lost, upon the young king, with whom died the future of reform.[1] His son Jehoahaz, crowned king immediately thereafter, was dethroned by Necho, and after a three months' reign was taken captive to Egypt. "Weep ye not for the dead," exclaimed Jeremiah, "do not bemoan him; weep rather for him that goes away, for he shall return no more, and not see his native land again!"[2]

The death struggle of Judah began. Necho had installed as king Jehoiakim, another son of Josiah (608–598). Judah became an additional prize for Egypt in her struggle against Babylon. In order not to be crushed between two formidable adversaries, Judah had need of much political skill and much loyalty. Josiah's successors possessed neither the one nor the other. The policy of the prophets was to remain faithful to Babylon, with whom Judah had been allied since the time of Hezekiah, and who had delivered the world from Nineveh. Josiah fell at Megiddo, a victim to this policy.

[1] 2 Kings xxiii. 29; 2 Chronicles xxxv. 24, 25.
[2] Jeremiah xxii. 10.

It was the policy of Jeremiah, who doubtless had approved, perhaps counseled, Josiah's course; for otherwise, instead of weeping at his tomb, he would, according to his usual style, have hurled anathemas against him. Egypt, however, was obliged to retreat in the great duel with Babylonia. Egypt's sole power lay in the memory of her past, so that Babylon against Egypt represented a powerful reality fighting with a shadow. Necho, defeated at Karkemish, fled from the Euphrates up the Nile; Nebuchadnezzar appeared before Jerusalem, and received the homage of Jehoiakim. Though their political duty was clear, the young men who succeeded one another on the throne of Jerusalem did not perceive it. They intrigued with Egypt, worn out as she was, and gave ear to her promises, leaning upon the reed that pierced their hands. Three years later, after his submission to the Chaldean, Jehoiakim threw off the yoke, and refused to pay tribute. This was the beginning of the end. A first deportation, and the pillage of the temple cut short the rebellion (598). Jehoiakim died during the war; his son Jehoiachin, aged eighteen, after three months' reign and siege, was carried captive to Babylonia to die. The last son of Josiah, and the last king of Jerusalem, Zedekiah, renewed the mad attempt; which brought about the siege of Jerusalem, the capture and destruction of the city, the burning down of the temple, the deportation of the upper classes (588 B. C.).

From the first days of Jehoiakim, it was quite evident that not only the external policy of Josiah was abandoned, but also his internal policy, the policy of prophetic reformation. Necho, in installing Jehoiakim, had imposed a heavy tribute upon him; and in order to obtain the necessary gold, Jehoiakim was obliged to oppress the people. The reconstruction of the country would have necessitated many modest virtues, — first and foremost, economy. He thought only of building himself new palaces, in the manner of the kings, by means of statute labor. And yet the law of Jehovah said, "Thou shalt not hold back the wages of the laborer;" and Jeremiah came to the door of the palace crying, "Woe unto him that builds his house by unrighteousness, and that uses his neighbor's service without wages. Shalt thou perchance be king to hold up thy head in palaces of cedar? Thy father ate and drank also, but practiced justice and charity; blessed be he! He exercised right to the poor and the lowly; blessed be he! Therefore thus says Jehovah concerning Jehoiakim, the son of Josiah, king of Judah: Wailers shall not lament for him, saying: *Ah, my brother! ah, my sisters!* they shall not lament for him, saying:

Where is my lord? where is his glory? He
shall be given the sepulchre of an ass, to be
dragged and thrown far outside of the walls of
the city."[1] And he hurls at royalty and the
ruling classes Jehovah's ultimatum: "King of
Judah that sittest upon the throne of David,
thou and thy servants, and thy people that enter
in by these gates! — thus saith Jehovah: Exe-
cute justice and charity; deliver the despoiled
from the hand of the oppressor; do not mal-
treat, do not oppress the stranger, the orphan,
and the widow; neither shed innocent blood in
this place.[2]

"If ye do according to these words, then
shall there enter again by the gates of this
palace, kings who will seat themselves near David, upon his throne, mounted upon chariots
and horses, they with their servants and their
people.

"But if ye hear not these words, I swear by
my name, saith Jehovah, that this house shall
be given up to desolation. I have already consecrated destroyers against thee, each with his
weapon, who shall cut down thy fine cedars,
and cast them into the fire."[3]

Jehovism remained the religion of the state,
but a religion devoid of meaning. "Run ye to

[1] Jeremiah xxii. 13–19.
[2] The seat of the Court at the palace gates.
[3] Jeremiah xxii. 1 *sq.*

and fro through the streets of Jerusalem, search
in the public places. If ye can find but one
man that does good and seeks right, I will
be merciful. But even while saying Jehovah
lives, they swear falsely."[1] The blows with
which Jehovah strikes them leave them insensible. The common people, says the prophet,
sin perhaps through ignorance, because they
know not the ways of the Eternal. I will go
unto the great men who know; but the great
men are even worse in regard to brutality and
luxury: "I fed them full, and they went to
houses of debauch; they are stall-fed and las-
civious stallions; *every man neighed after his
neighbor's wife.*"[2]

They think it possible to expiate everything
with burnt-offerings and sacrifices. Did God
ask burnt-offerings and sacrifices of their fathers
when he brought them out of Egypt? When
they came to the temple to prostrate themselves
before the altar, they said to themselves: We
are saved! Is this temple, then, to which I
have attached my name, become a mere robber's den? Well then, let them go to Shiloh[3]
and see what Jehovah has made of the sanc-

---

[1] Jeremiah v. 1 *sq.*

[2] Jeremiah v. 8. A good definition of the theatre or novel
of to-day.

[3] The oldest and most celebrated of the sanctuaries of Israel.

tuary of Israel; he will do to Judah as he has
done to Israel, and to the temple of Jerusalem
as he has done to the sanctuary of Shiloh.[1]

From day to day the breach grows wider, the
disillusion and anger reach an extreme. And
just at this time Jehoiakim, yielding to the
encouragement of defenseless Egypt, challenges
Babylonia. This was Judah's sentence of
death. Then Jeremiah begins to toll the final
knell. Judah's wound is incurable; there is
no balm in Gilead.[2] Let the mothers teach
their daughters wailings, for death mounts by
the windows, invades the palaces, strikes down
the children in the street, and the young men
on the public places.[3] The vague and constant
threat of dismemberment, ruin, and exile, that
the prophets had for two centuries held over
the crimes and sins of their people, became
finally a dread and imminent reality, and it was
the blinded king who brought it upon himself.
"Because ye have not heard my words, behold
I will enlist all the tribes of the north, and with
them Nebuchadnezzar, the king of Babylon, my
servant, and will bring them against this land
and its inhabitants. And I shall cause to cease
among you the voice of mirth and the voice of
gladness, the voice of the bridegroom and the
voice of the bride, the sound of the millstones,

---

[1] Jeremiah vii. 11–14.
[2] Jeremiah viii. 22.
[3] Jeremiah ix. 20 *sq.*

and the light of the torches."[1] And from day
to day he goes to the door of the temple, and to
the door of the palace, to announce the inevitable catastrophes which he sees already present, and in announcing them he seems to invoke
them. He is exposed to the jeers of the people,
whom he frightens and angers by his predic-
tions of misfortune; to those of the soldiers,
whose indignation he arouses; to those of the
false prophets, in quest of easy popularity, who
please the people by predicting impossible victories. But God makes of him a column of
iron, a brazen wall, against Judah, her kings,
her chiefs, her priests, and her common people.
For a while, however, he grows weary of the
cruelty of his rôle, and of the outrages that are
heaped upon him. "Woe is me, oh my mother,
that thou hast borne me, a man of strife, at war
with every one, and whom every one curses."[2]
He would remain silent, to escape from the
inner voice, from the yoke of the divine mission; but Jehovah beguiles and compels him.
He is the laughing-stock and the terror of
every one; for each time he raises his voice he
is obliged to complain, to announce violence
and perils, and the word of the Lord merely
brings shame and opprobrium upon him.
"Then I said: I will no longer speak of him,
I will no longer speak in his name: but his

[1] Jeremiah xxv. 9, 10. [2] Jeremiah xv. 10; xx. 14 *sq.*

word was in my heart, like a burning fire shut up in my bones; I was worn out with keeping it, and I could not do otherwise." [1]

For the first time Jerusalem is taken (598); the higher classes are deported to Babylon. The poor little king Jehoiachin goes to expiate, in exile, the folly of his father: "As I live, saith the Eternal, though Jehoiachin the son of Jehoiakim, king of Judah, were the signet upon my right hand, yet would I pluck him hence. . . . And I will cast thee out, thee and thy mother that bare thee, into a strange country, where ye were not born, to die there. And the land whereunto their soul desires to return, thither shall they not return. Wherefore is he cast out, he and his race, into a land which they know not? Wherefore shall none of his blood sit upon the throne of David? Because the shepherds of the people of God have permitted their flock to go astray and be scattered. . . . But God will gather his erring sheep, and give them shepherds, who shall let them pasture without losing any of them." [2]

A new reign began; and the very uncertainty of the future gave rise to a last fresh hope. The new king, Zedekiah, son of Josiah, was weak but well-intentioned. One of his first acts seemed to herald a new Josiah, and to prove that the policy of reform would again

---

[1] Jeremiah xx. 9 *sq.* [2] Jeremiah xxii. 24 *sq.;* xxiii. 1 *sq.*

prevail, the prophetic programme be realized. The book of Deuteronomy restored the legal freedom of every Hebrew slave who had served for six years. Zedekiah called together the grandees and all the slave-owners, and proclaimed the emancipation of the slaves, who were thereupon set at liberty. But on the morrow succeeding this night of the fourth of August, the wealthy already regretted their generosity, which had perhaps been wrested from them in an unguarded moment. The act of enfranchisement was rescinded, and the slaves returned to their former condition. It was one of those incidents that suddenly show the depth of the abyss to which a society has fallen, incapable of being saved, and it drew from Jeremiah a terrible cry that heralds the irrevocable decree of divine justice: "You have made your brothers return to slavery, you have refused to proclaim their liberty; verily I, — by the word of Jehovah! — I will abandon you to the liberty of the sword, of pestilence, of famine!"[1]

Zedekiah in turn falls into the snare of the Egyptian alliance, and soon the Babylonian troops again encamp in front of Jerusalem, this time without hope of pardon. Egypt has abandoned Judah in the hour of peril. And Jeremiah resumes with fresh frenzy his preaching of death. He is begged to question Jehovah,

[1] Jeremiah xxxiv. 17.

to ask of him some of those miracles to which
he had accustomed them of old. Balaam, called
upon to curse Israel, blessed; Jeremiah, called
upon to bless, could only curse. Jehovah shall
come himself to combat Judah, to strike man
and beast with the pestilence, to deliver his offi-
cers and the people to Nebuchadnezzar the king,
to be exterminated without pity and without
mercy. Zedekiah secretly sends for Jeremiah
and asks: "Hast thou anything to tell me
from Jehovah?" "Yes, that thou shalt be delivered to the king of Babylon." And he
taunts them with the advice that they followed:
"Where are now your prophets who have misled
you, who prophesied unto you that the king of
Babylon would not come again against Jerusalem?" Though cast into prison, he continues
before the people who flock to hear him:
"He that remaineth in this city shall die by
the sword, by the famine, and by the pestilence,
but he that goeth forth to the Chaldeans shall
be saved." The chiefs of the army beseech the
king to have him put to death, "for he weakens
the hands of the men of war, and of the people,
by speaking such words to them." They let
him down into a pit, where he sinks in the mire
to his arms, and when he is raised up, the
only words that can be forced from him are:
"The surrender or the destruction of Jerusalem." No orator has ever made use of more

eloquence and heroism, in preaching resistance to
the utmost, than did Jeremiah in urging surrender and the abnegation of the national honor.
Judged by our modern laws and customs, Jeremiah was a traitor. He was a traitor also in the
eyes of the last chiefs of the army of Jerusalem.
But what constitutes precisely the unheard-of
grandeur of the man is that this traitor to his
country was a patriot of patriots. Jeremiah
is by no means a saint or a fanatic who would
destroy the terrestrial city for a celestial one.
Although Christianity proceeds from the prophets, there is nothing Christian in this sense
even in Jeremiah; no more than in any other
of the prophets. What he dreams of, as did all
his predecessors, is a Jewish nation on native
soil, with the national capital, — Jerusalem;
with a national dynasty, — that of David; with
a law of justice, of piety, of morality, — that of
Jehovah. These enlightened men understood
what folly it was for insignificant Judah to
attempt to play a political and victorious rôle
in the midst of the great military monarchies of
Asia and Africa. Israel was not at all equipped
for the part of persisting for centuries in
the bloody path of force and of chance; of
intriguing with one nation to-day, with another
to - morrow ; of behaving in the manner of
other nations, — devouring one's neighbor, and
being devoured by him in turn. Her princes

and chiefs may have thirsted for it, but her talons were not sufficiently powerful. The prophets had in mind for her a different part, — to raise, in the midst of the nations, the standard of the eternal law. "I have placed you as a light in the midst of the nations." At the very moment when this dream became embodied and real, when the law that was destined to bring about justice and peace in the world mounted the throne of Judah, at that moment childish fools and intriguers, politicians and charlatans, dragged Israel to her mental and moral ruin, and, for the pleasure of playing at the game of diplomacy, destroyed both the temporal nation and its universal mission for all time. If Jeremiah had allowed himself to perish at the time of the destruction, or if he had hidden his despair in his heart, and had said to himself that it is scarcely generous to triumph at the sight of the perishing people, and had witnessed the ruin of Jerusalem in silence, the world would perhaps be no worse off than it is to-day, but humanity would have missed the sound of words which can still save her, and which have consoled her for twenty-six centuries. The Decalogue and the Sermon on the Mount could never have emanated from Babylon, nor from Athens or Rome. Jeremiah displayed the unparalleled heroism of fighting against his country false to herself, for the benefit of

a future country which was not yet born, and
which as yet existed only in his heart and in
that of some disciples. He would doubtless
have preferred, as he unceasingly preached, a
prompt submission to Babylon, which, by insur-
ing the existence of the nation, would have
made reform the rallying point of the temple
and of political tradition; but since rational
counsels were powerless, destiny had to take its
course, and an entirely new future be prepared
by the present annihilation of the nation. A
new nation shall arise out of the one destroyed.

From the time of the first deportation, that
of King Jehoiachin, Jeremiah was convinced that
the Judah of the prophetic ideal could not take
root in the Holy Land until the actual Judah had
been uprooted. The first exiles rebelled at the
idea of an indefinite exile; they dreamed of a triumphant return to their brethren, and the patriotic prophets talked of a miraculous intervention
in their behalf. Two of them, Ahab and Zedekiah, were cast by Nebuchadnezzar into a fiery
furnace.[1] The aggressive foresight of Jeremiah
was more successful than were the king's execu-
tioners in dispelling these idle illusions. Letters
from him circulated among the exiles, discouraging them with regard to their own country,

---

[1] Source of the legend of the three friends of Daniel cast
by Nebuchadnezzar into the fiery furnace, who were protected by God. Jeremiah xxix. 22; Daniel chap. iii.

begging them to accept the exile in Babylonia, to plant and to build, to marry and to multiply there, and not to allow themselves to be seduced by the prophets who held out false hopes. At the end of seventy years the Lord, faithful to his promises, would bring them back again to their native land. The prophet's idea revealed itself with remarkable clearness; the span of a human life[1] had to intervene between the condemned nation and the nation of the future; it was necessary, as at the time of the other " Exodus," that no child of a corrupt nation should enter into the promised land. A new race was needed, nourished entirely by the prophetic teachings, far from the troubling influences of old factions, far from worldly ambitions, and from all political traditions, so that an absolutely new nation might be produced, fashioned according to the heart of Jehovah and of the prophets. Then Rachel, who weeps at Ramah for the loss of her children, will weep no more, and shall be consoled.[2] Jehovah will bring them all back from the lands whither his anger has scattered them; he will again lead them into the Holy Land. And he will make a new covenant with the house of Israel and the house of Judah, but not again like the one he made with their

---

[1] " What is the number of our years? Seventy or at the most eighty." — Psalms xc. 10.

[2] Jeremiah xxxi. 15.

fathers at the departure from Egypt, and which
they broke; for he will put his law in their
bosom and write it in their hearts, so that he
shall be their God and they shall be his people.
And Jerusalem shall be rebuilt, never again to
be destroyed.[1]

That very year Jerusalem and the temple
were burned. King Zedekiah had his eyes
plucked out before Nebuchadnezzar, after his
sons had been slaughtered in his presence.
New troops of exiles bent their steps across
the desert towards the provinces of Babylonia
(588).

VI.

Among the first exiles was Ezekiel, a man
brought up in the school of Jeremiah. He was,
like Jeremiah, a priest, but more imbued with
the sacerdotal idea; not through caste prejudice,
but because every material rallying point was
lost in the sudden downfall of the nation, and
it became imperative to have a visible sign of
unity, a symbol of future nationality. A sacred
nation cannot be created by the State; it requires a ritual. Sacerdotal development was
the necessary consequence of political annihilation.

Ezekiel is considered the most obscure of the
prophets. In fact, he often carries to an extreme

---

[1] Jeremiah xxxii. 36 *sq.*

limit the processes of symbolism in which the ancient prophets delighted. From the bizarre and
fantastic spectacle presented to his eyes by the
art and civilization of Chaldea he absorbed
a number of complicated and strange images.
He is the father of the Cabbala,[1] and he is
the first to fill the foaming cup of the *Apoca-
lypse* in order to pass it over to Daniel, Enoch,
John of Patmos, and many others. But beneath obscure and puzzling symbolism, his
thought is developed with an amount of clearness and logic displayed by no other prophet.

As long as Jerusalem stood, as long as the
struggle between Israel and Babylon continued,
Ezekiel echoed Jeremiah's cry of malediction, —
echoed it in Israel, which was torn between
the old, commonplace, carnal world that would
not die, and a new world, animated with the
divine spirit, striving to disengage itself from
the corpse to which it was tied. He sees Jehovah's sword taken from the scabbard, and
drawn against the wicked and the just, from
north to south. Jerusalem relies in vain upon
her senseless prophets who mislead her — jackals howling in the ruins.[2] "If they ask thee,
Wherefore groanest thou? thou shalt answer,
For a message, which when it comes [3] shall melt
every heart, shall enfeeble every hand, shall

---

[1] Ezekiel i.   [2] Ezekiel xiii. 3 *sq.*
[3] The news of the destruction of Jerusalem.

humble every spirit, paralyze every knee. The
sword is sharpened for slaughter and carnage,
furbished that it may glitter; it is sharpened
and furbished to be given into the hand of the
slayer. And it shall come upon my people,
upon the princes of Israel. Because Judah is
become dross, Jehovah shall gather her into the
midst of Jerusalem, as in a crucible, to melt
her in the fire of his anger."[1]

The fatal crisis, so long foretold, comes at
last: Jerusalem is in ashes. And now all the
wrath of Ezekiel falls; for now the hour is
come to prepare the country of the future.
Jehovah wished not to destroy his flock, but
only the bad shepherds. The shepherds of Israel fed themselves, instead of pasturing their
sheep.

"You have nourished yourselves with wool;
you have slain those which were fat; and have
not given pasture to the flock.

"You have not strengthened the weak, healed
the sick, nursed the wounded, led back the
wandering, sought the lost; you have ruled
them with force and with cruelty.

"And now they are scattered, because there
is no shepherd, and they have become the prey
of all the wild beasts."[2]

Therefore Jehovah delivers his sheep from
the mouth of the bad shepherd, and will

[1] Ezekiel xxi. 7 *sq.*; xxii. 18 *sq.*   [2] Ezekiel xxxiv. 1 *sq.*

himself pasture them. He shall gather in all countries the flock that was scattered on the day of storm, and bring it to pasture on the hill of Israel, under the care of her ancient guides. "And I will set up one shepherd over them, who shall feed them, my servant David, and I, Jehovah, will be their god, and my servant David a prince among them." [1]

In the royal interregnum, the prophet succeeds the king; it is for him to revive the soul of the nation. The Lord has established him as a sentinel responsible to the house of Israel, for the man who has received the revelation of the Lord, and keeps it to himself, is equally culpable with the man who violates it. "When I say unto the wicked, *Thou shalt die*, and thou givest him not warning to enlighten him, and turn him from his wicked way, to save his life; he, the wicked man, shall die for his sin, but thee will I hold accountable for his blood." [2] For a new justice shall enter the world, and shall abolish the terrible hereditary fatality that requires each generation to expiate the faults of the preceding, and Jehovah to punish the sinner unto the fourth generation. It shall no longer be said: "Our fathers have eaten sour grapes, and our teeth are set on edge." [3] "The son shall no longer die for the sin of the fathers,

---

[1] Ezekiel xxxiv. 23. [2] Ezekiel iii. 17 *sq.*

[3] Ezekiel xviii. 2; comp. Jeremiah xxxi. 29.

the guilty alone shall die: to the righteous shall
be dealt righteousness, and to the wicked wickedness. And if the wicked turn from his wickedness, and do that which is right, he shall not
die, he shall live; for Jehovah takes no pleasure
in the death of the wicked, but that he should
return from his ways and live." [1]

And in this manner the future way is prepared by this same Nebuchadnezzar who destroyed Jerusalem. All the enemies of Judah,
all those, great and small, who oppressed or
betrayed her, or led her into temptation, or ap-
plauded her downfall, perish under the stroke
of the divine instrument, — Ammon, Edom, the
Philistines who howled with joy when the sanctuary was profaned, the country laid waste, the
people exiled; Moab, who exclaimed, "Where
is Jehovah? You see indeed that Judah is like
other peoples;" [2] Tyre, the jealous, who exclaimed, "She is broken, the gate of the nations, and it is to me that they now look for
aid;" Tyre, the beautiful, the rich, the learned,
the mistress of the ocean, the centre of commerce of the world, into which flowed the gold
of Tarshish, the horses of Armenia, the stones
of Aram, the ivories of Damascus, the flocks
of Arabia, the perfumes of Sheba, the slaves of
Javan. For thirteen years she is besieged by

---

[1] Ezekiel xviii., imitated from Jeremiah xxxi. 27 *sq.*
[2] Ezekiel xxv.

Nebuchadnezzar, and now that she goes down
into the sea with her wares, her sailors, and her
mercenaries, the lament shall arise: "Who was
like unto Tyre, to her who perished in the bosom
of the ocean?"[1] And then comes the turn of
Egypt, the traitress, who by deceitful alliances
caused the destruction of Judah. "To thee, now,
Pharaoh, king of Egypt, great crocodile cower-
ing in thy river! But I will put a hook in
thy jaws; I will attach to thy scales all the
fish of thy river; I will drag thee into the desert, thee and all the fish of thy river, and thou
shalt remain stranded upon the coast, and I
will give thee as food to the wild beasts and
to the birds of heaven."[2] And Pharaoh slain
goes down to Sheol and is consoled at finding
there the heaped-up corpses of Elam, Meshech,
Tubal, Edom, and the Zidonians, and at the
very bottom of the abyss Asshur and her multi-
tudes, slain by the sword for having brought
slaughter into the land of the living.[3] Perhaps
in the depths of the prophet's heart there already arose a hymn of triumph over the future
downfall of the instrument of all this vengeance,
the great Chaldean slayer. For were there not
some among his victims of greater worth than
he? The faults and the follies of Israel and
of the world had rendered inevitable the un-

[1] Ezekiel xxvi., xxvii., xxviii.   [2] Ezekiel xxix., xxxi.
[3] Ezekiel xxxii.

bridling of the monster that chastened them, but
already there were prophets who thought that
Jehovah had chosen an atrocious avenger.

"Art thou not, from everlasting time,
O Jahve, our God, our holy one,
who preserveth us from death ?

"Jahve, thou hast established [1] him as avenger
Rock, [2] thou hast appointed him to chastise.

"Thou, whose eyes are too pure to look upon iniquity,
who canst not suffer the sight of evil,
how canst thou then behold these perfidious men ?
how keep silent when the wicked devoureth the man
        more righteous than he ?

"Thou hast reduced mankind to the state of the fishes,
of the reptiles of the sea, that have no King.

"These people fish for them with their fish-hooks,
catch them in their nets,
gather them in their snares,
then are they content, they leap for joy.

"Shall we see them always empty their nets
to begin again to slay the nations, without pity ?" [3]

And the scheme of Jehovah and the prophets unfolds itself with clearness and calm

---

[1] The Chaldeans.

[2] The word *sour* (rock) almost became one of the names for
God.

[3] Habakkuk i. 12–17. [Darmesteter reproduces Renan's
beautiful translation. — TR.]

audacity: "When those of the house of Israel dwelt in their own land, they defiled it by their conduct and their crimes. And I poured my fury upon them for the blood that they had shed upon the land, and for the idols with which they had polluted it, and I scattered them amongst the nations. . . . And I will gather you out of all the countries, and bring you back into your own land. And I will put a new spirit within you. I will take away from your bosom this heart of stone, and put there a heart of flesh, and you shall dwell in the land that I gave to your fathers; you shall be my people, and I will be your God."[1] What! the day after the defeat, the dispersion, the ruin, shall there be room again for a nation of Israel, for a Jewish country, for a new Jerusalem? Yes! And the prophet saw himself transported in spirit to a valley covered with bones, and the Eternal asked him: "Son of man, can these dead bones revive? Lord Jehovah, thou alone knowest. Well then! Prophesy upon these bones, and say to them: Oh, ye dry bones, hear the word of Jehovah. I will cause breath to enter you, that you shall live; I will put sinews upon you, and flesh and skin, and put breath in you, that you shall live and know Jehovah." And while the prophet prophesied according to the command, a great noise arose,

[1] Ezekiel xxxvi. 17 *sq.*

and the bones came together with a crash.
And he beheld the sinews, and the flesh forming, and the skin spreading over them. But
there was no breath in them. And God says,
"Prophesy unto the wind and say: Come from
the four winds of the earth, oh breath! and
breathe into these corpses of the slain, that they
may revive! And the breath entered into them
and they returned to life, and they stood upon
their feet, an exceedingly great concourse. And
God said, These bones are the house of Israel.
Israel says to herself: Our bones are dried, our
hope is lost, there is an end to us. . . . Well
then! say to them, Thus saith the Lord Jehovah: I will open your graves, and cause you
to come up out of your graves, and I will put
my spirit into you, that you may come back to
life, and I will place you in your own land;
then shall you know that I, Jehovah, have
spoken it and have done it."[1]

Five years ago, while in India, I met three
rabbis, one from Warsaw, one from Jerusalem,
and the third from Bokhara, who were making
a tour of Asia, seeking alms for their brethren.
The one from Jerusalem told me that, in the
course of his wanderings through Persia, he
had found, to the north of Teheran, a village
named Gilead, entirely peopled with Jews, de-

[1] Ezekiel xxxvii.

scended from the bones resuscitated by Ezekiel.
He did not know that he himself was one of
these, and that all Israel descends from these
corpses revived by prophecy.

Thus the prophet, transported in thought to
the Jerusalem to come, reconstructs its temple,[1]
describes its proportions and forms, organizes
the future priesthood, the new cult, lays out
the geographical plan of the reorganized kingdom, and divides it among the tribes that have
come back from the four corners of exile. This
plan of the constitution of the future, full of
material impossibilities, is half ideal, half alle-
gorical. One part, that concerning the priesthood and the cult, has become reality; the other
is still a shadow. The whole is summed up in
the final word of Ezekiel: "And the name of
the city shall henceforth be, *Here is Jehovah.*"

VII.

The seventy years demanded by Jeremiah
were not required to make the new nation.
Two generations had scarcely passed away when
Babylon fell in turn, and Cyrus reopened to the
exiles the road to Palestine. The work of education of the prophets was accomplished (536
B. C.).

---

[1] Recently restored by Messrs. Perrot and Chipiez.

The prophetic cry that for two centuries accompanies all the great events of history, com-
ments on and explains them in the name of
Jehovah, was uttered by a great poet, whose
name has remained unknown, and who is of all
the one, perhaps, whose voice has reached the
farthest, for his imagery and his metaphors
created a new god. By general accord, he is
known as the second Isaiah, because the com-
pilers of the Bible have put his work after
that of Isaiah, who lived a hundred and fifty
years before him, but whose pupil and successor
he evidently is.

The acclamations with which he salutes Cyrus do not at all recall those with which Jeremiah saluted Nebuchadnezzar. The Chaldean
came in order to accomplish the necessary destruction, the Persian comes for deliverance and
restoration. Nebuchadnezzar was the instrument of the vengeance of Jehovah, Cyrus that
of his mercy. In the interval between the two,
the transplanted remnant of Israel had grown
into the way of the Lord; the dispersion had
purified the sin of Jacob.[1]

When the news spreads that Cyrus was
marching against Babylon, a cry of joy and
triumph arose in the heart of the prophets.
The restoration, so long foretold, is about to be
accomplished ; the last act of the prophetic

[1] Isaiah xxvii.

drama begins; the divine plan shall be carried
out.   Everything bends before a liberator sent
by a God whom he does not know.   God desires to repeople Judah and to rebuild Jerusalem; therefore he takes Cyrus by the hand, goes
before him, makes the crooked places straight,
breaks in pieces the gates of brass, cuts asunder
the bars of iron, delivers to him the hidden
treasures.[1]   The god Bel falls; Nebo is over-
turned, and all the golden idols are saddled upon
the beasts of burden, whom they weary with
their weight.[2]   The Eternal has broken the staff
of the wicked, the rod of the oppressor; the
whole earth breaks forth into a cry of joy; even
the cypress trees rejoice, and the cedars of
Lebanon that he hewed down for his palaces :
" Since thou art laid down, the axe shall no
longer come up against us."   And in Sheol all
the spectres of the tyrants of old, whom he cast
down, rise up to receive the new-comer and ex-
claim: "See, thou art also become wounded as
we, thou art become like unto us!   Thy pomp
has come down to Sheol, and the voice of thy
lyres! And those that see thee now, say: What!
Is this he who caused the earth to tremble, and
empires to shake ? "[3]

How could Israel lose heart and say: "My
fate is indifferent to Jehovah, God has forgot-

---

[1] Isaiah xlv. 1 *sq.*   [2] Isaiah xlvi. 1 *sq.*

[3] Isaiah xiv. 4 *sq.;* an imitation of Ezekiel xxxii.

ten me "? "Could a woman forget her suckling
child, a mother the fruit of her womb? They
may forget, but I, Jehovah, will not forget
thee.[1] Dost thou not therefore know, Israel?
Dost thou not then understand that Jehovah is
always God? That he has raised up from the
Orient one upon whose heels follows victory?[2]
And thou, Israel, my servant, thou whom I
have chosen, seed of Abraham, my friend, thou
whom I have taken from the ends of the earth,
whom I have called from the day that thou
wert still in leading-strings, fear nothing, for I.
am with thee, I am thy god.[3] Those that wish
thee harm shall be confounded. Fear nothing,
thou worm Jacob, poor little people of Israel."[4]

For the sufferings of Israel, transformed by
triumphant prophecy, are no longer, as at the
time of Jeremiah and of militant prophecy, the
expiation of her faults, the ignominious punishment for her sins; they are the price of salvation of the human soul. Jehovah had placed
his spirit in Israel, through her to acquaint
the nations with justice. It is therefore not
in vain that Israel suffered, that she was despised and rejected of men, a people of sorrows,
acquainted with suffering. Sent by the Lord
to preach his word, she was not rebellious, and
recoiled not from the stain of sorrow. She gave

[1] Isaiah xlix. 14. [2] Cyrus.
[3] Isaiah xli. 1 *sq.* [4] Isaiah xli. 14.

her back to those that struck her, her cheek to those that insulted her, and hid not her face although reviled and spat upon.[1] As the lamb that is led to the slaughter, as the sheep is dumb before the shearer, she opened not her mouth, and therefore she shall not die. Men believed her stricken of God, whereas it is to reclaim them from their sins that she was afflicted, it was for their salvation that she was chastised.[2] And she neither grows weary nor discouraged that justice may be established upon the earth; and the far-off islands await her instruction. Jehovah makes Israel the legislator of nations; the nations that know her not shall hasten to her. She shall lead the stranger to her holy mountain; for the house of Jehovah shall be called a house of prayer for all people.[3]

And the poet sees the dawning of a new world where all the past shall be forgotten, where cries of distress shall be no longer heard, and where man shall sin no more; where mothers will no longer in bearing children suffer a sudden death, where men shall not be cut off in the prime of life, where the youngest shall die at the age of a hundred, and where the sinner shall not be cursed for longer than a hundred years.

[1] Isaiah l. 5, 6. [2] Isaiah liii. 2 sq.
[3] Isaiah lv. 4, 5; lvi. 8.

VIII.

Stirred up by these great hopes, which, six
centuries later, were thought to be realized
under new forms and symbols traced back to
the metaphors of the prophet, a portion of the
exiles again took up the staff of pilgrimage,
took down the lyres that hung on the willows
of the rivers of Babylon, crossed the wilderness, and ascended the mountain of Zion, singing: —

"When the Eternal brought back the captives of Zion,
    we were as in a dream.
. . . Then our lips filled with mirth, our mouth with
    shouts of triumph !" [1]

And then Israel attempted to convert the
prophetic dream into reality, and to organize,
in place of the former prosaic country, a country at once terrestrial and divine, material and
ideal.   Reality soon brought a terrible awakening, silencing all shouts of triumph.

A day came when, in the presence of actual
disappointments, the nation was divided, and a
party arose, saying, "The kingdom foretold is
not of this world."   The prophet's conception
became an image and an allegory, and Christianity, accepting a dogma borrowed from Greek
philosophy, one which prophetic Judaism had

[1] Psalm cxxvi. 1, 2.

always ignored, — the belief in the resurrection and in future rewards and punishments, — set aside the problem that was troubling the conscience of Israel, by transferring its solution to another world.

This is not the place to examine how and why the time came when one portion of humanity ceased to be content with the Christian solution. The new birth of science in the sixteenth century, the destructive philosophy of the eighteenth, and the Revolution, brought back the question to the same position in which it had been placed by the ancient prophets, — the realization of justice on earth without the support of a reward beyond the tomb. In consequence, humanity finds itself, after twenty-seven centuries, facing the same problem that presented itself at the time of the shepherd Amos and King Jeroboam II. For this reason, these old pages still appeal so strongly to minds that have thrown off belief in gods and the other world, with all the other beliefs in which they had been cradled for eighteen centuries. "All of us," says the great historian of our moral crises, "all of us who seek a god without priests, a revelation without prophets, a covenant inscribed on the heart, are in many respects the disciples of these old deluded thinkers." Nay, not deluded, for they sought God in their hearts and found him. Their Jehovah was, after all, only the dominant conscience of certain men deified, the human conscience projected heavenward; and to-day, in the religious ruin of the century, that conscience is always present, always ready, with its gloom, its uncertainties, its good intentions, to respond to the cry of strong minds. The prophets were the first to utter this cry, and they did so for all time. They uttered in words of inextinguishable ardor the cry of a noble instinct, in a form so simple, so universal, so free from the fleeting fancies of religious poetry, so purely and triumphantly humane, that, after twenty-seven centuries, disciples of Voltaire upon hearing it wonder to find their own conscience bow before it. The historical power of the prophets is exhausted neither by Judaism nor by Christianity, and they hold a reserve force for the benefit of the coming century. The twentieth century is better prepared than the nineteen preceding it, to understand them, and they can still say to-day as of old: "The word issuing from my lips will not return to me without effect."

It is true that the horizon of modern humanity is not that of the seers of Ephraim. Humanity now has an additional torment which troubled them but little, the scientific torment, which no moral revelation can heal, and which the prophets do not speak. It springs not from the heart of man, the source of all certainty, but from his lack of heart; it comes down upon him from the stars, it ascends to him from the depth of the ages. It is for science, with its slow and progressive revelations, with its beautiful waking dreams, to pour, drop by drop, its balm upon a wound that will always bleed. Still, the lights of science are cold, like those of a polar sun, and for souls instinctively bad, its balm is a narcotic or a poison. It will not be wholesome or vivifying unless it find again in the moral instinct the sap and warmth of life, and unless it is employed in realizing God in man.

Nineteen centuries have passed since the noblest spirit of Rome, in the presence of the vileness of the gods and of the priests, uttered a cry of outraged intelligence: "Nor does piety consist in showing one's self constantly, with veiled face, before a stone, and approaching all the altars, nor in prostrating one's self on the ground, and stretching out open hands towards the sanctuaries, nor in sprinkling the altars with the blood of beasts, but in contemplating the universe with a calm mind."

" Nec pietas ulla est velatum saepe videri
   Vortier ad lapidem, atque omneis accedere ad aras
   Nec procumbere humi prostratum, et pandere palmas
   Ante deum delubra, neque aras sanguine multo

Spargere quadrupedum, nec votis nectere vota :
Sed mage pacata posse omnia mente tueri." [1]

And eight centuries before Lucretius, the
god of the shepherd Amos exclaims: "I hate
your feast days, your holocausts I despise;
from your offerings of fat beasts I turn away
my eyes. Away from me with the noise of your
songs, that I may not hear the sound of your
lyres! But let righteousness gush forth as
water, and justice as a never-failing stream."

The religion of the twentieth century is to be
found in these two cries: it will arise out of the
fusion of prophecy with science.

---

[1] Lucretius, *De Rerum Natura*, book v. ll. 1197-1202. — Ed.

AFGHAN LIFE IN AFGHAN SONGS.

On the night of the 7th of April, 1886 (Wednesday, eleven P. M.), as I was sitting in the garden of my bungalow at Peshawer, gazing at the stars and the silver moon, I heard my Afghan *chaukidar*,[1] old Piro, of the Khalil tribe, muttering in a broken voice, fragments of a song that sounded like a love-song. I asked him to repeat the song to me; this he modestly declined to do for a long time, but at last he gave way, and began:—

"My love is gone to Dekhan, and has left me alone :
I have gone to him to entreat him.
'What is it to me that thou shouldst become a Raja at
     Azrabad?'[2]
I seized him by the skirt of his garment and said: 'Look
     at me!'"

Here old Piro stopped, and neither for love nor for money could I prevail upon him to go on; his *répertoire* was exhausted. But my interest had been awakened, and from that night I resolved to collect what I could of the Afghan

[1] As life and property are not very safe at Peshawer, it is usual to keep an armed watchman, called *chaukidar*.

[2] Hyderabad, a favorite place of resort for Afghan adventurers and *soldats de fortune*.

popular poetry; the field was new and unexplored: English people in India care little for Indian songs.

I had gone to the border to study the Afghan language and literature, but I had soon to recognize that the so-called Afghan literature is hardly worth the trouble of a journey from Paris to Peshawer. It consists mainly of imitations and translations from the Persian, Arabic, and Hindustani. For a time, under the Moguls, an original and free spirit permeated those imitations, and Mirza Ansari, the mystical poet, or Khushhal Khan, prince of the Khatak tribe, would be accounted a true poet in any nation and any literature. But these are rare exceptions, and the theological lucubrations of the much-revered Akhun Darveza, that narrow, foul-mouthed, rancorous, and truly pious exponent of Afghan orthodoxy, the endless *rifacimenti* of Hatim Tai, the most liberal of Arabs, of Ali Hamza and the companions of the Prophet, or the ever-retold edifying story of Joseph and Zuleikha, all seem as if they had been written or copied by mediæval monks or unimaginative children.

The popular, unwritten poetry, though despised and ignored by the reading classes, is of quite a different character. It is the work of illiterate poets; but it represents *their* feelings; it has life in it, — the life of the people; it is simple, because the natural range of ideas of an Afghan is simple and limited; it is true to nature, because it represents those ideas without any moral bias or literary afterthought. Sometimes, therefore, it is powerful and beautiful, because it renders simply and truly powerful passions or beautiful feelings.

During a few months' stay on the border I collected about one hundred and twenty songs[1] of every description, — love-songs, folk-lore, hymns, romantic songs, and political ballads. If we want to know what an Afghan is, let us put all books aside and receive his own unconscious confession from the lips of his favorite poets. The confession, I am afraid, would not be much to their honor on the whole, but it will be the more sincere. This is the value of the wild, unpremeditated accents of these people: a poor thing it is, but it expresses their nature.

I.

THE AFGHANS AND THE DUMS.

The Afghans[2] are divided into three independent groups: —

---

[1] To be published, with text, translation, and commentary, in the *Bibliothèque Orientale* of the French Asiatic Society. [Since published by the Société Asiatique under the title "Chants populaires des Afghans" (1890). — ED.]

[2] *Afghan* is their Persian name: their Indian name is *Pathan;* their national name, *Pukhtun* or *Pushtun*.

1. The Afghans under British rule, or what we may call the Queen's Afghans, who inhabit the border districts along the Indus, Dera Ismail Khan, Bannu, Kohat, Peshawer, and Hazara. They were conquered in 1849, with the Sikhs, their then masters.

2. The Afghans of Afghanistan proper, or the Emir's Afghans; the only part of the race that forms something like an organized power.

3. The Afghans of Yaghistan, "the rebel or independent country;" that is to say, those Afghans who do not belong either to the British Raj or to the Emir, but live in the native national anarchy in the western basin of the upper Indus, — Svat, Buner, Panjkora, Dher, etc. The Afghan of Yaghistan is the true, unsophisticated Afghan.

Our songs were collected in the British districts of Peshawer and Hazara, but most of them express, nevertheless, the general views of the Afghans to whatever part they belong; for though there is no real nationality amongst the Afghans, yet there is a strongly marked national character, and, though nothing is more offensive to an Afghan than another Afghan, still there is nothing so much like an Afghan as another. Moreover, many of these songs come from Yaghistan, or Afghanistan. Songs travel quickly; the thousands of *Powindas* that every year pass twice across the Suleiman range, bringing

the wealth of Central Asia and carrying back
the wealth of India, bring also and carry back
all the treasures of the Afghan Muse on both
sides the mountain; and a new song freshly
flown at Naushehra, from the lips of Mohammed
the Oil-presser, will very soon be heard upon
the mountains of Buner, or down the valley of
the Helmend.

There are two sorts of poets, — the *Sha-ir* and
the *Dum*. With the *Sha-ir* we have nothing
to do; he is the literary poet, who can read,
who knows Hafiz and Saadi, who writes Afghan
Ghazals on the Persian model, who has composed a Divan. Every educated man is a
Sha-ir, though, if he be a man of good taste,
he will not assume the title; writing Ghazal
was one of the accomplishments of the old
Afghan chiefs. Hafiz Rahmat, the great Ro-
hilla captain, Ahmed Shah, the founder of the
Durani empire, had written Divans, were "Divan people," — *Ahli Divan*, as the expression
runs. The *Sha-ir* may be a clever writer, he
may be a fine writer; but he has nothing to
teach us about his people. We may safely dismiss him with honor and due respect.

The *Dum* is the popular singer and poet, for
he combines the two qualities, like our *Jongleur*
of the Middle Ages. The *Dums* form a caste;
the profession is hereditary. The *Dum* is despised by the people with literary pretensions,

who fly into a passion when one of these ignorant fellows, flushed with success, dubs himself
a *Sha-ir.* He is not a Pathan by race, though
he has been *pathanized;* he is a low sort of
creature, whom the Khans and Sardars treat as
the mediæval barons might have treated the
itinerant *Jongleur,* — despised, insulted, honored, liberally paid, intensely popular amongst
the people.

The novice *Dum* goes to a celebrated *Dum*
who is a master, an *Ustad;* he becomes his
disciple, his *shagird.* The master teaches him
first his own songs, then the songs of the great
Dums of the present and past generations.
The *Ustad* takes his *shagirds* with him to the
festivities to which he has been asked, private
or public, profane or religious: he takes them
to the *hujra,* the "common house" or town-hall
of the village, where idlers and traveling guests
meet every night to hear the news that is going
round, and listen to any man that has a tale to
tell or a song to sing. The *Ustad* pockets half
the sum given by the host, and the other half
is divided between the shagirds. When a shagird feels he can compose for himself and is able
to achieve a reputation, he leaves his master
and becomes himself an *Ustad.* I am sorry to
say that *Dums* generally are not over-sensitive
about literary honesty: plagiarism is rife among
them. A *Dum* will readily sing, as his own,

songs of the dead or the living. It is the custom that poets should insert their names in the
last line; you have only to substitute your own
name for the name of the real author or of the
former plagiarist: people will not applaud you
the less, though of course the injured party
may retort with a satire or a stab. A good
Dum may die a rich man: Mira would hardly
open his mouth anywhere under fifty rupees.
He was an illiterate man; he could not read,
but he knew by heart a wonderful number of
songs, and could improvise. You would ask
him for a song in a certain shade of feeling;
then he would go out with his men, and an hour
afterwards they would come back and sing a
beautiful chorus on the rebab. His song of
"Zakhmé" is sung wherever there are Afghans,
as far as Rampor in Rohilkhand, and Haydera-
bad of Dekhan, and sets them a-dancing as
soon as the first notes are struck. It was sung
at the Ravul Pindi interview as the national
song of the Afghans, though it is nothing more
— or, rather, nothing less — than a love-song.
An Irish journalist — Mr. Grattan Geary, of
the "Bombay Gazette" — was struck with its
melody, and had it printed. It is, I believe,
the only Afghan song that has ever been published.[1]

[1] Two songs have been translated by Mr. Thorburn in his
book on Bannu, and another by Colonel Raverty in the Introduction to his Afghan Grammar.

The people piously inclined object to song, among the Afghans as well as elsewhere; and the Mollahs inveigh against the *Dums*. There is only one occasion when even a Mollah will approve of the song of a *Dum;* it is when the Crusade, or, as the Anglo-Indians say, the Crescentade, has been proclaimed; then is the time for the *Dum* to rehabilitate himself, as he sings the glories of the Sacred War, the bliss reserved to the *Ghazi*, the roses .that grow for him in the groves above, and the black-eyed houris that come from heaven and give the dying man to drink of the sherbet of martyrdom. But in spite of the Mollahs, the *Dum* is as popular in his profane as in his semi-sacred character. Song is a passion with the Afghans; in fact, one of the few noble passions with which he is endowed. Whenever three Afghans meet together, there is a song between them. In the *hujra*, during the evening conversation, a man rises up, seizes a rebab, and sings, sings on. Perhaps he is under prosecution for a capital crime; perhaps to-morrow he will be hunted to the mountain, sent to the gallows; what matters? Every event of public or private life enters song at once, and the *Dums* are the journalists of the Afghans. I fancy the *Dum* of to-day has preserved for us faithfully enough a picture of what the Bard was with the Gauls.

II.

AFGHAN HONOR.

The supreme law for an Afghan is honor; they have the idea, and have a word for it, — *Nangi Pukhtâna*, or Afghan honor. But the word does not convey with them the same ideas as with us, and needs explanation. The *Nangi Pukhtâna* includes a number of laws, of which the chief are *Nanavatai*, *Badal*, and *Mailmastai;* that is to say, Law of Asylum, Law of Revenge, and Law of Hospitality.

"By *Nanavatai*, or 'the entering in,' the Pukhtun is expected, at the sacrifice of his own life and property if necessary, to shelter and protect any one who in extremity may flee to his threshold, and seek an asylum under his roof."[1] As soon as you have crossed the threshold of an Afghan you are sacred to him, though you were his deadly foe, and he will give up his own life to save yours; as soon as you are out he resumes his natural right to take your life by every means in his power, fair or foul.

You know of the dramatic tale by Prosper Mérimée, of the Corsican father shooting his own child because he has shown to the gendarmes the room where an outlaw had hidden himself. The Afghans have the same tale, but

[1] H. W. Bellew, *Yusufzais*, p. 212.

a degree higher in dramatic horror, because here it is the son that does justice upon his father. It is the tale of "Adam Khan and Durkhani," a tale that has been popular for more than a century, has inspired, and still inspires, many poets; it is in fact one of the subjects that every poet must treat. There are of course an infinite number of versions; I give here the one that was sung to me, in September last year, at Abbottabad, by the poet Burhan, son of the poet Nadir.

Durkhani was in love with Adam Khan, and they had pledged their faith to one another; but Durkhani's father had promised her hand to the hated Payavai. The lovers determined to flee together: —

"They left by night, and stopped in the house of Pirmamai. Of many villages, Pirmamai was the lord.

"Pirmamai's son, Gujarkhan, was the friend of Adam Khan : they had in days before exchanged turbans together.

"Gujarkhan's renown of prowess extended far and wide ; there was no man in Mandan who was a match for him.

"Durkhani said : 'Uncle Pirmamai, take us under your guard ; if Payavai carries me away, my life is ruined.'

"Pirmamai : 'Fear not, Durkhani ! I shall not deliver thee without struggle unto the hands of Payavai.

"'I have a hundred horsemen, covered with cuirass, all men of war; I have twelve hundred men, with their guns ready.

"'They will all of them give up their lives under thy eyes; he shall not carry thee from me — what dost thou fear?'

"Durkhani said to Pirmamai: 'Thou art the master; I have entered into thy courtyard; thou art my father.'

"Pirmamai said: 'Durkhani, be not afraid. Between thee and me here is the Lord as witness.'

"Pirmamai took a solemn oath, and Adam Khan and Durkhani trusted him."

Payavai pursues them, and sends before him a messenger to Pirmamai. The messenger takes his seat tranquilly near Pirmamai and says: "I am come from Payavai. He says to you: 'Give me up Durkhani: here are six hundred rupees.'" Pirmamai tried the rupees, and treasured them in his house, and was one in heart with Payavai.

Adam Khan had gone to a hunting party; Pirmamai sends Gujarkhan to Mahaban; Payavai arrives; Pirmamai enters the room of Durkhani and says: "Durkhani, quick, get up; the enemy is come; all my men have been hanged." "For pity's sake," cries Durkhani, "give me not up. The Pukhtuns keep their word; they are under the law of honor." "You speak in vain," shouts Pirmamai; "Payavai is too useful to me." She cries, she struggles, she curses him. "The man without honor will be despised: that word will be remembered to the day of Resurrection."

"Gujarkhan was coming home from his journey : the skirts of his turban were floating from his shoulders.

"A man told him : 'Gujarkhan, thy father, has given up Durkhani to Payavai : Payavai has carried her a prisoner.'

"Gujarkhan cried out : 'Where is my father ? Tell me : fire goes out of my body.'

"Pirmamai stood under the shelter of a wall ; he himself heard these words.

"Quickly he sprang upon his horse and fled away ; sweat ran down from his forehead out of fear.

"Gujarkhan galloped upon a white horse ; he let him loose behind Pirmamai ; he let the two reins lie on the neck of the horse.

"He ran ten miles. O my friends ! the spittle grew dry in the mouth of Pirmamai.

"Gujarkham reached him with the end of his lance, and Pirmamai's ribs were pierced through from side to side.

"Pirmamai rolled down from his horse to earth : Pirmamai cried, and entreated Gujarkhan.

"Pirmamai said : "O Gujarkhan ! I am thy father : the deed that I wrought was done out of sheer madness.'

"Gujarkhan said : 'I swear it, I will not spare thee ; thou hast covered with shame generations of Pathans.'

"He drew out his Iranian sword, and hewed him down : Pirmamai's bones were ground into powder.

"Gujarkhan galloped back on his white horse, and disappeared : Pirmamai's flesh was devoured by jackals."

What are the feelings of an Afghan listening to the tale of horror? The poet himself, like the chorus of antique tragedy, gives expression to the verdict of public conscience in one word, without appeal. Burhán says: "Gujarkhan has done a Pathan's deed."

Badal,[1] or revenge, is the soul of Afghan
life. All the history of Afghanistan, both public and private, is one continued tale of *vendetta*.
However, it chances that I have not in my collection any song of vendetta illustrating this
side of Afghan life in a manner sufficiently
characteristic to deserve quotation. Suffice it
to say, that vendetta is with the Afghans what
it is with the Corsicans, the Albanians, all
primitive mountaineers: it is hereditary and
not to be prescribed.

Even on British territory the law is powerless against the *Badal;* it is one of the crimes
for which no witness will be found to speak
before the judge in Kachehri. There is hardly
an Afghan in the mountain who has not a foe
who aims at his head, and at whose head he
aims. It happens not seldom that an Afghan
Sepoy from Yaghistan — many Afghans from
over the border enlist in the native contingent
— asks for leave for private business; that
means that there is up there some wolf's head
which he has to take. There is a story of an
Afghan Sepoy who, not having joined his *pal-
tan* in due time, complained bitterly of the
iniquity of his officer, who had dismissed him

---

[1] *Badal*, or retaliation, must be exacted for every and the
slightest personal injury or insult, or for damage to property.
Where the avenger takes the life of his victim in retaliation
for the murder of one of his relatives, it is termed *kisâs*.
Bellew, *loc. cit.*

from service: "I had a duty of Badal to perform; I had to kill a foe. The scamp absconded
for weeks: what could I do?"

Mailmastai is a virtue of a less stern character; it is hospitality in the widest meaning of
the word. The Afghan is bound to feed and
shelter any traveler who knocks at his door;
even infidels have a claim upon his hospitality.
The laws of *mailmastai* are binding on the com-
mune as well as on the individual; the *hujra* is
the home of those who have no home. Even in
British districts the chief of the village, the
Malik or *Lambardar*, raises a special revenue
— the *malba*, or hospitality tax — for the en-
tertainment of passing travelers. Whether
rich or poor, the duty is the same for all. The
poor entertain poorly, the rich richly. It happens not seldom that they run into debt, and
fall a prey to the Hindu money-lender, for fear
they should deserve the name of a *shúm*, a
miser, — the worst insult to an Afghan, especially to an Afghan of high rank. Old Afzal
Khan, of Jamalgarhi, of the royal family of
the Khataks, will be remembered for a long
time amongst his people because he is a *shúm*,
and poet Mahmud sang a cruel song of him.
Here is his story; it is the old story of the end
of a great name.

Afzal Khan was born in the first years of

this century; he is descended in direct line
from the prince of the Khataks, Khushhal
Khan, the great warrior and great poet, who
for years in his mountains defied Aurengzeb
and the Mogul empire, and "who, as he boasts,
was the first to raise his standard in the field
of Afghan song, and subjugated the empire of
words under the hoof of his battle-steed."
About 1830 his cousin, Khavâs Khân, received
the investiture of Akora at the hands of Runjet
Singh, the Sikh suzerain of the now British
Afghans: Afzal Khan stabbed him with his
own hand on his way home from Lahore. He
rendered service during the Mutiny; his income
was 3,629 rupees, 822 of which were a pension
from government for loyal service. Afzal Khan
was a rich man; he had a great name; he had
in his house the original manuscripts of Khushhal Khan; he had his enemies' blood on his
hand; he had everything necessary to deserve
him the esteem of his own people; but he was
a *shúm*, and Mahmud has made his name immortal in a satire. This satire is in the form
of a dialogue between pupil and master, *shagird* and *ustad :* —

PUPIL : At Jamalgarhi lives Afzal Khan.

MASTER : Tell me about him. He boastfully praises
himself and his sons every moment.

PUPIL : No guest is welcome to him.

MASTER : May God, therefore, bring distress upon
him !

PUPIL : Yes, ever invoke a curse upon a miser !

MASTER : He is evil-natured, evil-tongued, evil-mannered ; there never was, never will be, a miser such as he.

PUPIL : When from a distance he sees a guest coming,

MASTER : He says to him : ' Wherefore do you come ? '[1]

PUPIL : He kills him with questions from head to foot.

MASTER : He has no fear, no respect of the Lord.

PUPIL : He never lets a guest rest on a bed in the hujra.

MASTER : His mouth is always open as an empty well.

PUPIL : He has no teeth, his mouth is black as an oven.

PUPIL : He who will cut him into pieces,

MASTER : Will be a Ghazi, and it is a scamp he will kill.

MASTER : Let him vanish from my eyes ; he sets all his kith and kin a-blushing.

PUPIL : There will never be such a shameless fellow as Afzal Khan.

MAHMUD says : I wag my tongue upon him freely in the bazaar.

The curse of the poet was not lost. Last year in May I saw the poor old scamp, in chains, pleading for his life before the Sessions Judge in Kachehri. He was charged with traitorous murder; his two sons and two servants were with him in the dock. As witnesses were speaking, the five accused men did not cease from muttering prayers and telling their

---

[1] A question never to be asked from a guest until his needs have been attended to.

beads, in order to make the depositions harmless and turn the heart of the judge in their favor. Afzal Khán was acquitted, but one of his sons and one of his servants were sentenced to death. When I left, the appeal was pending at Lahore. I am afraid by this time the grandson of Khushhal Khan has been dangling for a long time; the English in India have a foible for hanging big people: it sets a good example.

I must say that public opinion amongst the natives underwent a revulsion in favor of Afzal Khan. They would have welcomed with pleasure the news that the old *shúm* had been stabbed by any man of his kith and kin; but it was hard to see justice done upon him by a Firangi. Besides, the murdered man had spoken slightingly of Afzal Khan's daughter-in-law.[1] That murder was the only fine trait in his life, the redeeming feature.

---

[1] " The abuse or slander of a man's female relations is only to be wiped out in the blood of the slanderer, and not unfrequently the slandered one, whether the calumny be deserved or not, is murdered to begin with." Bellew, *Yusufzais*, p. 214.

III.

AFGHAN HONOR.

What the Afghan honor is, we know; the ballad of Muqarrab Khan will teach us what it is not.

Muqarrab Khan is the ideal of the Afghan politician in Yaghistan. He was the chief of the Khedu Kheil, an important tribe, divided into two clans, the Bam Kheil and the Osman Kheil. He succeeded his father, Fatteh Khan, in 1841, at Penjtar, and helped the English during the annexation of Penjab. He took refuge with them in 1857, as his subjects had expelled him on account of his tyranny. He lived a long time at Peshawer on an allowance of three rupees a day. Then he entered into negotiations with the Amazai tribe, and with their help retook Penjtar in 1874. His enemies submitted; the *Jirga*,[1] composed of eighty men, came to receive him. The Coran was brought for them to take their oath upon it. Just at that moment the Amazais broke into the hall, and all the Jirga was massacred. After many vicissitudes, again an exile and a conqueror, turn by turn, he came once more, two years ago, to sit a refugee at the hearth of the English. The commissioner, Colonel Wa-

---

[1] The Council of the Elders.

terfield, gave him a plot of ground on free rent. "The old man is so old," said the commissioner to me, "that he will not long be a charge upon the budget of India."

Here is the tale of the massacre, as told by the poet Arsal: —

"Firoz[1] said to the Jirga : 'We will make peace at present for policy's sake. We will send away the Amazais, the Khan will remain alone, and then he will hear what we have to say.'

"The Jirga made peace ; but a thought of treason lay in the heart of each of them : 'We will sack Ghazikot.' Ghazan was a partisan of the Khan ; he informed him of the plot.

"Ghazan informed him to the full of all that was going on ; he told him : 'Put not thy trust in them ; the Jirga has decreed thy death. Slaughter them each and all, that thou mayest have no longer to weary thyself concerning them !'

"The Jirga and the Khan met together. My support is in the merciful God ! With them were Ghulám and Sheik Husein : may their face be black before the Lord !

"The Khan said : 'Firoz ! Thou committest treason every day. Take me to Penjtar ! I, the prince of this land, go from door to door as a beggar.'

"Firoz answered : 'Thou art our Khan. Come, make no havoc amongst us. We will bring back prosperity to thy house. We will give thee Penjtar. Between us and thee here is the Coran.'

"The Khan said frankly : 'You take oath in my hands now, and yet you will afterwards conspire against me. You will betray me when my army is dispersed.'

[1] The Chief of the Anti-Muqarrab party.

"The Jirga answered: 'Why should we play the traitor? Thou art our Khan for ever.'

"The two chiefs kissed one another, they sat down in the midst of the Jirga. . . . The Amazais broke in, a tumult arises, all disperse. The Khan has broken his promise, belied his own word. It has made all the world deaf and blind.

"The Khedu Kheil had been taken unawares; they did not understand what was being done; they were put to the sword, O my friend. *This* was written in their destiny.

"With the help of the Amazais, the Khan slaughtered the Khedu Kheil. There was mercy for no one; no one escaped. Amongst the victims was Mairu, who was the *malik* of the Mada Kheil; he was cut to pieces with the Persian swords.

"The night went. In the morning the news spread. *Some were indignant, some were glad.* It was a great sor-. row with the Osman Kheil; their time has passed away."

The poet does not precisely approve of Muqarrab; but if you look coldly at things, who is the good Afghan who in his stead would have not done the same? In the struggle for life, a man's word is only a weapon, and an oath is a hunting net as good as any other or better. The Jirga of the Khedu Kheil had forgotten that terrible maxim of their nation: "When thou hast reconciled thyself with thy foe, then beware of him."

IV.

THE KLEPHT.

The Afghans have a noble maxim, worthy of any Stoic: "If thou hast, eat; if thou hast not, die."[1] Unfortunately they do not live up to it, and in practice it becomes: "If thou hast, eat; if thou hast not, take." The ideal of a man is to live upon his neighbor. The Afridis of the Khaiber Pass lived for centuries upon the plunder of the caravans, till the British Government enlisted these hereditary robbers as regular gendarmes, and compounded for their right of plunder by a regular annuity. The Ghilzais, who are just now making life rather uneasy to the Emir, proudly interpret their name as "Son of robber," and live according to the etymology. When a child is born, his mother bores a hole through the mud wall of the hut, and makes it pass through, saying: "*Ghal zai* — be a good robber, my child." The Kashmiris, who were for seventy years under the Afghan yoke, have described in one line the morals of those strictest among Mussulmans, and the worst amongst plunderers: "To pray is piety (*qarz*), to prey is duty (*farz*)." In the British territory, though the idea of law and order has made remarkable progress,

[1] Thorburn, *Bannu.*

and people, who formerly were wont to settle their quarrels according to the prescriptions of the Nangi Pukhtána, are not seldom willing to have them brought to Kachehri, yet the Klepht is still a national hero, and a favorite subject with popular poets. One died three or four years ago, whose name is still on the lips of all. This is his story as it was told to me.

Naim Shah was born near Cherat, a military station in the Khatak mountains. His brother was insulted by the Sikh Phul Singh, who was Kotval, or chief of the police station, at Nau-shehra, an important cantonment on the Kabul River, with two regiments. He lodged a complaint with the British commandant; the complaint was discarded; then he applied for justice to his brother. Naim Shah wrote to the Kotval, saying: "You have harmed my brother, I will harm you." The Kotval and the General laughed; but on the same night Naim Shah broke into the town with a hundred men, looted it, entered the *kotvali*, sat as a judge, had time enough to have one of his enemies sentenced and shot. The noise awakens the commandant, who arrives from the distant cantonment just in time to see him fleeing down the river. He pursues him there for hours in vain. "Naim Shah was not a fish to hide himself in the river;" he was a man of the mountain, and was already safe in his Khatak den, while they were still hunting him down the river.

Once upon a time Naim Shah met "the General Sáb."[1] The General was one of his great admirers; he said to him: "Will you enter my service?" "With pleasure," was the answer; "but you must first put to death the Kotval of Naushehra." The General objected to the condition, and the negotiation was stopped; but he sent him, as a token of esteem, a gun, a sword, a pistol, two hundred rupees, and a milch cow. Naim Shah was touched with the proceedings; but this did not prevent his slaughtering an entire picket at Chahkot; he retired peacefully, carrying with him some twenty Martini guns, — quite a fortune for a poor Afghan robber.

The government at last had recourse to the unfailing method: they put a prize of 3,000 rupees on his head. Naim Shah, taken by surprise while asleep at Kohi, was wounded to death before he could defend himself. All the poets mourned his death; here is one of their songs, equal to any of the Klepht songs in Fauriel: —

" They fell down upon him unawares, he was captured ;
Náim Sháh was the falcon of the black mountains, he was
      the man of the great heart. The report of the
      guns burst unexpectedly upon him.
It was the hand of God that fired the guns, for *he* was
      stronger than a Nawab. He opened his eyes from
      his sleep, and this time the Tiger's shot missed.
The Tiger spoke in this manner : ' O that the fight were

---

[1] Sáb, the popular pronunciation for Sáhib.

in the open field ! This is the regret left iu my heart.' Death had taken him to Kohi : who could help him ?

Death said : 'Go not further : here is the place, under this vine.' The foes came upou him from above, from below ; they were men without the fear of God. He gave up the ghost.

What Fate has written cauuot be altered : they were meu without the fear of God. May curses rain upon them !

As he had still breath left in his body, the Thánadár[1] came by.

The Thánadár said to him : 'Tell me, why did you sleep untimely ? So did the guns devour thee from afar.'

He expounded the matter to the Thánadár, and breathed his last.

He expounded all the matter as it stood. They took him to the *koti*[2] at Peshawer. All people heard the news : they looked at the face of Náim Sháh :[3] all the people of the town were there.

All the people met at the *koti :* O hero, thy house is empty ! No hero ever will appear who is like unto Náim Sháh. The Engriz Government was sorry for his death.[4]

His mother came out of the house,[5] she stood before the Engriz bareheaded. I am sorrowful for it ; black, black is my grief !

YASIN says ; they heaped the earth above him."

---

[1] The chief of the police station.

[2] Police station.

> [3] Nequeunt expleri corda tuende,
>   Os hominis,"

But here even Hercules feels with Cacus.

[4] Of course they would havp liked to keep him alive for the gallows.

[5] A thing which an Afghan woman never does.

V.

LOVE AND FAMILY SONGS.

Love-songs are plentiful with the Afghans, though whether they are acquainted with love is rather doubtful. Woman with the Afghans is a purchasable commodity; she is not wooed and won with her own consent, she is bought from her father. The average price of a young and good-looking girl is from about 300 to 500 rupees. To reform the ideas of an Afghan upon that matter would be a desperate task. When Seid Ahmed, the great Wahabi leader, the prophet, leader, and king of the Yusufzai Afghans, tried to abolish the marriage by sale, his power fell at once, he had to flee for his life, and died an outlaw. There is no song in the world so sad and dismal as that which is sung to the bride by her friends. They come to congratulate — no, to console her, like Jephthah's daughter; they go to her, sitting in a corner, and sing: —

> " You remain sitting in a corner and cry to us.
> What can we do for you ?
> Your father has received the money."

All of love that the Afghan knows is jealousy. All crimes are said to have their cause in one of the three *z's: zar, zamin,* or *zan —*

money, earth, or woman; the third *z* is in fact the most frequent of the three causes.

The Afghan love-song is artificial; the Afghan poet seems to have been at the school of the Minnesinger or the troubadours. It is the same *mièvrerie* which seems almost to amuse itself with its love — more witty than passionate, a play of imagination more than a cry of the heart. They would have felt with Petrarch or Heine, *si parva licet componere magnis*. There is much of the *convenu* and of the poetical commonplace in their songs, as there is in those of their elder brothers in Europe. You will hardly find one in which you do not meet the clinking of the *pezvan* (the ring in the nose of the Afghan beauty), the blinking of the gold *muhurs* dangling from her hair, the radiance of the green mole in her cheek; and the flames of separation, and the begging of the beggar, the dervish at her door, come. as pilgrim of love; and the sickness of the sick, waiting for health at her hand; and the warbling of the *tuti*,[1] sighing by night for his beloved *kharo* bird. Yet in the long run one finds a charm in these rather affected strains, though not the direct, straightforward, all-possessing rapture of simple and sincere emotion. It is difficult to give in a translation an idea of that charm, as it can

---

[1] The *tuti* is the Indian parrot; he is supposed to be in love with the *Maina* bird, whom the Afghans called *Kharo*.

hardly be separated from the simple, monotonous tune ever recurring, as well as from the rich and high-sounding rhyme for which the Afghan poet has the instinct of a modern Parnassian. The most popular love-songs are those of Mira of Peshawer, Tavakkul of Jelalabad, and Mohammed Taila of Naushehra. Here is the world-known "Zakhmé" of Mira: —

" 1. I am sitting in sorrow, wounded with the stab of separation, low low !

She carried back my heart in her talons, when she came to-day, my bird *kharo*, low low !

2. I am ever struggling, I am red with my blood, I am your dervish.

My life is a pang. My love is my doctor ; I am waiting for the remedy, low low !

3. She has a pomegranate on her breast, she has sugar on her lips, she has pearls for her teeth :

All this she has, my beloved one ; I am wounded in my heart, and therefore I am a beggar that cries, low low !

4. It is due that I should be your servant ; have a thought for me, my soul, ever and ever.

Evening and morning I lie at thy door ; I am the first of thy lovers, low low !

5. Mira is thy slave, his *salâm* is on thee ; thy tresses are his net, thy place is Paradise ; put in thy cage thy slanderer.

6. He who says a ghazal and says it on the tune of another man, he can call himself a thief at every ghazal he says. — This word of mine is truth."

I shall give only one other ghazal, which derives a particular interest from the personality of its author, as well as from a touch of reverie and quaint lunacy, rarely met in Afghan poetry. When I visited the prison of Abbottabad, in company with the assistant-commissioner, Mr. P., I saw there a man who had been sentenced to several months imprisonment for breaking a Hindu's leg in a drunken brawl. The man was not quite sane; he told Mr. P. that he was not what he was supposed to be; that he was a king, and ought to be put on the *gadi*. His name was Mohammadji. Next day I was surprised to hear from a native that Mohammadji was a poet, an itinerant poet from Pakli, who more than once had been in trouble with justice, for he was rather a disorderly sort of poet. Here is a ballad, written by the prisoner, and which is quite a little masterpiece, "in a sensuous, elementary way — half Baudelaire, half Song of Solomon:" —

"Last night I strolled through the bazaar of the black locks; I foraged, like a bee, in the bazaar of the black locks.[1]

Last night I strolled through the grove of the black locks; I foraged, like a bee, through the sweetness of the pomegranate.

I bit my teeth into the virgin chin of my love; then I breathed up the smell of the garland from the neck of my Queen, from her black locks.

Last night I strolled in the bazaar of the black locks; I foraged . . .

[1] See Baudelaire, *La Chevelure* (" Les Fleurs du Mal," xxiv.).

You have breathed up the smell of my garland, O my
friend, and therefore you are drunken with it ; you
fell asleep, like Bahrám on the bed of Sarasia.[1]
Then thereafter there is one who will take your
life, because you have played the thief upon my
cheeks. He is so angry with you, the *chaukidar*
of the black locks.

> Last night . . .

" Is he so angry with me, my little one ? God will keep
me, will he not ?
Stretch out as a staff,[2] thy long black locks, wilt thou not ?
Give me up thy white face, satiate me like the Tuti, wilt
thou not ?
For once let me loose through the granary of the black
locks.

> Last night . . .

" I shall let you, my friend, into the garden of the white
breast.
But after that you will rebel from me and go scornfully
away.
And yet when I show my white face the light of the lamp
vanishes.
O Lord ! give me the beauty of the black locks.

> Last night . . .

" The Lord gave thee the peerless beauty. Look upon
me, my enchanting one ! I am thy servant.
Yesterday, at the dawn of day, I sent to thee the messenger. The snake bit me to the heart, the snake of
thy black locks.

> Last night . . .

---

[1] An allusion to a popular tale of Bahrám Sháhzáda.
[2] To protect me.

"I will charm the snake with my breath ; my little one,
    I am a charmer.
But I, poor wretch, I am slandered in thine honor.
Come, let us quit Pakli, I hold the wicked man,[1] in hor-
    ror.
I give to thee full power over the black locks.

"MOHAMMADJI has full power over the poets in Pakli.
He raises the tribute, he is one of the Emirs of Delhi.
He rules his kingdom, he governs it with the black locks.
Last night I strolled through the bazaar of the black
    locks ; I foraged, like a bee, through the bazaar of
    the black locks."

Poor Mohammadji, as you may see from the last stanza, was already seized with the mania of grandeurs before he entered the prison at Abbottabad, though he dreamed as yet only of poetical royalty. If these lines ever reach Penjab, and find there any friend of poetry amongst the powers that be, may I be allowed to recommend to their merciful aid the poor poet of Pakli, a being doubly sacred, a poet and a *divana*,[2] and one who thus doubly needs both mercy for his faults and help through life.

There is a poetical *genre* peculiar to Afghan poetry; it is the *misra*.[3] The *misra* is a *distique*, that expresses one idea, one feeling, and is a complete poem by itself. Poets, in poetical *assauts*, vie one with another in quoting or

---

[1] Her husband.   [2] A lunatic.

[3] A friend points to the remarkable similarity of the Afghan *misra* with the *stornello* in the popular poetry of Italy.

improvising *misras.* They refer generally to love and love affairs, and some are exquisitely simple: —

" My love does not accept the flower from my hand ; I will send her the stars of Heaven in a *Jirga.*"

" Thy image appears to me in my dreams, I awake in the night and cry till the morning."

" I told him : There is such a thing as separation, and my friend burst into laughter till he grew green."

" When the perfume of thy locks comes to me, it is the morning that comes to me and I blossom like the rose."

" O letter, blessed be thy fate ! Thou art going to see my beloved."

" My honor and my name, my life and my wealth — I will give everything for the eyes of my beloved."

" Strike my head, plunder my goods, but let me see the eyes of the one I love, and I will give my blood."

" Red are thy lips, white are thy teeth, so that at thy sight the angels of heaven are confounded."

" — Red are my lips, white are my teeth ; they are thine. To the others the dust of the earth ! "

" O my soul ! at last thou wilt become dust ; for I have seen the eyes of my friend, and they were friendly no more."

"Were there a narrow passage to the dark niche in the
grave, I should go and offer flowers to my love."

"O master builder! his grave was too well made; and
my friend will stay as long as time lasts."

Of the inner family life, popular song is rather
reticent. Of the brutality of man, the slavery
of woman, the harsh voice, the insult, the
strokes, the whipping at the post, the fits of
mad jealousy without love, it has nothing to
say. Women, however, have also their poetry
and their poets, the *duman;* but that poetry
goes hardly out of the walls of the harem. I
was fortunate enough to gather some fragments
of it, though less than I should have liked. A
child is a child even to an Afghan mother:—

"Your two large eyes are like the stars of heaven:
Your white face is like the throne of Shah Jahan:
Your two tender delicate arms are like blades of Iran:
And your slender body is like the standard of Solomon.
       My life for you! Do not cry!"

   "O Lord! give me a son who says 'Papa! papa!'
   Let his mother wash him in milk!
   Let her rub him with butter!
   They will call him to the mosque.
   The Molla will teach him reading,
   And the students will kiss him."

   "Dear, dear child! a flower in your hat!
   It shines like a sprig of gold!"

The following is a nursery rhyme which I

believe is unparalleled in the whole of the nursery literature; it is history as well as a lullaby.

In the time of the Sikh domination, I am
told, a Sikh carried away by force a Yusufzai
girl, and took her to Lahore. Her brothers
went in search of her, and after a year found
at last the place where she lived. She had a
child by the Sikh. She recognized them from
the window, put the child in the cradle, and
while her husband was drunk asleep, she rocked
the child with a lullaby in which she informed
her brothers of all they had to do. The Sikhs
are gone, but the lullaby is still sung: —

" *Swing, swing, zangutai!* [1]
   Come not, ye robbers. Come not by the lower side :
      come by the upper side, sweet and low.
Swing, swing, zangutai!
   There are two dogs inside ; I have tied them with rims.
Swing, swing, zangutai!
   There is a little basket inside, full with sovereigns.
Swing, swing, zangutai!
   There is a bear [2] asleep ; come quickly therefore.
Swing, swing, zangutai!
   If he becomes aware of you, there will be no salvation
      in your distress.
Swing, swing, zangutai!
   The infidel is a drunkard, he does not perceive the
      noise.
Swing, swing, zangutai! "

But every life must end with *voceros.*
During the agony all the family surround the

---

[1] *Zangutai:* berceaunette in French.   [2] Her husband.

dying, and repeat the sacred formula, *Ashhadu:*
"I bear witness that Allah is God, and there is
no other God. I bear witness that Mohammed
is his servant and apostle." Thus the dying
soul is kept in the remembrance of God, and
brought to repeat the *Ashhadu*, and dies in
confessing God, and is saved. In the moment
when his soul goes, an angel comes, and con-
verses with him, questions him, and, recognizing a good Mussulman, says: "Thy faith is
perfect." Then the men leave the room; the
women sit around the dying bed; the daughter,
sister, or wife of the deceased, standing before
the dead, repeats the *vocero* for an hour, and at
each time the chorus of women answer with a
long, piercing lamentation, that thrills through
the hearts of the men in the courtyard, and
creates the due sorrow.

Here are some of the *voceros:* a mere translation cannot of course render the effect of those
simple plaints, which derive most of their power
from the accent and the mere physical display
of emotion.

For a father: —

"Alas! alas! my father!
  I shall see you no more on the road.
  The world has become desolate to you forever."

For a mother: —

"O my mother! the rose-hued,
  You kept me so tenderly,
  I shed for you tears of blood."

For a husband: —

> "You were the lord of my life :
> Then to me a king was a beggar :
> This was the time when I was a queen."

For a daughter: —

> "O my daughter ! so much caressed,
> Whom I had kept so tenderly,
> Now you have deserted me,
> This world is the place of sorrow."

VI.

AFGHAN POLITICS — THE AMBELA CAMPAIGN — THE AFGHAN WAR.

About the romantic and religious literature of the Afghans there is too little or too much to say. I come at once to a subject of more particular interest. What is the echo of political events in the popular literature?

The history of Afghanistan could be traced in songs from our days back to the days of Ahmed Shah, the founder of the Durani empire; even farther, to the time of Akbar. Not all those songs are contemporary with the events, but they embody at least an old tradition, and sometimes, through the happy habit of plagiarism, are authentic relics of the past. The wars with the Sikhs, the quarrels of the Barukzai Sardars, the crusade, miracles, and death of

Seid Ahmed, have all left poetical records, still preserved in the memory of the older poets of the day and soon to be buried with them. I leave these older songs of mere antiquarian interest and come to the question of actual interest: What have the poets of the more recent period to tell the people in the British districts, Afghanistan and Yaghistan? or better, What do these people expect their poets to tell them about their masters, allies, and foes, the Engriz?

It is characteristic of the one-sidedness of the English, that neither Kaye, the author of that otherwise beautiful and thorough history of the first Afghan war, nor Mr. Hensman, of the "Pioneer," the reporter of the last Afghan war, seems to have had the slightest suspicion of the all-powerful influence of popular poetry in either case. Imagine a German writing a history of the French Revolution without mentioning the "Marseillaise." Songs, moreover, with singing, non-writing people, are the only reliable documents which remain to prove their true feeling. Mohammed Hayat, the assistant political agent in Cabul during the last war, who knows the Afghans well, was not mistaken when he ascribed the rising of the Afghans in 1839 to the preaching of the Mollas and the songs of the poets. What the Molla preaches, the poet sings; and when the Molla has preached and

the poet sung, the turn of speech goes soon to
the gun.

I could unfortunately procure no songs of the
first war: I must pass at once to the most popular cycle of historical ballads now in existence,
— the cycle of the Ambela campaign. That
campaign, not much known to the general English reader, I suppose, is not yet forgotten on
the Penjab border, and has left amongst the
Afghans more vivid recollections than even the
last war, though more than twenty-five years
have elapsed since then.

In 1824, as the Sikh infidels were holding
the Penjab, a Seid from Bareilli, Seid Ahmed,
preached a return to the primitive purity of
Islam; he established himself amongst the tribes
of Yaghistan with a small band of devoted men
from Hindustan, and on the 20th of December,
1826, preached the Sacred War, and the conquest of the infidels from the Sikhs to the
Chinese. After wonderful successes, he perished in an encounter with the Sikhs. But the
colony of "Hindustani fanatics," as they are
called, which he had brought with him, remained there, receiving recruits, arms, and
money from their brothers in Bengal, ever
ready to fight the good battle. In 1849 the
British took the place of the Sikhs in the hatred
of the Hindustanis as well as in the empire of
Penjab. From 1850 to 1857 they had to send

sixteen expeditions against the rebel camp at
Sitana, whence plundering raids were contin-
ually directed across the border. In 1863, after new outrages, it was decided that an expe-
dition should be sent to expel them from their
den, and on the 19th of October a well-equipped
force of 7,000 men entered the then unknown
Ambela Pass, under the orders of General
Chamberlain.

The Ambela Pass turns round the inexpugn-
able Massif of Sitana, but it belongs to neutral
tribes.   Chamberlain thought it inopportune
to inform them of his plans, lest the Hindustanis should have time to prepare for resistance; he hoped he could reach Sitana in a day
or two, burn it down, and then retire at once
into British territory. . The Afghans did not
view things in that light; when they saw 7,000
men, with 4,000 mules of baggage, draw near
the pass, they took fear; they believed their
own independence was in danger, and blocked
the road.   Chamberlain was obliged to stop;
four days later, the 12,000 fighting men of
Buner took the gun; and the Sahib of Svat,
the highest religious authority of Indian Islam,
though a bitter foe to Seid Ahmed's doctrine
and party, which to him smacked of Wahab-
ism, proclaimed the Sacred War. For two
months all Yaghistan came pouring upon the
pass; and in spite of repeated reinforcements,

Chamberlain remained for weeks at the entrance of the pass without advancing a step. The English historians speak of a point that was taken, lost, and retaken three days together; it is known still amongst the Afghans by the name of *Katal garh*, the Castle of Slaughter. The Afghans charged the gunners with sticks, and stopped with their mantles the mouths of the guns. British pluck and diplomacy at last exhausted the constancy of the allies; jealousy crept in; the coalition melted like snow; "double rupees" hastened the decomposition; and at last the Jirga of the Bunervals volunteered to guide the British army to the Hindustani camp. Chamberlain, with his new unexpected allies, went to Sitana, burnt the camp, and came back through the fatal pass without firing a gun. But he had left at the entrance one tenth of his army.

That campaign ended officially in a success, — not a very decisive one, since the Hindustanis are still at the door, waiting for the time; but to the Afghans it was a victory of the Afghans and Islam, and they sang triumphant songs, of wild and epic eloquence, which after twenty-five years still fill the echoes of the mountain: —

"On the top of Katalgarh the Firangis came to long grief: there were cries of terror. Night came upon them : when they saw the Ghazis, despair fell upon them.

"On the top of Katalgarh the Firangis had collected

their troops ; from afar the Bunervals pounced upon them like falcons ; I was astounded with their rush.

"The youths wore red girdles and two-colored buckles; cries rose from every side; rifle bullets rained like rain.

"Rifle bullets rained as fine rain. The Deputy said to the Commissioner : 'They have with them a powerful Fakir,[1] against whom there is no fighting.' The regiments of the White[2] cried aloud, on account of the Pir : 'When shall we be delivered ? They storm our ramparts ; we cannot stop the Ghazis ; the sword leaves no trace upon them.'

"O Master ! I say unto thee : 'Blessed be thy native place, the sacred land of Buner and Svat !'

"The General cried out : 'I have no breath left in my body. O disaster ! My army is cut to pieces. I shall not endeavor again. Where is the use ? In vain have I tried to reduce Svat.'

"O Lord ! make there a *carion*[3] out of that recreant from Lahore : he will be thrown back and broken. Some fled away on all-fours : the Ghazis butcher the others, they will not reach Chimla.

"They plunge into the thickets, but they will not be saved for all that, the ruffians, the snakes. They do not dare to face the Ghazis in the fight ; the Ghazis have made them flee along the valley. Islam has made a great feast upon them.

"For six months[4] the Firangis have fought on the banks of Surkavi ; they have perished wholesale. From the top of a high rock the Master has pronounced the *tekbir*, for he is the butcher that slaughters them."

[1] The Sáhib of Svát.

[2] The *Gaurá*, or British troops ; the native contingent are called *Kálá*, the black.

[3] A *murdar*. The Infidel dies a *carion ;* the Faithful one dies a *sháhid*, a martyr.

[4] In fact, for two months.

To realize all the frantic eloquence of the last line, one must remember that every head of cattle that is slaughtered is supposed to be a sacrifice to Allah, and is made sacred to him with the *tekbir* — *Allah Akbar* ("God is great").

The old Fakir, the Sahib of Svat, was the ideal centre of the struggle. It was said that he had come riding on a horse at the head of forty thousand horsemen. As he most prudently kept at safe distance from gunshot, they said that he had the gift of making himself unseen: —

"The shadow of the hero's gown overshadows the Ghazis.

"Flee away, O Firangis! if you want to save your life. The Sahib comes riding and the Akuzais follow. In the Ambela ravines lie the White with their red girdles and their disheveled hair.

"The mercy of the Lord was on the Babaji,[1] for he threw back the Firangis as far as Calcutta!"

Unfortunately traitors have crept amongst the Ghazis: —

"Through the intercession of the Prophet and Master, accept this prayer of mine : make lame in both feet whoever makes war upon me, throw illness on his family, call his family, call calamity upon him.

"Let Zaid Ullah Khan,[2] of Dagar, tremble before Dagar, O Lord."

It is well known in Dagar that Zaid Ullah's name is *Nihang*.[3]

---

[1] The father, the Sahib.   [2] One of the first who deserted.
[3] A crocodile ; a hypocrite.

" As the Ghazis had met, he went in the dead of night and made it known to the Firangis. He told James :[1] ' To-day thy life is in great danger.'

"James answered : ' Zaid Ullah, I will heap thee with favors. Thou shalt have from me in perpetuity fivepence a day.' "

The last Afghan war produced also a plentiful crop of songs, though I do not find any in my collection that can compete with the savage eloquence of the Ambela songs. They breathe hate and scorn enough, but hardly anything better. Here are fragments that may give an idea of the general tone : —

" The Firangi set out in a rage ; he wants to wage battle ; he has collected an army. But Havâs[2] has received their money, and he serves loyally the Engriz.

" Havâs let himself be bought ; he is not ashamed of his bad renown. Before the Lord his forehead is black. He told Kamnari : ' I shall serve thee loyally.'

" Havâs is a traitor ; he nourishes treason's self in his veins. Great is the•glory of the Ghazis ! Glory to the Ghazis who have solidly seized the sword.

" The *Lat*[3] has spread rupees with full hands ; the Ghazis cried with shame. He has filled with them the Afridis, who feed on the flesh of the dead.

" The Mohmands are numerous, like dust ; the Ghazis have hurried forward with forced marches, and I have sung.

[1] The Deputy Commissioner.
[2] The *malik* of the Afridis, who opened the Khaiber Pass for the English.
[3] *Lat*, Lord ; the commander-in-chief.

" But there were no chiefs, no munitions. Had they been all of one accord, had they all met on one point, had they camped at Bash Balag, the Firangis would not have taken Lalpura.

" But some went over to the worship of the recreant ; they received money from him, they became the foes of the Prophet.

" For five farthings they denied Islam : their forehead is already black for the day of doom.

" Whoever is a Mussulman, whoever is of good faith in Islam, goes to the sacred war, gives up life and goods for the law of the Holy Prophet, and is not afraid of the impious."

The murder of Cavagnari — or, as they pronounce it, Kamnari — is often alluded to, generally as a fine feat of Islam. The current native report is, that an Afghan regiment came to ask their arrears of pay from the new Emir, Yaqub Khan, who directed them to Cavagnari, as being the real master in Cabul. They were sent back by Cavagnari to the Emir, and again by the Emir to Cavagnari, who ordered his men to fire at them, though they were disarmed; then all the city rose, and the massacre followed : —

" Mohammed Yaqub Khan was the son of the Emir ; he was not a child — he was great, clever, and learned.

" He called for Kamnari ; he gave him Bala Hissar ; [1] Kamnari stayed there for a few days.

" A band of *ardel* [2] came to the castle to present a pe-

---

[1] The fortress in Cabul.

[2] *Ardel*, a corruption of the English *orderly*.

tition to Yaqub: 'Our pay has been left near your father,[1] we are in urgent need of it.' Yaqub cursed them with anger. They went to Kamnari, the Infidel. The true Ghazi, it is with the sword he fills his hunger.

"There was a tumult; the Firangis were slaughtered in Cabul; the Emir did not know of it.

"The Emir was angry; he called for the soldiers; the soldiers said: 'The massacre was done by Mohammed Jan Khan.'

"Mohammed Jan Khan said: 'I confess it; I have killed that madman with my own hand. I cut his throat; my knife grew blunt.'

"The news came to Company.[2] He flew into a passion, and said: 'Lat Rapat,[3] go at once.'

"Rapat went through the Kurum valley towards Cabul. May God save us from that reptile!

"Rapat, like a reptile, entered the heart of Yaqub Khan; Yaqub left Cabul.

"Mohammed Yaqub, to save his life, went to Rapat, turning his back to Islam.

"He made Yaqub a prisoner, he sent him down to the plain. Hindustan became his country, and he forgot his native place. Was he drunk with wine or drunk with blang?[4] no one knows.

"But the Ghazi Mohammed Jan Khan collected the Ghazis. He went into the open field and pursued Rapat. Rapat was lost and all amazed, and he said to Mohammed Jan: 'You are my lord, I am your slave.'"

This Mohammed Jan, whom the poet most gratuitously, I am glad to say, credits with the

---

[1] Shir Ali, the former Emir, overthrown by the English.
[2] John Company has survived himself in Afghanistan.
[3] *Lat Rapat*, Lord Robert (Sir Frederick Roberts).
[4] *Khánazáda ghulám.*

murder of Cavagnari, was a home-born servant
of Yaqub Khan,[1] and he was with the Emir's
brother, Ayub, the sword of the nation, as the
old Molla of Ghazni, Mushki Alam, was its
voice and soul.

"Mohammed Jan was the leader, and so was the Sá-
hibzadá Mushki Alam. Company had to mourn on that
account.

"Whoever has courage to fight face to face, let him
slaughter that ruffian.[2]

"Mohammed Jan Khan stretched out the hand against
Rapat ; he uncovered the locks of his head.[3] May God
give him victory !

"They had many battles in Cabul — battles to the
death — with gun and sword.

"When he had driven them from Cabul, he marched
on Ghazni ; he fought a great battle. There were white
men, there were black men, but he made them all blood-
red.

"Ayub Khan and Mohammed Khan encamped both of
them in the field ; they kissed one another in the battle."

Mohammed Jan fought to the last. However, when all was over and Abdulrahman was
on the throne, he announced his readiness to
submit and recognize the new Emir. But Abdulrahman trusts more to the dead than to the
living. Mohammed, enticed by the unworthy
son of the Sahib of Svat, Miyan Gul Kalan,
presented himself to the Emir, who had him

---

[1] When he put himself into the hands of Lat Rapat.

[2] "That ruffian" is Company.

[3] A great insult to a Hindu.

put to death. But one day, as the Emir was riding through the bazaar of Jelalabad, he heard these lines: —

"The Ghazi Mohammed Jan Khan, martyr, has passed from this world. The Emir had him put to death. He was taken by treason.

"Since Emir Abdulrahman sits on the throne at Cabul, man has lost his faith in man."

The Emir, stung to the quick, alighted from his elephant and did not disdain to go to the poet and apologize before him. I wonder what sort of songs are ringing now in the bazaars of Ghazni and Candahar.

I shall conclude with a Persian song that was sung at Cabul in the time when General Roberts was besieged in his camp at Shirkhan; many of its lines have again an interest of actuality. To understand them one must remember that Ayub Khan, who is now again to the front, and has just left his prison at Teheran to try his chance, is the brother of the late Emir Yaqub, now a prisoner in India at Dehra Dun; that little Musa Khan is the son of Yaqub, and was proclaimed Emir in his place by Ayub and Mohammed Jan. If Abdulrahman falls, Musa will reign under the regency of Ayub. He has been for years the hope of the Ghazis, and popular legend is already busy about him. People from the exile court at Teheran, who come to Peshawer, tell in the bazaar that he is always repeating to his uncle: "Uncle, let us declare war on the English; either they will kill me or I will deliver my father."

" Yaqub Khan is the man of Right,
    Come, boy, and get the grapes ! [1]
Musa Khan is the Emir of the Afghans, Come, boy . . .
Abdul Rahman is the child of the Russians,[2] Come,
    boy . . .
Cabul has become Hindustan,[3] Come, boy . . .
Shame will be the lot of our wives,[4] Come, boy . . .
But there is still one great battle to be fought, Come,
    boy . . .
The signal will come from Iran, Come, boy . . .
The plain is all red with flowers,[5] Come, boy . . .
The red roses are the blood of martyrs, Come, boy . . .
Double rupees fly about on every side, Come, boy . . .
Herat belongs to Teheran, Come, boy . . ."[6]

[1] Bullets. The boy is General Roberts.

[2] He is no longer so.

[3] A British province.

[4] English morality is supposed to be in Afghanistan what French morality is supposed to be in England. The rising of 1839 is ascribed by native tradition to an "English lord" having debauched the wife of one of the first Afghan chiefs, Abdullah Achakzai. Abdullah killed them with his own hand, and called his people to revenge. An *ordre du jour de moralite* by General Roberts recommends the soldiers to avoid the indiscretions committed during the first occupation of Cabul, in order to remove the prejudice of past years, "and cause the British name to be as highly respected in Afghanistan as it is throughout the civilized world." H. Hensman, *The Afghan War of* 1879-1880, p. 68.

[5] Grown out of the blood of martyrs.

[6] This song was published in the *Civil and Military Gazette* of Lahore as an "Afghan Nursery Rhyme" (April 15, 1880).

Is Herat again the proposed price of Persian assistance? Will the next Afghan Frontier Commission have to draw the Perso-Afghan line east of Herat?

I must say here that not all the political songs of the Afghans evince such feelings of desperate aversion. Though in the songs from Afghanistan and Yaghistan there is no love lost on the British, the songs from the British districts are often in a rather different spirit. Mahmud, the author of the scathing satire on Afzal Khan, quoted above, is a stanch supporter of the British Raj, and has written a ballad on the justice of the English: —

"The Sâhibs have the same law both for the weak and for the strong. They practice to perfection justice and equity, and make no difference in a lawsuit between the strong and the weak.

"The man of honor they treat with honor, and they shield not the thief, the scamp, the gamester. They wield royalty as it becomes kings, and take tribute from Rajahs and Nababs."

It must be confessed that the loyal poetry of the Afghans has not the same go and swing as that which is not loyal. They are at their best in satire, which, however, can be loyal too. What indictment of the dilapidations in the Commissariat could be shorter and sharper than these lines, written after the last Afghan War: —

"Everybody has bought the *tatoos* [1] of the Commissariat; for four *annas* [2] the camels of the Commissariat.

"In fine dress, boots on their feet, a cane in hand, strout about the *munshis* [3] of the Commissariat.

"Their fathers and grandfathers did not know what an ass is, and here they are driving in *tam tam*,[4] the rich men of the Commissariat."

It is time to conclude. The reader may already have drawn his conclusion for himself. The songs, on the whole, confirm, by the Afghans' own confession, the rather unfavorable estimate which was suggested by their history in the last fifty years. A strong race, nothing like the mild Hindoo, — of a strong, but mixed metal; a sense of honor that can do without truth; the half-conventional virtues of the savage; real love ignored; the respect of the weak a weakness. A sense of religion that teaches no charity, no self-control, no self-improvement, and is best gratified in the damnation of alien creeds. As to the intellectual side, no high imagination, a limited range of ideas, but at the same time one of the highest of all gifts — one which effete Europe has lost — simplicity and directness of expression. Politically, none of the virtues that make a nation, the clan and the family divided against themselves, and the word cousin [5] meaning "deadly

---

[1] *Tatoo*, a pony.　　[2] Five pence.　　[3] Clerks.
[4] A light open carriage.　　[5] *Tarbur*.

foe;" the foreigner hardly worse hated than the countryman, and played off against him. The Englishman hated as an infidel, despised as unreliable and immoral;[1] in the impending struggle for the Empire of Asia, no help to be hoped except for cash, no promise to be trusted except on bill of exchange; in fact, no permanent and sincere support to be expected, because the fields for loot lie across the Indus, not across the Oxus. It must be said, in fairness to the tribes, that sixty years ago Christians could travel safely through Afghanistan, that the present desperate feelings were created in 1838 by the wanton aggression of Lord Auckland, the Liberal, and that, while they were slowly dying out,[2] they were revived ten years ago by Lord Lytton, the Conservative, too intensely, perhaps, for any hope to be left of stemming again the current of hatred and distrust. It may be added, however, as a reassuring symptom of a negative kind, that the name of Russia is not yet on the lips of the singing politicians of Afghanistan, and that the "Divine Figure from the North" is not yet looming on the horizon of their hopes.

---

[1] This, of course, applies chiefly to the Afghans of Afghanistan and Yaghistan. Those of the British districts know more of the British and know better.

[2] During the Mutiny, the British Empire was saved by the neutrality of Afghanistan and the active support of the Afghan districts.

RACE AND TRADITION.

I.

THE historical sciences in this century have subsisted on a single idea, that of race. When one lives on a single idea, one is at last apt to die of it. The idea of race, after having revived, or rather created, modern history, has for some time begun to render it sterile and to pervert it; it has had its day, and ought to give way to a new idea, that of *tradition*.

The idea of race was developed and formulated in the first quarter of this century. The discovery of Sanskrit, and the creation of comparative grammar brought about the recognition of the existence of a well-characterized family of languages, the *Aryan* or *Indo-European*. Its various members, Sanskrit, Persian, Greek, Latin, Slavonic, Germanic, and Celtic, being essentially identical in their material elements, their form and general structure, are manifestly one and the same tongue, which in the course of time was slowly and in diverse manners modified, according to the various places to which it was carried. On the other hand, it has for a long time been known that Hebrew, together with Arabic, Ethiopic, Syriac, and Phœnician, forms a family no less clearly characterized, the *Semitic*. This family, whose circle, enriched by recent discoveries, now includes the Assyrian and the Himyaritic, is absolutely distinct from the Indo-European family. Apart from the system of sounds which is dissimilar, the roots and vocabularies are unlike, the word-formations follow other laws, and the arrangement of phrases follows a different movement. May not these two families in a prehistoric epoch have proceeded from one and the same type? The question has been before us for half a century, and is still open to hypothesis rather than to definite solution. Viewed from the historical side, and in the form in which these families appear to us, they are strangers to one another, despite certain vague indications that seem to point to a primitive common parentage.

The religions of the peoples that spoke these languages present, at first sight, the same points of similarity and the same differences, less accentuated, it is true — possibly because of our imperfect knowledge of these religions, and of the more fleeting and less tangible character of the phenomena in question. A written or spoken word is a definite and palpable fact, about which it is possible to reason, and upon

which it is possible to lean. This is less so
in the case of a religious idea, which is a fact,
often dull and obscure, existing only in one's
conscience, where it is produced and where it
most frequently takes refuge. It is difficult to
follow the thought of our contemporary, of our
every-day neighbor, who speaks our language,
and lives under our eyes in the same material
and moral atmosphere. How can we flatter
ourselves that we can discover, at a distance of
thirty centuries, the thought of peoples so different from us, with nothing to guide us but
the remains of mute monuments, or the uncertain echo of ancient and badly-deciphered texts,
with regard to which even scholars are at odds.
Nevertheless, and in spite of the general wave
of speculation upon ancient religions, it certainly appears, at first sight, that the religions
called Aryan form one group, and those called
Semitic, another. In the former there is encountered everywhere, under the same name in
some, and occasionally under different names,
one god of heaven, and various goddesses of the
waters; everywhere an exuberant polytheism,
all the forces of nature deified, a rich dualistic
mythology of storm-gods fighting against demons: divinities of forests, of rivers, of mountains, nymphs, dryads, apsaras, peris, elfs,
nixen, — a whole nation of gracious or formidable spirits hovering about us at all times. On

the other hand, among the peoples speaking a Semitic language, everywhere apparently, severe unity, everywhere a Baal, a Moloch, or a Jehovah, crushing nature with the blaze of his isolated splendor.

Upon these striking contrasts the theory of races was built. The Aryan language and religion are the expression of a race, — the Aryan; the Semitic language and religion are the expression of another race, — the Semitic; different and irreconcilable expressions, because they are the outcome of two distinct and irreducible forces.

The Aryan and Semitic groups are the only ones that have been closely studied. They are not the only families of languages and religions in the world, but the indications resulting from a superficial examination of any of them would only confirm the inductions furnished by the more complete study of these two. There is, for instance, a Chinese family absolutely independent of the other two. Now, ethnologically, it strikes one at once that the physical type of the Chinaman is absolutely different from that of the Aryan or the Semite.

The theory of races gave a strong stimulus to the progress of science; for in attempting to follow it to its last ramifications, it was necessary to lay bare the facts in all their details. But as often happens, with their usual ingratitude towards the human mind, the facts evoked by theory turned against it. Suddenly it was seen — and the suggestion seemed almost a stroke of genius — that a man is perfectly capable of acquiring a language which was not his father's. An Englishman born in Paris will talk the slang of the boulevards quite as well as a Parisian of ten generations; the sons of German emigrants in the far West do not murder the Queen's English any more than does a Yankee, son of the Pilgrim Fathers. Languages disappear, while the people that spoke them remain, — a proof that they learned others. The Gauls of Julius Cæsar after the lapse of several generations supplied the bar of Rome with barristers. Not only does Mr. Parnell, an Englishman by blood, vindicate in English the hereditary rights of the Celtic race, but so do the purest of the pure Irish, the O'Briens, the McCarthys, the O'Donnells, the O'Donoghues. Scarcely 150,000 Irish people speak Irish. The Magyarized Germans speak and write their adopted language as correctly as do the pure Tartars. The people of the Aryan language are not therefore necessarily Aryans; they may have learned it from the Aryan conquerors, and forgotten their own.

The history of Celtic antiquity proves that the Celtic element was superficial, a simple, dominant aristocracy, beneath which there was

the ancient, non-Celtic layer, vanquished and
reduced to slavery by the conquerors.[1] Without the guidance of history, the Celts of northern France, the Iberians of southern France
and Spain, the Gètes and nameless tribes of the
lower Danube might have been regarded as
Latins, Romans by blood, sons of the *Quirites.*
What Rome did in historical times, in Gaul,
in Spain, in Roumania, might, and indeed must
have happened there and elsewhere, in prehistoric epochs.

Aryan peoples is therefore only a convenient
expression for *people of the Aryan language;*
just as *Semitic peoples* signifies simply *people
of the Semitic language. Aryan peoples* signifies, people in whose language in ancient times
all the roots were dissyllabic, with whom "father" was called *patar* (Zend, *patar;* Greek
and Latin, *pater;* Sanskrit, *pitar;* Germanic,
fadar; Celtic [*p*]*athar*); with whom "god" was
called *deva ;* with whom the genitive denoted the
name of the possession, and the objective preceded the verb. *Semitic peoples* means people
in whose language the roots were monosyllabic,
with whom "father" was called *abu ;* with whom
"god" was called *El*, the genitive denoting the
name of the thing possessed, and the objective
following the verb. But a man could say *patar*
for "father" and still be descended from an-

[1] See the excellent work of M. d'Arbois de Jubainville.

cestors who said *abu*. Language and race are
equivalent expressions at their origin, — but at
their origin only. Let us suppose that two
couples, of the anthropoids so fashionable at
present, produce two species of humanity in two
islands separated by oceans, each one of these
species making its own language, and both languages becoming diversified with time, according
as the group that speaks it extends, multiplies,
and branches out. So long as no meeting takes
place between the two groups, the difference of
language will correspond exactly to that of race;
but as soon as the two groups meet each other,
as soon as they mingle in whatsoever degree or
manner, be it by conquest or by alliance, race
and language cease to be parallel. One of the
two languages may perish, without the least
mixture of race, the least alteration in the two
primitive types; the cry of one of the two anthropoids may, after centuries, drown the cry of
his rival, without a drop of blood passing from
the veins of one into those of the other. Con-
versely, the two races may mingle and coalesce,
and the primitive types yield to a third and new
type, whereas the two languages may continue
their independent course. In historical times,
the word that issues from the lip is no longer
an indication of the blood that courses in the
veins.

On the other hand, in religion, the terms

Aryan and *Semitic* tend to lose even the conventional sense that they may retain in linguistics. Since the creation of Semitic epigraphy and the discovery of Babylon and Nineveh have introduced us into the intimacy of the Semite gods, we are astonished to see how little they really differ at bottom from their Aryan neighbors. The monotheistic idea, that was believed to be the basis of the Semitic spirit, belongs really only to the Jews, and in a minor degree to the Arabs, half Judaized and half Christianized by Mahomet. In ancient times, the religions of the Semitic language show the same polytheism as do those of the Aryan language, and the same poetical chaos. More than this, in proportion as we become better acquainted with the religions of Greece, the Semitic imprint becomes more manifest. In those times there was no conversion from one religion to another, because religion did not consist of universal and absolute dogmas, but of details, of practices, of histories. Religions were national and local, not universal. But, without abdicating one's own religion, one borrowed to an indefinite extent from others. A religion was added to one's own; strange gods were worshiped, because it is well to have friends in every camp. The believer always had a large place in his heart open to unknown gods; the jealous god did not yet exist.

The Greeks, an artistic and inquiring people, borrowed largely from all sides. Adonis, for whom the Athenian ladies wept, came from Syria. Later, Cybele and Attys with their timbrels came from Phrygia, and Serapis came from Egypt to give advice and to cure. In an earlier period, the Phœnicians, those great draymen of the ancient world, brought to the Greek Pantheon a mass of gods and goddesses and myths that soon lost the stamp of their origin. Without going to the length of such "semitizing" scholars as Ernest Curtius, who do not hesitate to make the entire Greek mythology merely a chapter of the Phœnician, it is difficult, in spite of the dangers of method that these new views already display, to close one's eyes to the daily increasing evidence. Though Greece was not obliged to wait for the Phœnicians in order to have a goddess of love, it is none the less true that it was in the wake of a Phœnician bark that Anadyomene of Cythera rose from the foam. Heracles is by name and origin an Aryan god, who easily recognized his brothers in the Vedas; nevertheless, in the course of his long history and wanderings, he has been clothed more than once in the garb of a Syrian god. In his apotheosis the hand that applies the torch to the stake is by no means the hand of the *Devas*, or of the Indian *Vritras*, struggling in the storm-cloud; it is the hand of the Zidonian Melkarth,

—of the sun, dying at the end of his annual course, to reappear with new life.

Thus we see the barriers separating the two Pantheons diminish day by day, and it might appear for a moment that the differences separating them are not such as imply two essentially different forces. There is no fundamental difference, but only one of form. From the present position, the distinguishing characteristics of these two families seem to be the predominance of storm-myths in the Aryan mythology and of season-myths in the Semitic. Both are developed under the idea of the struggle between good and evil, and under a visible form; but the one took as a starting-point, and for the *mise en scène*, the struggle of gods and demons, quarreling over the waters, and the light in the storm; the other, the struggle of spring and winter, of life and death in nature. One was developed about a more dramatic incident, giving birth to a poetical situation; the other portrays a regular law, which makes the struggle slower and more solemn. But each has retained the traces of the favorite prejudices of the other, the Aryan of the season-myths, the Semitic of the storm-myths. There is nothing there which reveals, at the origin, irreducible forms of thought, nothing of that which is generally understood by the fatal instinct of race.

Therefore neither the one nor the other of

the two classes of facts, upon which the existence of two races, Aryan and Semitic, has been
based, justifies the hypothesis maintained. The
facts of the second order, the religious, are in-
sufficient to establish two series of this kind,
and have no ethnographical significance. They
might have had, in a time that lies beyond the
horizon of history; they no longer have, in the
historical period. The starting-point of humanity lies so far off, and history, in trying to go
back to it, comes to a standstill so quickly,
that in no civilization, least of all in the Aryo-
Semitic, does it touch upon the part taken by
race. It reaches only to the results of the action of ten races, superimposed and amalgama-
ted, and which learned enough from each other,
and forgot enough, to present the appearance of
an irreducible unity of thought. Wherever we
imagine that we see the factor of race, there is
simply *tradition*, transmitted and modified from
one race to another.

II.

M. Ernest Renan, in a lecture which has
become famous,[1] demonstrated this opposition
of tradition to race by an example which is

---

[1] *Le Judaïsme comme race et comme religion.* Lecture delivered to the Cercle St. Simon, in January, 1883. Paris, Calmann Levy.

more forcible than mere arguments. The example was all the more conclusive inasmuch as
it is the one ordinarily cited as the typical illustration of the triumph of race, — the example of
Judaism. The proposition maintained, or rather
the facts set forth, by the illustrious Orientalist
are as follows: —

Judaism is generally considered a fact of
race, and one speaks of the Jewish race as one
speaks of the Jewish religion. One imagines
that a Jew of 1891 is a descendant of a Jew
of David's time; that the entire genealogy of
a Jewish family, whether the starting-point be
Paris, London, Vienna, Warsaw, would, if
traced back far enough, lead us to some village
of Palestine after having made the circuit of
the world. Religion and race are supposed to
be mutual supports to such an extent that at
the present time Judaism is still represented
by a physical type, and its adherents recognized
by their countenance. Such at least is the popular theory.

History proves that this is not the case. Beneath the actual religious unity of what is called
the Jewish race, there is hidden an infinite diversity of races. It is true that there was a
time when the racial type was definitely fixed
by persecution, imprisonment in the Ghetto,
absolute sequestration from the rest of the
world. But, up to that time, the blood of

Jewish society was being constantly renewed by a process that had gone on for centuries. M. Renan does not go back to the historical origin of this society, but takes up the thread at the time when Judaism, in the historical sense of the word, was constituted, when the national religion had become a universal one, the time of Isaiah and the prophets. In going back beyond this time, it would not be difficult to show that many foreign elements had entered into the blood of the primitive tribe of the Beni-Israel. At the flight from Egypt, they dragged with them "a mixed multitude," and in Palestine they found established a numerous population, only a part of which was exterminated in the conquest. In this double mixture, the first of which at least was very close, the primitive blood must have been transformed and renewed. Nevertheless, during centuries after the conquest of Palestine, the religion of the Jews remains purely national and local, as are all the religions of the time. They worship a God who belongs only to them, but who is not the one God. Religion has no occasion to leave the frontiers of the Jewish country, nor to spread among foreign races. The scene changes with the prophets. They rise, about the eighth century before the Christian era, to proclaim a new doctrine, a unique God, to the world, and a law of justice for all men. They create universal

religion, — a religion without analogy up to that
time, and whose dogmas and orders could and
must find an echo in every human heart, whatever the blood that courses through it.   The
disdain for sacrifices and cults, for vain forms
and lifeless images; the direct communion of
man with God in reason and in right; the communion of man with man in justice and charity;
an ideal resplendent with terrestrial happiness
that awaited humanity at the end of its career,
— all these strange novelties, still new to-day
despite all our philosophy, burst for the first
time upon the world in the lightning words of
the prophets.   From that day, religion was separated from race; from that day, too, there
begins a new order of phenomena that had
never as yet been produced, — the phenomena
of conversion.

Upon the return from the Babylonian exile,
numerous foreign elements mingle with the old
Jewish substratum, — Babylonian elements that
came from Chaldea with the exiles, Palestinian non-Jewish elements that commingled with
them.   But grafting on a much larger scale
took place during the Græco-Roman period.
It is well known from authentic sources that a
large part of the Greek population of Antioch
was converted to Judaism.   The Jewish colony
of Alexandria, one of the most considerable of
the time, was essentially of Hellenic blood.   At

Rome, the movement of conversion attracts the attention of statesmen, who abandon the attempt to stop it, and leave the matter to the satirists. Judaism attempted what Christianity accomplished. "The result is, that from this time," as M. Renan says, "the word ' Judaism ' possesses no special ethnographical significance. Conformably to the prediction of the prophets, Judaism became universal. Every one was admitted."

The triumph of Christianity and the Talmudic reaction which follows arrest this movement, without, however, suppressing it. It maintains its force in the Orient and in western Europe in the first part of the Middle Ages. The founding of Islam had been preceded, and in part prepared, by the conversion of a portion of Arabia to Judaism. There was a Jewish kingdom of Abyssinia, whose remains are still found in the Falashas of our days. In Russia, in the eighth century of our era, a whole Tartar nation, the Khozars, following the example of their king, embraced Judaism. Closer to us, on our own soil, in the fifth century, Gregory of Tours, in his combat against the Jews, sees in them only heretics, — not foreigners; the Jews of Gaul are to him merely Gauls professing Judaism.

There follows from this "that there is in the whole of the Jewish population, such as it exists in our day, a considerable portion of foreign blood, very much as among all other races, and that this race is far from being the ideal of a pure *ethnos*, as it is usually considered to be because of its opposition to mixed marriages." The permanence of the Jewish type, or, to speak more exactly, of the Jewish types, — for there are several, — is a secondary, not a primary fact. Given a human mass taken at hazard, unexpectedly isolated from the rest of the world and reproducing itself, it will be found that at the end of a certain time "the types will be reduced, massed in some degree, concentrated into a certain number of types, that by prevailing over others will persist and become fixed in an immutable form." It is the Ghetto that detached and fixed the Jewish types. It is the Ghetto, too, that produced that unity of habits and customs which we are wont to regard as the result of race, and which in reality is the mark of a religious minority concentrated and thrown back upon its own resources. "There is a psychology of religious minorities, independent of race."

The deductions of M. Renan's argument are various and of different kinds, some possessing present interest;[1] others of a general and universal bearing, already previously pointed out

[1] They are still interesting, since Anti-Semitism is triumphant in the entire west of Europe (1891).

by M. Renan in his admirable lecture upon the formation of the French nationality.

From the other side of the Rhine, this strange crusade of Anti-Semitism, that recently astonished Europe like an awakening from the Middle Ages, has endeavored to justify itself by history. Political hatreds and commercial rivalries, in combination with the laments of inquisitors, have been clothed with scientific formulas, and shopkeepers' quarrels have come to be regarded as the symptom of the supposed eternal collision between two races, — between two worlds, the Aryan and the Semitic. The rhetorical duel between court-preacher Stoecker and deputy Lasker [1] is interpreted as the old duel of Scipio and Hannibal, of Adrian and Bar-Kochba, of the Crusaders and Saladin. Germany is the ensign of the Aryan race, raised against the encroachments of the rehabilitated Semitic race.

"Historical spirit" is a beautiful thing, but it is easier to abuse the term than to apply it properly. It takes a strange ignorance of facts, and a singular docility in regard to words, to make of the Jew the type of the Semite. Judaism is born in a Semitic medium, but it is the most absolute reaction imaginable against the religion, the manners, the traditions that prevailed in that medium; it is the living pro-

[1] 1883.

test of broad humanity against the tribal idea.
Here is revealed the social danger contained in
this word " race," when it is snatched from the
hands of science by the would-be men of affairs,
and thrown out to the masses. Through it
every struggle takes on a character of bitter
and undying hatred, because the combatants
are persuaded that there exists between them,
not a momentary and accidental hostility, but
an irretrievable and fatal one. War between
these parties is supposed to be inevitable and
eternal, since the cause is always present, and
extends from the remote past to the distant future. Two organisms, two instincts, two irreconcilable souls, are supposed to be engaged in
the struggle; not two men, but two vertebrates
of a different order. Rapid or gradual extermination can alone put an end to the struggle.
In the same way, during the War of Secession,
the scholars of the South published "manuals
of anthropology" in which the monkey occupied
the intermediate place between the negro and
man.

What is still stranger is that, in the bloody
battle of words of the century, the scientific
subdivision of races and racial instincts involves a subdivision of the hatreds and fatali-
ties of war and destruction. The movement in
Germany would prompt the Aryans to make an
assault upon the Semitic world, but the Aryans

are subdivided into secondary races which must
in turn hate, fight, and exterminate each other
by reason of the secondary hostility of their
instincts, — the Germanic race against the Slavonic, the Germanic against the Latin. Humanity is merely a cruel and regular network
of hatreds and sub-hatreds, interwoven with the
hierarchy of races, and entangled by science
and by war.

If the form of human thought in historical
times was really an unchangeable expression of
the first race, a permanent state of war, with
no other outcome than extermination, would be
the inevitable lot of humanity. Happily this is
not the case, and among the infinite causes of
the struggles that engage civilized nations, —
struggles for outlets and for means of subsist-
ence, clashings of pride, metaphysical quarrels,
— the vague and obscure antipathies of race
occupy the very lowest place. What is taken
for them is merely the clash of colliding traditions. The clash of traditions, however ancient
and deeply rooted, cannot produce a state of
ceaseless warfare, since two opposing traditions,
when brought into contact, end either by an
adaptation of the one to the other, if they be
equally strong and sound, or by the *conversion* of the one into the other. The law of the
equilibrium of temperature reigns in the moral
as well as in the physical world. The struggle

of races can end only upon the battlefield and by extermination. The struggle of traditions, though carried to the battlefield, can find its definite solution only in the depths of thought and conscience. The extinction of a tradition does not involve the extinction of the race that possessed it, but its moral reconstruction, and generally the rejuvenation of its forces and of its aims.

It is not just to estimate a scientific theory according to the amount of good or bad that it does in the world. Truth, in the hands of the unintelligent or the shrewd, can do as much harm as error. In the domain of history, however, when a theory that has not been invented with a secondary thought of edification or benevolence, but which is the natural and spontaneous product of disinterested research, points the way to progress, there is a strong probability of its being the truth. The movement of the humanity of to-day is merely the result of accumulated impulses, movements condensed from centuries of history and prehistoric times. The fusion of races involved in the unity of tradition is due to a proper instinct regarding the past, and is at the same time a prognostication of the future.

In this light the words uttered in the Cercle Saint Simon are profoundly true. Some of these words may be the means of deliverance

for millions of oppressed, and, by the same
stroke, the beginning of a new career for their
oppressors.   In the Anti-Semitic movement of
Russia, the vague idea of an opposition of race
has brutalized the antipathies due to purely
economic, political, and social causes.   The mass
of Russian Jews have a Russian foundation
(Slav and Tartar).   Russia has in this case
to deal, not with a race but with a tradition.
She can neutralize the dangers of the situation
by suppressing the artificial causes that created
these dangers, such as isolation, confinement,
placing beyond the pale of justice.   And she
will do well to assimilate the good and the powerful in this tradition.   Let this new idea once
enter into her policy, and one of her plagues
and stigmas will soon disappear.

In the constitution of modern nations, race
is, in the same way, the secondary and inferior
element.   It may be remembered with what
eloquence M. Renan showed how France formed
the indissoluble alloy of her nationality by the
fusion of her heterogeneous elements, melted in
the fire of the soul, fanned by the wind of history.   A nationality is all the more solid the
more elements that are mixed with it, each
bringing to the crucible the quality of its metal;
one resistance, another brilliancy: —

"Tres ignis torti radios, tres alitis austri
    Miscebant operi, flammisque sequacibus iras."

Of other European nationalities, one of the strongest, presenting the most perfect cohesion with the greatest variety of aptitudes, is certainly the English people. This is what the author of "Robinson Crusoe" wrote two centuries ago, in answer to the attacks of the *true-born English-man* against the invasion of the Dutch element that followed in the wake of William of Orange:

> " These are the heroes that despise the Dutch,
> And rail at new-come foreigners so much ;
> Forgetting that themselves are all derived
> From the most scoundrel race that ever lived ;
> A horrid crowd of rambling thieves and drones
> Who ransacked kingdoms, and dispeopled towns ;
> The Pict, and painted Briton, treach'rous Scot,
> By hunger, theft, and rapine, hither brought ;
> Norwegian pirates, buccaneering Danes,
> Whose red-haired offspring everywhere remains ;
> Who join'd with Norman French, compound the breed
> From whence your *true-born Englishman* proceed." [1]

The satirist's compliments aside, there remains a basis of historical truth that explains the greatness of England. A race manifests its proper genius, in all its brilliance and all its soundness, when there is mingled with it a spark of foreign genius. The misfortune of Germany — what constitutes her momentary strength, and will bring about her lasting weakness in the future — is, that the element of race is better preserved there than elsewhere.

[1] *The True-Born Englishman,* De Foe.

Hence, narrowness of spirit, lack of proportion in her intelligence, of justice in her heart. She lacked that fruitful struggle of contrary forces that limit their excesses by complementing their energies, and that, in recognizing their mutual rights, enlarge the innate narrowness of man, with the result of producing something that has the extent and variety of Nature herself. Germany has remained, and still remains, a thing strangely powerful and painfully incomplete.

IN regard to every great mind that leaves a deep impress on its age, the curiosity of contemporaries asks two questions. On the one hand it inquires, "How was this mind formed, and what was the genesis of the thought which it expressed?" On the other hand it asks, "What lasting and fruitful element has it contributed to its generation and those which come after?" This double problem has a fascinating interest in this particular instance on account of the personality of the man, one of the most attractive and complicated characters which have appeared since Montaigne, and because of the extreme importance of the questions to which he devoted his life. Endowed with the most manifold gifts, — a savant, a philosopher, a poet, — no one exerted a profounder influence upon the doctrine, the thought, and the imagination of his countrymen; no one, perhaps, has been so insufficiently comprehended both at home and abroad. He has been stupidly criticised and stupidly praised. Men have been arrested by the apparent contradictions in his thought, in which there seemed to triumph in turn the most elevated idealism and the most absolute skepticism; by this stoical life which wrapped itself more than once in the formulas of Epicurus; by this science which seemed always preoccupied by a fear that its affirmation or its negation might be taken too seriously. He was denounced as one of the moral dissolvents of the century, and yet from his lips there fell some of the highest and gravest words to which our generation has listened. By a supreme contradiction, those who came near to M. Renan, those especially who studied him with some care, have rendered their testimony to the unparalleled sincerity of his thought, which always was expressed as it appeared to himself, and was never sacrificed either to the desire of popularity, or to fear of the powers that are, or of public opinion, or even, great artist though he was, to the search for artistic effect. In order to solve the enigma of this manifold soul, we need only follow it in its history and in its work. The task is easy: the work is before us, and the essential element of this history, the critical period which formed it, M. Renan himself has described to us in the clearest and frankest of Confessions.[1]   I

---

[1] *Souvenirs d'Enfance et de Jeunesse* (Paris, 1880), to which should be added the pages, of which only a few copies were printed, devoted to the memory of his sister, *Henriette Renan,* "a Souvenir for those who knew her:" Paris, September, 1862. These pages, the most touching that ever came from the heart of the writer, will doubtless soon be made public.

shall be excused for devoting myself mainly to
the Renan of the early years; one may say that
after twenty-five M. Renan no longer changed,
and that all the qualities, all the essential ideas,
all the general views, and the greater part of
the special views which made him original and
powerful, are shown in the first pages which he
wrote on leaving the seminary, with all the consciousness and all the clearness that they were
to have later on.

I.

Brittany is the country of fairies. It is the
corner of France which has preserved the ancient faith in its greatest purity, not only the
Christian faith, but also the old popular religion older than the church, the roots of which
go deep down into the period of mythology and
paganism. Its true temples are the country
chapels, with their local saints and their bizarre
images and their legends, which are more Dru-
idical than Christian, and are much more
closely related to the Richis and the Devatas of
India than to the canonized saints of the established church.

Here M. Renan was born of a family of sailors. These people, cradled in the eddies of a
terrible sea that rarely smiles and is always
solemn, and in the mysteries of their super-
stitions and legends, are more grave, more spir-

itual, and more profoundly thoughtful than any
other people of France. Renan was still a
child when his father perished at sea. He was
reared by his mother, who was of Gascon de-
scent; she added to the Breton faith a fund of
gayety, verve, and gentle irony that were foreign to Brittany. She gave her son his profound and sincere faith in the teachings of the
church and also his imaginative faith, amused
and semi-skeptical, in the creations of the popular religion. She was a living folk-lore; "she
loved these faiths as a Breton and smiled at
them as a Gascon." To his education in this
naïve and earnest environment, so different from
that of our great cultivated and commonplace
cities, Renan attributed later his historical faculty, and his gift of reviving spiritual conditions
different from those of our own day. He had
there acquired "a kind of habit of seeing under-
ground, and of hearing noises beyond the reach
of other ears."

His first masters, the good priests of Treguier,
that old city of convents, chapels, and churches,
were such models of tranquil faith and spotless
virtue as the provincial clergy of France often
exhibit. By their lessons and by their example
they taught him that Christianity sums up
every ideal, and that the spiritual life is the
only noble life. When, in 1838, led by the report of Renan's success as a scholar in the

college of Treguier, M. Dupanloup, in search of
brilliant recruits for the church, called him to
the seminary of Saint Nicolas du Chardonneret,
he carried there a perfect docility and an entire
faith, thus far untouched by any disturbance
from within or from without. Reared in a
confined atmosphere, where no breath of the
profane world came, he had had none of those
encounters with the modern spirit which suffice
with so many other Frenchmen to shake and
destroy their traditional faith, while they have
no part in the work of their own conversion.
We do not divest ourselves of our faith; it is
torn from us by the wind which blows upon the
age, and those who lose their beliefs through
the labor of their own minds only are as rare
as those who form their own beliefs. The few
men who are the real makers of their own in-
credulity have generally been stranded on the
arid shores of reasoning; it is upon the anti-
nomy between the teachings of revelation and
those of science that their faith makes shipwreck, or upon the logical impossibilities which
appear on every side as soon as faith seeks to
justify itself. The spiritual crisis which threw
M. Renan out of the church was quite different.
It was entirely of a philological and critical
order; it was the sense and the date of some
lines of Hebrew which fixed his destiny. It
was the crisis of Robert Elsmere forty years

before "Robert Elsmere." An excellent Hebraist of St. Sulpice, the Abbé Le Hir, a man of great learning and acquainted with the critical labors of the Germans, but who had a profound faith not to be in any way uprooted, which allowed him to dismiss without trouble and by an *a priori* process every conclusion of science which conflicted with Orthodoxy, had initiated the young seminarist into the study of Hebrew and of German exegesis. This was the cause of the shipwreck. Renan had never been arrested by an objection to the doctrines of the Trinity and of the Incarnation viewed in themselves; he had accepted every dogma on faith in the revealed texts. But now the philological study of these very texts showed him that they cannot be revealed, since they swarm with contradictions and have all the characteristics of ordinary human literature. The Book of Daniel is an apocryphal document belonging to the time of the Maccabees: the infallible church is mistaken, then, when it makes this the work of a prophet in the time of Nebuchadrezzar and exults in the realized prophecies which it contains. The history of Christ rests upon the Gospels; the Synoptics contradict the Fourth Gospel and contradict each other; there is no reconciliation possible, and it is impossible to accept them all together. The New Testament founds its dogmas upon citations from the Old

Testament: these quotations are inaccurate, or
have not the sense which was given them, so
that the two Testaments cannot be equally inspired. The skepticism which rests entirely
upon the exercise of the logical faculties always
appears to be a kind of begging the question in
the eyes of the religious critic, and has no convincing effect upon him: the claims and the
merits of faith are precisely that it rises above
reason, and so all the arrows darted by abstract
reason are necessarily *telum imbelle sine ictu.*
But it is not the same with doubts as to facts,
with historic doubts; for if the word which
establishes the faith is a word human, change-
able, contradictory, and born out of historical
circumstances, the dogma and the book dissolve
together.

The young man who on the 6th of October,
1845, having recognized that he could no longer,
without denying his conscience, keep the name
of Catholic and of Christian, descended the
steps of St. Sulpice never to ascend them again,
had as little in common with the frivolous and
incredulous world in which he was to disappear
as with the world of belief which he had left.
Voltairianism, which was then the religion of
France, was unknown or profoundly antipathetic
to him. Although much later M. Renan recognized not only the substantial gratitude which
we owe to the Encyclopædists, but also the pro-

found and just views in which their frivolous
exegesis sometimes anticipated by a century the
most recent criticism, the Voltairian spirit had
had no part in his conversion. He even compared more than once, not without a little regret, the slow and painful manner in which he
had effected the emancipation of his thought
with the easy and painless fashion in which any
gamin of Paris reaches his independence. Did
it need six years of Hebrew and of German
exegesis pursued in doubt and trembling in
order to reach at last as a doctrine the postu-
late of Gavroche! The historian of the ideas
of this century will not be able to share this
regret. That redoubtable but superficial polemic of the eighteenth century which assured
the right of free thought, even to those very
persons who are now the most disdainful of it,
was an admirable weapon in the contest with
the worst of oppressions, — that which tortures
in the name of charity and brutalizes in the
name of intellect. But, this task done, it remained singularly ineffective; it has nothing to
establish in the moral order, and nothing to
teach in the scientific order, and it can neither
explain nor satisfy the religious sentiment. In
its necessary work of destruction, in destroying
the fantastical and murderous vegetation which
was choking the thought of Catholic peoples, it
laid the axe upon the very germ, upon the root

of the moral life. M. Renan, if he had been
emancipated at fifteen by the methods of the
day (fifteen is the critical age for faith, in
French education), would doubtless have showed
the world, sooner or later, the incomparable
artist that was in him; the literary chimes
which he carried in his head from birth would
certainly have sounded, early or late, but to
what tune? He might perhaps have been attracted by Greece, which later exercised so
powerful an attraction over his imagination, or
by pure science, which is the finest field for
poetry next to history. But we should not
have had the advantage of this unique experience, the like of which was never before seen in
France, and which was to give us, in the end,
the first historian of the religious sentiment.

"In order to comprehend a religion," M.
Renan loved to say, "one must have believed it
and have left it." Doubtless this in itself is
not sufficient, and everything depends on the
manner in which one leaves the religion behind
him. Lamennais also had believed in Christianity and had left it; nevertheless, only at
the end of his life and many years after his
stormy conversion did he do it justice. He
had left the faith on the battlefield of life
moved by indignation and anger; he did not
leave it by the royal road of criticism and history. He detested, the very day when he

ceased to adore, and his hatred, eloquent and noble like his love, was, like that, sterile and blind. The young seminarist who bade the church farewell in 1845 left it without hatred and without anger, through very respect for it, obeying solely the command of an enlightened conscience, which forbade him to commit the sacrilege of serving a God who still possessed his heart but no longer mastered his reason. Leaving religious illusion behind, he remembered all its magic spells and all its evasions, but also all its charm and all its benefit. Knowing why he no longer believed, he knew also *how* he had believed; why he did right to believe, and how the lost faith had answered for a time the noblest instincts of his nature. For this reason, when he wrote the history of past beliefs he had only to interrogate himself to find again in his own consciousness the secret of their nature and their power.

His state of mind at this time was that of the liberal Protestant theologian or of the Unitarian. "For two months," said he, "I was a Protestant." During the last Holy Week which he passed at St. Sulpice, confiding the decision which he had already taken and the anguish of the approaching separation to one of his friends who had taken orders, he wrote: "This Holy Week above all has been sorrowful for me; for every circumstance which withdraws me from

my ordinary life plunges me again into distress.
I console myself by thinking of Jesus, so beautiful, so pure, so ideal in his suffering, whom I
shall always love, whatever view I take of his
nature. Even if I should come to abandon
him, it would please him, for it would be a
sacrifice at the altar of conscience: God knows
what it would cost me." For him, as for the
extreme left of Protestant theology, Jesus was
no longer more than the ideal man, the most
divine expression of human nature, and he
dreamed of a neo-Christianity freed from all
dross of superstition, preserving its moral effi-
cacy, and capable of remaining or becoming
again the great school of humanity and its
guide in the future. He believed himself still
a Christian. He recognized very quickly, however, that he was no longer such, and that the
symbolic and esoteric Christianity of Protestant
Germany is only an equivocation. It has no
substantial immorality in it, for it is not due to
politic and worldly calculation: its most common source is a very respectable and very religious feeling, a sincere and profound attachment
to ancient forms, and a touching gratitude for
the dreams which formerly gave the ideal its
surest wings. It is, moreover, a beneficent
equivocation; it favors in every sect the exercise of free investigation, it deadens the shocks
of dogma; it facilitates religious peace by crea-

ting the illusion that the esoteric Christianity
of thinkers and the miraculous Christianity of
the masses are one and the same thing, and that
Dr. Harnack and Dr. Stoecker are both Christians.   Finally, it allows the highest layers of
thought of the age to penetrate the lower layers
through the medium of a common tradition and
common watchwords, and permits the new wine
to fill the old skins.   Happy is the country and
the time in which this confusion can take place.
It is not now possible, however, in Catholic
countries.   Long before Renan saw clearly into
his thought, his teacher in theology at the little seminary of Issy, M. Gottofrey, an ardent
and sectarian nature with the intuitions of the
inquisitor, — struck by the logic and the force
and the argumentative power his young pupil
brought to the discussion of theological subjects,
— divined the hidden monster, and raised the
cry which terrified Renan without enlightening
him: "You are not a Christian!"   There is no
way under Catholicism to escape the letter, to
take refuge in allegory: for Catholicism there
is no essential difference between rationalism,
Euhemerism, the mythology of the schools, and
the brutal Voltairian negation; and we must
avow that there is none substantially, and in
the face of positive religion.   The Catholic does
not comprehend and he cannot accept, that
esoteric attitude which is the negation not only

of Catholicism but of Christianity itself, for the liberal theologian who volatilizes the Christ into a moral metaphor, and reduces the entire Christology to an allegory and a symbol, just as the liberal theologians of Neopaganism were wont to do in the case of Jupiter and Hera, is not a Christian.

At the time when M. Renan left St. Sulpice, he was still only a pupil of Germany. He took from her not only a system of exegesis, but also a philosophy which for the time replaced for him the faith of his fathers. He has often described the profound impression which was made upon him at the age of eighteen by his first initiation into Goethe and Herder: "I felt that I was entering a temple." What impressed him at the first in this philosophy was that reconciliation of the high religious spirit with the critical spirit which holds out to the Protestant the agreeable prospect that he can be a philosopher without ceasing to be a Christian. The foundation of this philosophy is the notion of ' Becoming,' of the perpetual transformation of things which never are, but are always on the way to being; a view eminently historical, elevated, and sanctified by the feeling of an active ideal which moves onward to its realization through this incessant flux and metamorphosis. In its Hegelian form especially, this philosophy lends itself admirably to the task of reconciling the most respectful religious conservatism with all the demands of history; the Christ being the realization in time of the unconscious and hidden deity who, in the panorama of the universe and the ages, seeks to come to consciousness, and who finds it at last in humanity, in the bosom of humanity, in the consciousness of the Christ. But M. Renan was too much of a Frenchman in intellect to delay long over these formulas of a too precise mysticism: moreover, through a bankruptcy which still weighs upon Germany, they were to end, under pretext of the ideal, in the deification of brute fact, in the divine right of the strongest; to be logical, they should have laid down as the last term of the Infinite in its march, not the Christ upon his cross, but Hegel in his professorial chair. Renan traversed the German systems without settling there; he drew from them only certain principles: from Hegel the idea of Becoming, and from Herder the idea which corrects and complements ' Becoming,' the rôle of spontaneity in creation.

Scarcely entered into lay life, Renan encountered influences which were to enlighten the obscurity that his Catholic education and his German initiation had left in his thought. Thrown upon the streets of Paris without resources and without a future, in this desert of men he had for support only his determination to live in the truth and for the truth. He obtained the position of supervisor in a school of the Quartier Latin, where he earned his board and lodging by two hours' work a day, and had the remainder of his time free for his own tasks. Among the pupils of the institution, there was a young man eighteen years old who already displayed the aureole of genius, — Marcellin Berthelot. He already possessed the encyclopædic mind, the concentrated ardor, the passion for truth, and the sagacity in discovery which were to make him one of the kings of science. Younger than Renan by four years, he imparted to him the revelation of science and the philosophy of the external world, as Renan had given him the revelation of the philosophy of the spirit. A deep friendship, which was to endure for forty years, was established between these two young men intoxicated with science, dreaming of a cosmogony, in their eager converse tossing about the fragments of the universe. Both were still Christians in imagination; but the exchange of ideas sufficed in a few months to relegate these vestiges of faith "to the department of their souls devoted to memory;" and certain inflexible principles were laid down which were to form the *inconcussum quid* of their faith. There is no break in continuity in the order of phenomena; there is no interruption in the laws of nature, which goes on without ceasing, following the impulse of its interior movements, while no external will, no supernatural intervention, can ever be detected in the world. Such were the necessary conclusions which followed from experience and the justified inductions of science during the three centuries since science was instituted. Analogous conclusions were necessary in the world of mind and in the history of man. Never has a miracle been proved; never has the intervention of an extra-human will been manifest to man; in every verifiable case, where such a deviation has been declared, the apparent deviation has been resolved into an illusion or a legend. The history of man and of his thought is only one chapter in natural history. In this way, M. Renan found himself brought back to the point of view of all French philosophy, of the great empiricists of the last century and of the idealists of the beginning of this century; but he added what was lacking in them, the religious sense.

While he continued the study of Semitic languages begun at St. Sulpice, he devoted a large part of his time to Indo-European studies and attended the lectures of Burnouf at the Collège de France. A new illumination, a new horizon opened before his thought, a third and more powerful awakening of his imagination and his intellect. No scholar made upon him so profound an impression as Burnouf; and no one was more deserving of the opportunity than this great mind that realized most perfectly the type of the modern savant whose discoveries are the result of the mere bringing together of facts honestly collected, and interpreted by the genius of good sense. A creative mind in the most diverse domains, — in the history of Buddhism, of the Vedas, of Zoroastrianism, — no one ever left behind him a shorter record of error, and we must come down to M. Pasteur to find a similar example of the reward which, in the hands of genius, awaits this irreproachable and patient method; but M. Pasteur labors in a field where this method has been applied for a much longer time and is more easily verified. "In hearing your lectures" (said Renan to Burnouf, in 1849, when dedicating to him the "Future of Science") "upon the finest of languages and literatures in the primitive world, I found the realization of what before I had only dreamed, science becoming philosophy and the highest results proceeding from the most scrupulous analysis of details."

It was not Burnouf's method alone which filled Renan with admiration, it was his entire view of the history of thought as manifested in language and religion. It was a whole branch of the human family that Burnouf spread out

before him with all its ramifications in time
and space, with its infinite variety and its fruitful unity. Again, it was a broad pencil of
light, of induction and analogy projected upon
the parts of the human forest which had hitherto remained in the dark. This was a method
to be applied beyond the Aryan world. Impressed by the treatise of Bopp, Renan outlined in thought a comparative grammar of the
Semitic languages.

Thus, in less than five years, there were
united in his hands the three elements, the three
metals, the fusion of which was to make of his
genius the most supple weapon, and, despite ap-
pearances, the one of greatest resistance since
the days of Goethe. He had drawn from Germany his system of exegesis, from the natural
sciences his view of the world, and from historical philology his method: from his own
treasury he brought forth the things which are
not borrowed, all the gifts of a pensive and
austere race; a vigorous curiosity and infinite
sympathy, espousing in imagination every form
of reality; inflexible attachment in science and
in life, to whatever had once been recognized
as just and true.

These diverse but not disparate elements were
fermenting in his mind, when the Revolution of
1848 broke out with its humanitarian dreams
and its bloody disillusions. This was a new

shock, which forced the student to interrogate
the depths of his conscience, and to take account of what he was before the world and
before God, to sum up the new faith which
had replaced in him the ruins of Catholicism,
and to which he was now to turn for guidance
in thought and life. The last two months of
1848 and the first four months of 1849 were devoted to the compilation of this confession. It
formed a large volume, which was intended to
appear in the same year, but was not published
until 1888, under the title of "The Future of
Science." It is one of those books which are
written only at twenty-five, when one is overflow-
ing with illusions and enthusiasm. It is the
enthusiasm of the young man who has had a
revelation of a great idea, of science, and who,
in the intoxication of the discovery, attributes to
it all the nobility of his own soul, adorns it with
omnipotence, and believes it capable of satisfying all the aspirations of humanity, of healing
all its miseries, and of taking the soothing rôle
which positive religion can no longer sustain.
Insufficiently developed, often difficult in expression, obscure through the plethora of thought
in a mind which has not yet learned to sacrifice
or reserve a part of its treasures, and which
gives itself forth entire, often retarded, after
the German fashion, by those considerations of
system, which require an apparatus of thought

too considerable for the substantial residue which
they leave, — this book has yet more than the
merit of being a curiosity, as M. Renan regarded
it when, forty years later, he took it out of his
desk "to show an entirely natural young man
but one afflicted by a serious brain fever, living
solely in his intellect and believing fanatically
in truth." This book is, in a certain sense, the
most complete that M. Renan wrote, and it
contains, more than in the mere germ, the whole
Renan whom we know. To be sure, in the course
of time he will lose his illusions as to the omnipotence of science; he will recognize that it
cannot of itself found a religion; that truth can
enlighten and direct only those who have already
in themselves a directing principle, either in the
innate nobility of their education, or in the
hereditary habits of virtue impressed upon them
by ancestors who believed. He himself will say
later that the virtue of skeptical ages is the
residuum left by ages of faith: "My life is
always governed by a faith which I no longer
possess." He will recognize that the dream
of Plato is only a dream; that philosophy is
not made to rule the world and to replace politics; and that it is not possible for science to
reconstruct the edifice which was built by the
spontaneous forces of nature. The fundamental optimism which penetrates these youthful
pages — these unmeasured hopes for the future

of humanity, considered as the purposed end of the development of nature, and remaining, in this semi-Hegelian conception, as it was before in the Catholic conception, the centre of the universe — will make way for a limited optimism which, under an objective view of things, is only the form that theoretical pessimism takes in a good soul enamored of the beautiful, and open to the innocent pleasures of life and knowledge. These pages bear the mark of 1848, in their democratic aspiration, in their conception of humanity as one single being, as a homogeneous body, all the members of which are capable of comprehending and realizing the same ideal. It is a long way from this book to the despondent pages of the "Dialogues philosophiques," and to that transcendent and cruel vision of progress making the immolation of a lower layer of humanity serve the coming of an elect race which will realize more fully the obscure dream of the hidden God.

Nevertheless, despite the corrections which age is to bring to these theories of youth, all Renan's essential ideas are already here, and it is upon this foundation, laid in his twenty-fifth year, that his whole doctrine was developed. For a long time this great Purana, left unpublished, was a sort of monumental quarry from which he drew, without exhausting it, raw material and polished stones, like those architects who built the Rome of the Popes from the stones of the Coliseum. Some of his most admired pages came from this quarry, and nowhere has he brought out more clearly his conception of the divine: "Beauty in the moral order, — that is religion. This is the reason why a dead and outgrown religion is yet more effective than all purely secular institutions; this the reason why Christianity is still more creative, consoles more sorrows, and acts more vigorously upon humanity, than do all the acquired principles of modern times. The men who will make the future will not be petty men, disputing, reasoning, insulting, — partisans and intriguers, without an ideal. They will be beautiful, they will be amiable, they will be poetic. . . . The word 'God,' possessing the respect of humanity, having a long office, and having been employed in noble poetry, its suppression would put humanity off the track. Although it is not very 'univocal,' as the scholastics say, it corresponds to a sufficiently definite idea; the *summum* and the *ultimum*, the limit where the soul stops in ascending the ladder of the infinite. . . . Tell the simple to live a life of aspiration after truth and beauty, and these words will have no meaning for them. Tell them to love God, not to offend God, and they will understand you marvelously well. God, providence, the soul, — these are so many good old words, a little awkward, but expressive and respectable, which science will explain, but will not replace to advantage. What is God for humanity if not the transcendent résumé of its supersensible needs, *the category of the ideal* (that is, the form under which we conceive the ideal), as space and time are *the categories of matter* (that is, the forms under which we conceive matter). All may be reduced to this fact of human nature: Man facing the divine rises out of himself, and is held by a heavenly spell, and his own petty personality is exalted and absorbed? What is this if it is not to adore?"[1]

Augustin Thierry, to whom M. Renan read his manuscript, dissuaded him from making his entrance into the literary world with this metaphysical epic in his hands. He advised him to send to the "Revue des Deux-Mondes" and to the "Journal des Debats" articles upon various subjects, in which he could publish by instalments a stock of ideas which, presented in one solid mass, would not have failed to frighten the French public. Thus "The Future of Science," put forth in sections and in a concrete, illuminated, and manageable form, entered little by little into intellectual circulation.[2] Yet

---

[1] This page was reproduced in an article on Feuerbach, *Etudes d'Histoire Religieuse,* [pp. 418, 419. — ED.].

[2] These articles, collected in volume form, furnished the material for the *Etudes d'Histoire Religieuse,* 1857, and for the *Essais de Morale et de Critique,* 1859. In the first of these

Renan's apprenticeship to learning was sufficiently advanced to enable him to begin his
scientific career proper. Such a nature was
necessarily led to take for ·its object the study
of the human mind. The great progress realized over the seventeenth and eighteenth centuries, for which the study of the human mind
was, above all, a logical analysis and a judgment *a priori*, has never been better expressed
than in the closing lines of the preface of his
book: "The science of the human mind should,
first of all, be the history of the human mind,
and this history is possible only through the
patient philological study of the works which
it has brought forth in different ages." It is
this history which formed the object of his research for the rest of his life.

II.

Thus at twenty-five M. Renan was what he
was to be later, what he will be always. His
philosophy is constructed, and his life and his
work will be its peaceful and uniform development. External circumstances may alter the
form and the expression, but not the essence.

volumes is found the article on "The Critical Histories of Jesus," which anticipates the method of the *Vie de Jésus*, and the
fine study of "Mahomet and the Origins of Islam" which
Dozy so greatly admired.

The critics, who are absolutely determined that
every man shall be placed in a category fixed
in advance, and are not at ease until they have
furnished each name with a label, like the apo-
thecary with his drugs, have often asked whether
M. Renan was a philosopher, a scholar, or a
poet. As he was plainly an incomparable
writer, they concluded that he was, above all,
an artist, and that in philosophy he was a reflection of Germany, and in science an amateur.
This shows that they but slightly understood
M. Renan. No writer of the century sacrificed
less to the delusive and barren idol of "art for
art's sake." In France, where the art of expression has always been the supreme gift, as
in the time of the Gauls, no one has more profoundly disdained and more decisively assaulted
that literary dilettanteism, that love of form
courted for itself and not pursued as the sincere
expression of an idea which deserves to be expressed, that obstinacy in despising the substance of knowledge and esteeming only style
and talent, which, from 1830 to 1860, paralyzed
science, gave a fatal blow to serious research,
and reduced intellectual culture to pompous and
superficial qualities, to the art of making aca-
demic phrases.[1] Science, philosophy, and art
are for him and in him, one and the same single

[1] See in particular, *Questions contemporaines*, 1868; and *Re-
forme intellectuelle et morale*, 1871.

thing, — the diverse aspects of truth sought, comprehended, and expressed.

It is not easy to sum up the work of M. Renan, so diverse is it in its subjects and in its forms. In the variety of his studies he resembles more a Greek philosopher than a modern specialist. A specialist in the proper sense of the word he never became. If the philosopher devotes himself to a limited field, this is reasonable because of the impossibility of embracing everything; by right the whole universe belongs to him. Classic antiquity, the Middle Ages, art, contemporary history, politics, — M. Renan invaded all these provinces; and if he devoted twenty years of his life to the history of Christianity, it was not solely because his ecclesiastical education predisposed him to it, but most of all because Christianity, with its roots in Judaism, led him through the most vital periods of the human soul, and allowed him to refresh himself from one of the most fruitful sources of the moral life of humanity.

The special work of M. Renan was done in the Semitic domain. It is a work essentially synthetic. Although he never ignored the value of detailed research, and although his historical works in particular presuppose an infinite number of minute investigations, things as a whole attracted him most — the monument which he sees behind the separate stones, the living being that he seeks under the fossil débris. His work as a scholar was, according to his own definition, "the study of the human race, supported by the philological study of its productions." It is thus philological and historical. It is summed up in his "History of the Semitic Languages," in his history of the "Origins of Christianity," and in the organization of the "Corpus Inscriptionum Semiticarum."

He started with pure philology and never abandoned it, — the study of languages being the first and indispensable instrument of the historical method. One comprehends an idea only when one can follow it in its original expression; the larger part of the errors which encumber religious history have proceeded from theologians or theorists who labor upon translations and cannot seize the idea in its nascent state. So all the great historians of ideas have begun with philology; so Burnouf, so Renan. It was, indeed, in Burnouf's lecture-room that the idea of a history of the Semitic languages originated. Dazzled by the light which the discovery of Sanskrit had thrown upon the languages of Europe and of half of Asia, by this unexpected bond uniting Greece to India and Gaul to Persia, and by this rediscovered relationship between so many supposed strangers, he resolved to do for the Semitic language what Burnouf had done for the Indo-European

tongues. In 1847, two years after leaving St.
Sulpice, he drew a sketch of what became his
"History of the Semitic Languages." Penetrated as he then was by the cosmogonic
spirit, he went back at once to the beginning
of things, and in the same year that he wrote
the "Future of Science" he published an essay
upon the "Origin of Language" (6th edition,
1882). This again is one of those subjects
which only a beginner attacks, and the Société
de Linguistique of Paris, of which M. Renan
was president, puts at the head of its programme a notice that the society does not admit communications concerning the origin of
language. "The true theory of languages,"
M. Renan himself will say later, "is their history." The origin of language, as the very
words show, is outside of experience, outside of
history, outside of science. But ⌈questions of
origin have such a fascination for a religious
soul that it always returns to wander around
the forbidden pit.⌋ According to M. Renan,
language does not owe its birth to a revelation
from on high, nor is it a reasoned invention of
mankind : languages are the immediate product
of the human consciousness. They have not
been created slowly and gradually by gropings
and successive approximations; man is naturally
a speaker as he is naturally a thinker. Speech
is a spontaneous work, like thought, like reli-

gion. It is not a rudimentary language, an incomplete vocabulary, a grammar on the way to
be made, which Renan places in the cradle of
humanity. Nascent humanity had gifts of creation and of reaction upon nature which were
blunted when it no longer had need of them.
The ancestors of our race had a special feeling
for nature which made them perceive, with a
delicacy which we no longer can understand,
the qualities which should furnish appellation
by signs. Nature said more to them than to
us, or rather they found in themselves a secret
echo which responded to all those voices from
without and rendered them in words. In short,
language, the history of which is the triumph
and the finest revelation of Becoming, was in
the beginning a creation of Spontaneity. We
feel here the influence of Herder's conceptions
of the dominant rôle which spontaneity plays in
human creations. Doubtless between animal
expression and human expression, science is
forced to admit as intermediary a spontaneous
human creation, analogous to those which take
place on every plane of life, and which mark
the progress of nature. The error consists in
attributing to this spontaneity of the earliest
time the product of a long development which
escapes us from the very fact that we know
nothing of spoken language except from the
moment when, by a happy chance, writing made

it known to us. To deny and to suppress this development, because we cannot trace it to its beginning, is to objectify our ignorance, and to say that nothing is going on in the street because the curtains are drawn.

If there is any order of phenomena which can throw light upon the ancient epochs of language, we must seek it in a parallel order of science, in writing. If we knew only the modern alphabetic forms of writing, its origin would offer a miracle analogous to that of speech, and perhaps still more astonishing; for here all the relations are purely abstract and all the elements are apparently arbitrary, while in language which has arrived at the highest degree of abstraction there still remain two natural elements, — exclamation and gesture. The ancient documents of Egypt, Assyria, and China have happily preserved for us the first concrete and natural element from which all the naked elements of abstract writing have arisen, — the *ideogram.* So, at the origin of language, is found the *ideophone* which escapes us, for what we call "roots" are only a late abstraction which grammar extracts from formed words. But the creation of an ideophone, that is, a sound once attached to an image (whether this be the image of a material object, or the image of the sentiment reflected in the expression and the attitude of the face), is sufficient to begin a language;

its career is then open to an infinite "becoming," which we cannot restore but which we
can conceive, and toward which induction allows
us to go back, up to a certain point, setting out
from the most ancient form accessible.

It is not a simple question of linguistic philosophy that M. Renan thinks to solve: it is a
grave historical question. Have the Semitic
and the Aryan languages the same origin, and
can we bring them into one and the same family? Many attempts have been made with this
end in view, without much success; nevertheless, the failure of these efforts does not pronounce decisively against the unity, for the
separation of the two branches might have been
too remote for the primitive relationship to have
left visible traces. M. Renan dismisses *a priori*
every attempt of this kind: the two groups of
languages are constituted according to a different type, and two types presuppose two creations; two independent acts in two different
centres have created two types essentially and
originally diverse.

This is a theory which by its very nature
escapes control, and which, in the present state
of knowledge and under the impossibility of
laying hold of the two families in really primitive epochs, science can neither verify nor refute.
But M. Renan extended it and carried it into
territory where verification is possible. At the

time when he entered upon his task, Germany
had just created, on the basis of comparative
grammar, the ingenious but frail edifice of comparative mythology, — an illusory science which
could not keep its promises, for it confounded
nomen and *numen*, and furthermore by assimi-
lating the common divine names, disregarded
the infinitely diverse revolutions of ideas which
had taken place in these names in the course of
time, amid the thousand accidents of history and
the manifold collisions of different races and
civilizations. As comparative grammar had
brought the family of Aryan religions and the
family of Semitic religions face to face, and as,
in fact, among Semitic religions, only the monotheism of the Jews and that of the Arabs were
known, monotheism was made the religious
mark of the Semites. M. Renan carried into
the religious domain his theory of the origin of
languages: religions have been created by a
sudden intuition of the race. The Semitic race,
like the Aryan, was in possession, from the first
days of its existence, of a certain type of language and a certain type of religion. "In religion and in language nothing is invented;
everything is the fruit of a position assumed in
the beginning, once for all." Hence a vast
antithesis which extends to every aspect of the
soul and of life. With the Aryans, we find the
epic, the myth, the legend, the drama, the ob-

jective imagination, the worship of nature; with
the Semites, we find personal poetry, the lyric
cry; the Aryans have founded the city, political life, and the nation; the Semites have known
only the nomadic and pastoral life; the Aryans
have created art and the Semites religion. We
know the good fortune which these simple,
clear, and imperative formulas have had: "You
inclose twelve hundred years and one half of
the ancient world in the hollow of your hand"
(Taine). They were too simple not to seduce
the public and popularizers at second hand, for
they offered an admirably clear outline and a
guiding thread through history. But they were
also too simple to accommodate the facts, and
in proportion as they were more closely examined, facts could hold up their heads. We will
not dwell here upon the doubtful and dangerous identification of the conception of race and
the conception of language: though there is no
longer an Aryan race (for the so-called Aryan
languages are obviously spoken by a multitude
of races which have nothing in common with
the creators of these languages), we may admit
that the peoples speaking a Semitic language
have, for the greater part, belonged to one and
the same family. But the progress of Semitic
epigraphy since 1845 has revealed the fact that
monotheism was only an exception with the
Semites; that with the Jews it was a late step

in reflection, and with the Arabs and Syrians an importation from the Jews and the Christians. The history of Assyria and of Chaldea has shown that the Semites could also found empires, and the library of Assurbanipal has given us fragments of epics. The Corpus itself, directed by M. Renan, has brought from ancient Carthage, from Phœnicia, and from pre-Islamic Arabia innumerable relics of an ancient Semitic polytheism. The Arabian desert is no more monotheistic than the Iranian plateau or the valley of the Indus.

These theories, which dominate the whole work of M. Renan, form the introduction to his "History of the Semitic Languages."[1] Through the effect which they had upon the ideas of this second half of the century, they belong to history; but the book itself belongs to science alone. Without doubt, if it had been written to-day, its limits would have been extended. M. Renan included only the classic Semitic languages, those of which scholars had a grammatical and literary knowledge thirty years ago, — Hebrew, Syriac, Arabic, and Ethiopic. Phœnician is the only purely epigraphic language admitted. In his "Recollections" of his youth he declares, with his usual frankness,

---

[1] See, also, his opening lecture at the Collège de France in 1862, and in the *Journal Asiatique*, 1859, " *Nouvelles Considérations sur le Caractère général des Peuples Semitiques et en particulier sur leur Tendance au Monothéisme.*"

that he never knew well anything but what his teacher of Hebrew at St. Sulpice, the Abbé Le Hir, had taught him. This is a great exaggeration, but it had a foundation of truth. His essential ideas were sketched early, and the facts which agreed ill with these ideas had great difficulty in getting themselves recognized. A history of the Semitic languages should have devoted one of its principal chapters to Assyrian. M. Renan dismissed it with a few lines, not being sure that the language was Semitic. Doubtless the uncertainties of decipherment to this day, and the unusual awkwardness which the Assyriologists showed in their exposition, went far to justify his attitude of reserve, and he was right in waiting for fuller light; but this reserve was due also to a purely theoretical idea, — that Assyrian, being expressed in an alphabet which was not Semitic, could not be a Semitic language. Here, again, dogmatic theory took precedence of fact.

In spite of these licenses and these omissions, the "History of the Semitic Languages" is one of the fine books of the century, a book the equivalent of which for the Aryan family is still wanting. It is not a comparative grammar, properly so called (the comparative grammar was to form a second volume, which has never appeared); it is a history proper, that is, it shows us these languages in the geographical domain which they occupied, in the vesture of writing which they adopted, in the ages through which they endured, in the historical, religious, and literary monuments to which they gave expression, and in the works that they have left. Of the second volume a few separate chapters have appeared; one chapter on the Semitic verb (Memoires de la Société de Linguistique de Paris); another upon the theophoric names (Revue des Etudes Juives, vol. v.). In these fragments, of much later date than the composition of the first volume, Assyrian has taken its due place.

The "History of the Semitic Languages," appearing in 1855, opened to the author the doors of the Académie des Inscriptions et Belles-Lettres, and made him the recognized master of Semitic philology in France. But he had published three years before a book of another order, which is not subject to the same theoretical reservations, and which is an admirable specimen of what he understood by "the history of mind." This was his doctor's thesis, "Averroès et l'Averroïsme." Up to this time, M. Renan had diffused over the most diverse subjects his vast curiosity, his breadth of thought, and a talent for exposition the personal character of which had surprised connoisseurs. Happily the necessities of life forced him to concentrate upon one subject and to apply his whole

strength. Being entirely without personal resources, and supporting himself by a very modest place in the National Library, he needed to
pass the University examinations before he could
hope for a situation which would free him from
pecuniary cares. He had passed the examination for a fellowship in 1848, and by the advice
of M. Victor Le Clerc, dean of the Faculty of
Letters, who had recognized his promise, he
aimed at the doctorate. The subject was the
best one that could have been chosen to give
the old Sorbonne an idea of the value and the
range of the new methods. It was a chapter
out of her own history, out of her own tradition,
that the young candidate brought to her from
the Orient. The scholastic philosophy derived
from Arabic philosophy, which was itself only
a reflection from Greek philosophy, and the
thought of our Middle Ages lived on scraps of
Aristotle. Certainly there is little in philosophy more barren and less original, and only by
revolting against it could Europe reënter the
world of the living. Nevertheless, it is interesting and consoling to see how under the rigid
shroud of traditional formulas individual genius
could stir, and, under the only form which the
time admitted, take up all the problems of philosophy. It is also curious to see through what
strange channels the intellectual curiosity of
Greece found its way to us, and preserved the

spark of fire under the ashes, until the days of
the Renaissance. M. Renan begins by writing
the history of this philosophy among the Syrians, for it was from the Syrians that the Arabs
received it.[1] He shows us how the Syrian Christians, pupils of the Greeks, accepted in the
fourth century, from the Alexandrians the ascendency of Aristotle, whose "Organon" they
translated; how Edessa became a peripatetic
centre; how the Nestorians, expelled from
Edessa in 486 by the Emperor Zeno, carried
Aristotle into Persia, and how one of them,
Paul the Persian, dedicated to Khosroes an
abridgment of the "Logic." The Arabic conquest, with the fanaticism which accompanied
it, interrupted only for a short time the course
of Aristotle's conquests; hardly a century and
a half had elapsed when the lay spirit took the
upper hand with the Abbassides, the heirs of
the intellectual curiosity of the Sassanides. M.
Renan shows the deceptive, uncertain character
of the term "Arabic philosophy," as applied
to the movement which went on under the auspices of the Caliphs. This philosophy had nothing Arabic about it except the language in
which it was expressed, Arabic having become

[1] *De Philosophia Peripatetica apud Syros. Commentationem
historicam scripsit E. Renan.* Paris: A. Durant. Compare a
series of articles upon the literature of the Syriac texts pertain-
ing to philosophy or gnosticism in the *Journal Asiatique*, 1880,
'82, '83, '85, '86.

the official and literary language. Not one of the so-called Arabic philosophers was of Arabian blood; they were all Persians; the dynasty which favored them came from the Eastern provinces of the caliphate, the provinces which preserved the Iranian spirit most purely, and the devotion of which led them to the throne. The Abbassides were Mussulman Sassanides, and the movement begun under Khosroes went on under the Abbassides with the same initiators, the Christian-Greek Syrians. The limit was no longer the "Organon." It was Aristotle entire that, after the time of Al-Mamun (813–833), passed from Greek into Syriac and from Syriac into Arabic. The Arabic translations will comprise Al-Farabi, Avicenne, Averroës, and all the Mussulmans who are to wholly supersede their Syrian masters. Averroës was the last great Arabic scholar. He came before the decadence of philosophical studies among the Mussulmans who were to find peace in the theology of Gazzali and to condemn rational science with him, because it teaches how to do without God. The works of Averroës had an infinitely greater reputation in the West than in the East; his name closed Arabic and began European philosophy. Adopted by the Jews of Spain and of the South of France, he was translated from Arabic into Hebrew, and from Hebrew into Latin, and thus was completed the circle which, by a strange series of détours, was to bring to the West a ray of Greek thought and prepare it for the Renaissance. By the middle of the thirteenth century almost all the work of the great Commentator was translated. A curious history, this, of the combats which raged over these texts falsified by the errors of four or five series of translators of every religion and every race, misunderstood by those who brought them as well as by those who received them, and which, nevertheless, served as a support and a pretext for the boldest and most liberal theories. Respected as a master by the Franciscans and the University, but denounced by the Dominicans as the chief of heresiarchs, this not especially original commentator of a badly understood doctrine became in the Middle Ages the representative of materialistic skepticism, the protestant for free thought against the theological yoke. When the Renaissance brings back the real Aristotle and the veritable spirit of Greek philosophy, Averroism, depending only upon its own slight worth, loses its vitality, and becomes an embarrassing and ridiculous débris. In the school of Padua alone it continued to lead a barren and insipid existence down to the seventeenth century.

The problems which had beset him at St. Sulpice remained for M. Renan the essential aim of science, and the ideal of his life as a

savant was always the pursuit of critical researches concerning Christianity, with resources
far larger than lay science offered him.   A fortunate opportunity took him in 1860 to the very
cradle of Christianity.   The Emperor Napo-
leon, inspired by a woman of a noble and free
spirit, his friend in childhood (Mme. Henriette
Cornu), whose secret and beneficent influence
was to be found in all the liberal and intelligent
measures that marked the second half of the
empire, charged M. Renan with a mission to
Phœnicia.   This mission was to make its mark
in the history of science and of ideas, not only
through its direct results, — rich as was the
archæological harvest gathered by M. Renan
on a ground apparently exhausted by many
wars and revolutions, — but chiefly through
the two great projects which came from it, the
"Origins of Christianity" and the Corpus.

During the last days of his mission, on the
heights of Ghazir in Lebanon, where he had
brought his sister, Henriette, in search of rest
and health, exhausted as she was by the voyage
and attacked by a malady which was to prove
fatal, Renan resolved to put in writing the
ideas concerning the life of Jesus which his trav-
els in Palestine had kindled in his mind.   "In
reading the Gospel in Galilee, the personality
of this great founder had forcibly impressed
itself upon me.   In the profoundest repose that

it is possible to conceive, I wrote, with the help of the Gospel and Josephus, a life of Jesus which, at Ghazir, I brought down to the last journey of Jesus to Jerusalem. Delicious hours, too soon vanished, may eternity bring you again!" These lines at once explain and sum up the human charm and the scientific originality of the "Life of Jesus." They emanate from a profound and penetrating feeling of the human personality of Jesus. His scientific predecessors (naturally, I do not speak of purely orthodox theologians) had made of the life of Jesus either an amalgam of arid rationalism and attenuated mythology, satisfying neither to reason nor faith nor history, or a creation of imagination and logic, due entirely to the mind of the believer, to his expectations and his prior beliefs; the life of Christ was written almost entirely in the thought of his own people, and it was almost superfluous that Christ himself had existed. The first of these conceptions was inadmissible for those who believe in the continuity of the laws of nature and history. The second, by suppressing the person of Christ, or drawing a veil before it, left a miracle greater and more astonishing than all those of the ancient faith. How could the Messianic hopes which filled the atmosphere of Judea in the time of Augustus have centred at a certain time around the person of Jesus, if

this person had not been more than a name, if
he had not been something potent, august, fruitful, capable of creating a faith; in other words,
if he had not acted, if he had not had a history?
Critics can find ' abundant objections to the
work of M. Renan, and they have not failed to
do so. Some reproach him with the inexact-
ness and the uncertainty of his facts, and the
contradictions in his characterization, or, in-
versely, with an excess of precision in the psychology of illusion, and that desire to explain
all the legends which leads us by a round-
about way to that rationalism so much decried.
Others will reproach him for not being acquainted with "the latest German criticism,"
which in the eyes of some is the unpardonable
sin (but there is so much latest German criticism!); with having given to the narratives of
the Fourth Gospel a questionable value; others,
finally, will make the reproach which can be
made, indeed, against all lives of Jesus, that
the writer has not studied sufficiently, and at
first hand, the Jewish environment where Jesus
was produced, — most essential to a thorough
comprehension of the subject. But making allowance for all these criticisms, and admitting
that M. Renan has not written the definitive
"Life of Jesus," and that a definitive life of
Jesus is only a dream, — since we know Jesus
only by documents late in point of time, and

impregnated with legends which veil his figure
and his life from the day after his death, and
even before it, — it still remains true that Renan drew nearer to the real Christ than any one
had done, for he is the first writer who brought
him back within the limits of historic humanity.
This human and therefore scientific conception
of the Christ was not in M. Renan the fruit of
reflection and study. It went back to his Catholic and French education. In that beautiful
page of the "Souvenirs" where he imagines the
Christ, in the midst of his struggles at the seminary, saying to him, "Abandon me in order
to become my disciple," he adds: "I can say
that from that time the ' Life of Jesus ' was
written in my mind. The belief in the pre-
eminent personality of Christ, which is the soul
of this book, was my strength in my struggle
with theology." A Catholic who ceases to believe in Christ "truly man and truly God " is
forced to choose clearly and without reserve between the Christ-man and the Christ-God. He
seizes the man Jesus with an instinct for reality
which no liberal theologian displays, and M.
Renan justified the lines, written several years
before he began his "Life of Jesus," when perhaps he was already dreaming of it: "One may
affirm that if France, better endowed than
Germany with the sentiment of the practical
life, and less inclined to substitute in history the

action of ideas for the play of individual passion
and character, had undertaken to write the life
of Christ in a scientific manner, she would have
exhibited a more vigorous method, and while
avoiding the transfer of the problem, after the
manner of Strauss, into the domain of abstract speculation, would have approached much
nearer to the truth." [1]

I am not competent, neither have I any right,
to judge the "Origins of Christianity" as a
whole. Such a whole raises a multitude of secondary questions of every order, and the subject itself leads to many divergencies, so that
it is impossible to expect a uniform judgment
from criticism. German criticism seems to have
been put off the track by the processes of M.
Renan's exposition; having taken as his object
the reproduction of the historical reality, as he
has restored it, in a continuous narrative, he is
content to name his sources, and takes for
granted the discussion which specialists should
be able to follow up on a hint. The German
critics have not always taken the trouble to do
this work for themselves (it demands a certain
measure of good-will), and they have often
treated M. Renan's work as a scientific fantasy
in which the imagination had as large a part as
research. French criticism, on its side, has
reproached him with the uncertainty of his con-

[1] *Les Historiens Critiques de Jésus.*

clusions; with the multiplicity of his conjectures and possibilities; with his abuse of "perhaps" and "it seems;" with all that atmosphere
of doubt in which floats the movement of a history that, nevertheless, had a definite reality.
A criticism less prejudiced than the German
would have recognized the immense labor which
the "Origins" presupposes and the solidity of
the substructure, especially from the time when
Christianity definitely separated from Judaism.
If the French critics had also taken the trouble
to refer to the sources indicated in the notes,
they would have recognized that these words,
"perhaps" and "it seems," never referred to
the matter of the history but to the manner;
and that the author never adds a material circumstance to the text, a detail to the picture of
manners, or a feature to the landscape. Never
does he suppose an important circumstance
which the text does not present or suggest.
"Origins are always obscure, and in order to
divine the effaced pages of these old histories, a
divination is needed into which there enters
something of the personal element. To know
exactly how things occurred is almost impossible; the end which criticism proposes to itself
is to discover the manner, or the manners, in
which they might have occurred." Perhaps M.
Renan sinned too often through excess of scru-
ples. The fear of taking sides between hypo-

theses equally plausible and equally uncertain
is the beginning of wisdom, but we must know
sometimes, through our very devotedness, how
to accept the rôle of imprudence; it is a sacrifice made in the interest of further progress.
An error resolutely adopted and clearly expressed is sometimes more profitable than a too
wise reserve; it refutes itself by its conse-
quences, clears the ground by so much, and
frees the horizon from one of the clouds which
serve to obscure it. We must take sides in
science as in life: it is the condition of movement and action. But with all its defects and
its weak points, this great synthesis will serve
for a long time as a point of departure to new
efforts of analysis; men may take it up again
in sections and replace many parts, but the history of knowledge, if it is just, will admire the
strength of this effort, the first ever made by
independent science, to present the story of the
heroic and creative periods of Christianity in
the continuity of their development.

In a collection of fragments of paper found
after the death of M. Renan, in which he was
in the habit of noting down at the moment the
thoughts and fancies which came to his mind,
there was discovered one containing these words:
"Of all that I have done I love the Corpus
best." This is a saying which will be comprehended with difficulty by the myriads of readers

of the "Life of Jesus," and it will not be well
understood even by the two hundred persons
who are acquainted with the Corpus, unless
they have been thoroughly penetrated by the
spirit of M. Renan. For Renan, the great
object in life, that which makes its nobility, its
dignity, and its worth, is to work for absolute
truth, for truth without alloy of error and free
from personal illusion. Now, in the present
state of science, all the restorations that we can
make of the periods of antiquity which are most
important to us, since they are creative forces
and we live on our inheritance from them, are
conjectural works in which the intuition of the
thinker is the great architect. But genius itself cannot reërect the edifice of the ages from
scattered débris of column shafts, in its full
extent and grandeur, in all its form and beauty;
it can only build a temple to its own glory. If
the instinct of its intuition has found the dead
reality, the felicity of this agreement is fully
known only to the gods, and it is felt by us and
by itself only through a vague and uncertain
pleasure. Nevertheless, these magnificent restorations, which have their full value in the
presence of the ideal, are not lost to science,
for they inspire the ardent search for relics, and
bring about the discovery of unexpected remains
which will one day permit new constructions
more reliable and nearer to the inaccessible

reality. There will thus have entered the eternal Pantheon, beautiful forms and noble images,
which humanity will come to adore, satisfying
its thirst for the ideal and its aspirations for
great things. Above this grand work, which
is the vision of a universe in fragments reflected
in a great soul, but a soul of individual color,
there rises imperceptibly, according to a realis-
tic philosophy, the obscure, impersonal, almost
anonymous labor of the worker who has put
aside the ego which limits his ambition for
disinterring facts, for exhuming realities, for
bringing us in contact with the things which
have been, for reducing the yawning abysses
which the poet's induction would fill up at
once. This is the work which has life, — life
from the past whence it draws all its substance,
life in the future which will be built upon it;
this is the work which succeeds, and through
which, however mute and incomplete, the savant
enters into full and perfect communion with the
truth that has been, and the conscience of the
universe.

It is a work of this kind which was realized in
the "Corpus Inscriptionium Semiticarum," and
for this reason it was very dear to M. Renan.
At the beginning of this century there scarcely
remained of Semitic antiquity more than one
document, the Bible. The rest of the Semitic
world was only a pale shadow, divined through

the Bible. Epigraphy called this world from
the limbo of shades. In 1842 the pickaxes
of Botta and Layard brought from the earth
ancient Assyria with its innumerable inscriptions, the decipherment of which will occupy
generations of scholars. Then came the turn
of Chaldea. In 1843 the chemist Arnaud discovered in Yemen the remains of that old Himyaritic civilization which had left only one legendary trace, the name of the Queen of Sheba.
In 1862 M. de Vogüé brought back from the
volcanic mass of Safa, in central Syria, four
hundred specimens of a new epigraphy. Phœnicia was still poor; but in 1846 the inscription of Marseilles, and in 1855 the inscription
of Eshmunazar, added two significant monuments to this epigraphy, until then so meagre
and sterile. M. Renan's mission, though richer
in sculpture than in inscriptions, nevertheless
added some important texts. The epigraphic
material thus accumulated gave a good view of
chapters of history of which men had had no
notion before. Was it not time to bring together all these scattered materials, and to put
them in the hands of investigators? Böckh's
Greek Corpus had shown the progress that one
might expect from a collection of this kind.
What unknown aspects of the life of the Greeks
and what new chapters in their history had been
revealed by simply bringing together the in-

scriptions discovered in every corner of the empire of the Greek language, and classifying them
according to their country and their date!

On the 25th of December, 1867, M. Renan,
in his own name and in that of MM. Saulcy,
De Longpérier, and Waddington, proposed that
the Académie des Inscriptions et Belles-Lettres undertake the publication of a Corpus of
Semitic inscriptions. The commission named
by the Academy was unanimous in recognizing
that the project was worthy, and that France,
through her domination in northern Africa,
through her scientific relations with Egypt,
Assyria, and Greece, through the numerous specimens of Semitic writing which she possessed
in her museums, through the quantity of material accumulated by her missions, and finally
through the tradition maintained in France
from the time of the founder of Semitic epigraphy, the Abbé Barthélemy, was called upon
to take charge of this task. On the 26th of
April, 1868, the first commission on the Corpus was named:[1] the preparatory labors lasted
fourteen years, and it was only in 1881 that the
first fasciculus of the work, so long expected,
appeared. This long delay had not been use-
less. According to its first calculations, the

---

[1] It embraced MM. De Saulcy, Mohl, De Longpérier, Renan,
De Slane, and Waddington. Only one of these six originators
of the work remains.

commission would have completed the Corpus in two volumes; the new treasures acquired after 1867 soon proved that these modest proportions would be greatly exceeded. In 1869 M. Halévy, who had been sent by the Institute to Yemen, brought back nearly five hundred inscriptions to add to the fifty of Arnaud and his predecessors, and this number has been tripled lately by M. Glaser. In 1874 M. de Ste. Marie disinterred at Carthage those thousands of ex-votos to the goddess Rabbat-Tanit, which, in spite of their discouraging monotony, compensated, through the multitude of their proper names, for the emptiness of their contents, and permitted the restocking of the Pantheon of the Phœnician gods with the names of their worshipers. Some years ago the peninsula of Sinai, explored by M. Benedite, supplied three thousand *graffiti*, which are for the Nabathean region what the Rabbat-Tanit are for Carthage. Huber bought with his blood the stele of Teima, the most precious monument of northern Arabia. In addition to the exploring movement which had its centre in the Institute, the Corpus received the support of Italian archæologists in Sicily and Sardinia, and of Charles Doughty in northern Arabia, and the brilliant discoveries of the German mission to Zinjirli brought into the limits of the Corpus regions which it had not expected to explore. Thus the

dimensions of the monument were extended in-
definitely; doubtless it will never equal in size
the Greek Corpus, for the Semites were less talk-
ative than the Greeks, and their most ancient
works passed through more eras of destruction.
But perhaps it will be a more potent instrument
of investigation and resurrection, since, instead
of embracing a single world like Böckh's Corpus, it extends to five or six different worlds, —
worlds at once different from one another and
closely related.

For twenty years M. Renan was the inspirer
of the Corpus and the central factor in its labors. Although he had, eminent collaborators
and his special part was chiefly limited to Phœnicia, his name will remain attached to a Corpus, the idea of which he conceived, the plan
of which he traced, and which he brought to
realization. The lines of the plan are great
and simple. The Corpus comprehends all the
ancient texts of Semitic tongues expressed in
the Semitic alphabet (this excludes the cunei-
form inscriptions, which are the subject of a
special Corpus).[1] These texts are classified according to the language, and for each language, according to a geographical division.
They are given in facsimile, in such a manner
that the student is brought as directly as possi-

---

[1] Of several Corpora rather: the most important is that in
the British Museum.

ble face to face with the monument, in a printed text and in a Hebrew transcription. This is the objective part. Then comes the subjective part, — the exposition of what science has done, or may do, with these materials. It comprises a complete bibliography of the works of which each text has been the subject; a translation, and a commentary briefly justifying the translation, indicating the doubtful points, and summing up succinctly the divergences from earlier translations or even from members of the commission. This commentary is to be as sober as possible, and it will shun scientific dissertation and the polemic style. Although the Corpus takes sides, since it gives a translation, it remains as objective as possible, even upon the shifting ground of interpretation; and as it places the student face to face with the matter to be interpreted, so it brings before him the previous efforts of science in all their diversity, without creating an orthodoxy and without imposing its own views.[1]

[1] The Corpus was begun independently on three sides at once. Of the first part, devoted to Phœnician inscriptions, one complete volume has appeared, and the first fasciculus of a second volume, comprising 905 inscriptions (from Phœnicia, Cyprus, Egypt, Greece, Malta, Sicily, Corcyra, Sardinia, Corsica, Italy, Marseilles, and Carthage). The progress of exploration is so active that the fasciculus containing the Egyptian inscriptions was hardly published when it was left behind by the discovery of some thirty Phœnician *graffiti* in the temple of Abydos. Of the Aramean part, under the direction of M. de

The single fact that he conceived, organized, and rendered practicable such a work as the Corpus is sufficient to demonstrate the superficiality of the criticism that would make of M. Renan a dilettante savant, too lordly to trouble himself with the details and the minute cares of scholarship. The ordinary critic cannot understand the union of two superiorities in the same mind; and as Renan was, above all, a synthetic and philosophic genius, such critics refused to acknowledge in him the virtues of the scholar enamored of detail, who knows that the single circumstance, the minute fact, is the foundation of science. On the contrary, we may say that only the synthetic genius feels and thoroughly comprehends the value of details and the necessity of microscopic analysis, since he knows better than does the ordinary scholar that no detail is insignificant, that not an atom may be safely neglected, and that a débris of stone, a half-effaced stroke of a letter, and a tattered piece of papyrus, may reveal the secret of the whole. So M. Renan's course on epigraphy, at the Collège de France, was a delusion and a snare for the crowd that was drawn thither by his reputation. I remember how the

Vogüé, a first fasciculus has appeared (with 149 inscriptions, from Assyria, Chaldea, Asia Minor, Adarbaijan, Greece, Arabia, and Egypt). Of the Himyaritic part, under M. Derenbourg's supervision, the first fasciculus contains 69 inscriptions.

[Several other parts have since appeared. — ED.]

hour was spent in staring at a certain stroke
of a letter (was it Daleth, or was it Resh?) in
the impressions of the Nabathean inscriptions
brought home by Charles Doughty. It was
in this course that the Corpus was sketched;
the auditors soon dwindled in number, but,
sitting round the little table in Hall IV., they
formed, so to speak, the first public and the
first body of critics of the great work.

III.

Thus far I have said nothing concerning the
skepticism which, in popular estimation, was
one of M. Renan's characteristics. This skepticism was only on the surface; it had no existence where the problems which go to make the
dignity and the worth of life were concerned.

M. Challemel-Lacour, whom the Academy
saw fit to choose as Renan's successor, — a man
of talent, but too deeply imbued with the classical and the political spirit, — said of him:
"Renan thinks like a man, feels like a woman,
and acts like a child." Did the poor young
Breton act as a child when he fled from St.
Sulpice because he believed that all which his
masters had taught him was, perhaps, not true?
It was, perchance, a piece of childishness, from
the worldly point of view, to renounce the
splendid future that awaited him in the church,

which has not a Renan to show the world every
day, and to face poverty, without resources,
without a future, sustained only by the conviction that it was impossible to live for anything
else than for an idea.   They who believe that
the first proof of manliness is to be sincere
with others, and with one's self, will think that
he was that day twice a man.   Did he act as a
child, or as a man, when he allowed himself to
be driven from the chair in the Collège de
France which had been the supreme object of
his ambition, rather than veil with one politic
word, or even with a discreet silence (which the
authorities would have accepted), the guiding
faith of his scholar's conscience and the assertion of the right of science, respectful but independent, to penetrate into the sanctuary of
religion?   The letter he addressed to the professors of the Collège de France, in regard to
the suspension of his lectures, is the most eloquent and forcible vindication of the rights
of human thought that French literature can
show since the "Provincial Letters" of Pascal.
Very indulgent to his fellow-men, and convinced that few of the things about which they
worry are worth while, there is one about which
he was inflexible, — duty.   If we seek for the
one motive of his active life, we shall find it in
the most abstract notion of duty.   This man,
who of all the virtues of St. Sulpice seemed to

exemplify politeness above every other, who
seemed always to seek for the word most pleas-
ing to his interlocutor, whoever he might be,
and who often carried the caresses of amiability
to a point where it seemed to assume the fea-
tures of irony, — this man, so supple and pliant
apparently, as soon as men wished to draw from
him a word or an act affecting his inmost conscience, became a bar of iron. Parties did not
love him, his view was too wide for them;
parties like only men who wear blinders and
have committed a section of their conscience
to their chief. Men were never sure of him;
he escaped just as they felt their hold secure:
he was neither republican nor royalist, neither
clerical nor anti-clerical, neither for Caliban
nor against him. He wished to see a France
where institutions should be free, where the
mind too should be free, and which, instead of
wasting in the vendettas of sectaries, or in the
pursuit of unrealizable or fatal utopias, the im-
measurable power of faith and devotion in which
she still abounds, should consecrate them to realizing before the whole world the national and
human ideal which she has confusedly beheld,
and which she has abandoned to the hands of
the conscienceless. He was not afraid to contradict himself, feeling deeply that in the anarchy of contemporary politics it was things and
parties which were contradicting themselves,

and not he who followed in the tempest the
unique, wavering, but unextinguishable light of
conscience.

M. Renan was bitterly reproached for some
imprudent words addressed to young men.
"Amuse yourselves," he said to the students,
not thinking, as an ingenuous ascetic, grown
old in toil, what the word signifies for the mass
of young men, and remembering only that he
had just pressed the cold hand of the young
and noble Stanislas Guyard, a victim of science
and thought.   He might have said, but he did
not say: "Look at me! I have worked long,
slept little, and played scarce at all; I am famous and poor, old and still in harness; I have
never recoiled before the most difficult duty; I
have ever set the Ideal before the Real, and sacrificed the Present to that Eternity of which I
cannot conscientiously recommend the evidence.
Go ye and do likewise." [1]   His so-called skepticism never derided the principles of morality:
it bore only upon the product of human thought,
that thought of which he was the apostle and
emancipator, the power of which he knew and
glorified, but the slightness of which before the
infinite — present, past, and future — he knew
better than others, since he thought more.
Morality was to him the only thing absolutely

[1] "Ernest Renan, A Pastel:" Mme. Darmesteter in *The
Albemarle*, May, 1892.

certain. "An impenetrable veil hides from us the secret of this strange world, the reality of which at once commands and overwhelms us; philosophy and science will forever pursue, without attaining it, the formula of this Proteus whom no intelligence can limit and no language can express. But there is an indubitable foundation which no skepticism will shake, and in which man will find, to the end of time, a fixed point in all his uncertainties; good is good; evil is evil. To hate the one and love the other no system is needed, and in this sense faith and love, apparently unconnected with the intellect, are the real foundation of moral certainty and the only means man has for comprehending, in some degree, the problem of his origin and his destiny."[1] Renan's point of departure was Kant's point of arrival. That categorical imperative, on which Kant reconstructed his metaphysic, he did not attain by dint of analysis and dialectic; he found it at the very basis of his life, in hereditary instincts, fortified by the religious discipline of his youth, in the impossibility of desiring aught else but the good.

We can thus see how little M. Renan is understood by the petty philosophers of dilettanteism claiming to be his followers, who would shelter their moral incapacity and their egotism

[1] *Essais de Morale et de Critique.*

behind formulas misunderstood and detached from a whole scheme of life, and would so make the world a prey to be exploited by their voluptuous intellect and their dainty senses. When, in another quarter, our neo-Christians veil their faces before Renanism, they forget that they are only faulty pupils of M. Renan, and that from him they learned the rights and the worth of the religious sentiment; one thing, however, they should also have learned from him and comprehended, — that the first condition of a religion is sincerity and spontaneity, and that faith cannot be commanded.

The mistaken judgments passed upon M. Renan are due to the fact that in his work he did not place the emphasis upon the Good, but upon the True. Men concluded that for him, therefore, science was the whole of life. The environment in which he was formed was forgotten, an environment in which the moral sense was exquisite and perfect, while the scientific sense was *nil.* He did not need to discover the moral sense, it was the very atmosphere in which he lived. When the scientific sense awoke in him, and he beheld the world and history transfigured by it, he was dazzled, and the influence lasted throughout his life. He dreamed of making France understand this new revelation; he was the apostle of this gospel of truth and science, but in heart and mind he never attacked what is permanent and divine in the other gospel. ⌉ Thus he was a complete man, and deserved the disdain of dilettantes morally dead, and of mystics scientifically atonic.[1]

What heritage has M. Renan left to posterity? As a scholar he created religious criticism in France, and prepared for universal science that incomparable instrument, the Corpus. As an author he bequeathed to universal art pages which will endure, and to him may be applied what he said of George Sand: "He had the divine faculty of giving wings to his subject, of producing under the form of fine art the idea which in other hands remained crude and formless." As a philosopher he left behind a mass of ideas which he did not care to

---

[1] The final words on M. Renan were spoken in these English verses, written the day after his death: —

VERITATEM DILEXI.

IN MEMORIAM — ERNEST RENAN.

"Truth is an idol," spake the Christian sage.
　"Thou shalt not worship Truth divorced from Love.
　Truth is but God's reflection : Look above ! "
So Pascal wrote, and still we trace the page.

"Truth is divine," said Plato, " but on high
　She dwells, and few may be her ministers,
　For Truth is sad and lonely and diverse ;
Heal thou the weakling with a generous lie ! "

But thou in Truth delightedst ! Thou of soul
　As subtle-shimmering as the rainbow mist,
　And still in all her service didst persist,
For no One truth thou lovedst, but the Whole.

MARY DARMESTETER, *Retrospect*, 1891.

collect in doctrinal shape, but which, nevertheless, constitute a coherent whole. One thing
only in this world is certain, — duty. One
truth is plain in the course of the world as science reveals it: the world is advancing to a
higher, more perfect form of being. The supreme happiness of man is to draw nearer to
this God to come, contemplating Him in science, and preparing, by action, the advent of a
humanity nobler, better endowed, and more
akin to the ideal Being.

AN ESSAY ON THE HISTORY OF THE JEWS.

I.

THE time is still distant for attempting a complete history of the Jewish people, pursued through the entire course of its development from its origin up to the present time, and covering every phase of this development, in religion, in philosophy, in language, in literature, and in the hazards of its material fortunes.

In the revival of historical science, which constitutes one of the glories of our century, the place accorded to the history of the Jewish people will grow in importance from day to day in proportion as the coördination of disjointed discoveries permits a clearer view of the outlines of the development of Aryo-Semitic humanity. The historian's special interest in the Jewish nation is due to its being the only one that is met with at every turn of history. In following the course of this nation's destinies, he is successively brought into contact with nearly all the great civilizations, and with nearly all the great religious ideas that have left their impress on the civilized world, from

the dawn of history up to the present time.
He sees in turn, in Israel's path, nomadic and
polytheistic tribes of primitive Semites, Egypt
and her priesthood, Syria and her gods, Nineveh
and Babylon, Cyrus and the Magi, Greece and
Alexander, Alexandria and her schools, Rome
and her legions, Jesus and the Evangelists.
Later, when, upon the destruction of the national unity, the Jews are scattered into the
four quarters of the world, the historian who
follows them into Arabia, into Egypt, into
Africa, and into all the countries of Western
Europe, beholds the panorama of Mahomet and
Islam, of Aristotle, of the Scholastics and their
philosophy, of all the science of the Middle
Ages and its commerce, of the Humanists and
the Renaissance, of the Reformation and the
Revolution.

Thus the history of the Jewish people comprises and implies that of the entire Mediterranean world from beginning to end, rarely
entering, and only by accident, into the political
and material aspects of history, but concerned
with the ideas, the religions, the social factors,
in short with the living forces of humanity.
The history of all other nations, even of those
exercising the longest and most remote influence, covers only a single epoch and a single
place. Each one appears and disappears; its
part was played in a single period, its history is

exclusively its own. The Jewish people, enduring through all times, has helped to shape all great events that have had their day: it is a perpetual and universal witness of all these dramas, and by no means an inactive or mute witness, but closely identified with them in action or in suffering. Twice it remodeled the world, — the European world through Jesus, the Oriental world through Islam, not to speak of an influence slower and more hidden, but none the less powerful, nor perhaps less lasting, that it exercised in the Middle Ages upon the formation of modern thought.

This great history could not have been attempted, nor even conceived, before this century, because of two necessary conditions that are only beginning to be realized in our day, the one of a moral, the other of a material character. On the one hand, as this history is, above all, religious, and as a consequence involves, in the present state of the human mind, a perpetual appeal to the most irritable of all the passions, it was necessary for liberty of thought not only to become a part of law and custom, but, what is much more difficult, to find an echo in the mind of the scholar. It was necessary for research to be freed from the corruption of sectarianism or of philosophical system, and for the history of religion to cease to be a battlefield. Not yet have all those engaged in these studies reached that degree of serene impartiality where facts are studied for the sole purpose of being understood, and where thought is carried to a height that will not permit of conclusions dictated in advance by the ephemeral prejudices of politics, of faith, or of metaphysics. Some, however, have reached this eminence, and they suffice to insure the continuance of science.

On the other hand, a succession of remarkable and unexpected discoveries was required to fill up the gaps of Jewish history, and to illumine its innumerable obscurities. The three great periods of this history — the first extending from its origin to the Return from the Exile, the second from the Return from the Exile to the Dispersion, the third from the Dispersion to the French Revolution — were all represented only by incomplete or inaccessible documents. For the first period we had but one book, the Bible, the work of ages, composed of fragments, of detached leaflets, where often a line, a word, is all that remains of a century. For the second period there was nothing but the Talmudic chaos, which the Jews alone were able to fathom, and in which they sought only subjects for edification and casuistry, and not historical instruction. For the third period, finally, there was the immense quantity of writings of the Middle Ages, in great part for-

gotten by the Jews themselves, and buried
in the dust of libraries. The situation was
changed by a double movement proceeding from
within and from without; from within through
the application of the historic method, by Jewish scholars, to the direct study of the Jewish
sources; from without through the discovery of
non-Jewish sources, throwing light upon and
complementing the Jewish sources.

In this way a whole series of new sciences,
creations of yesterday, Assyriology, Egyptology,
Phœnician epigraphy, have been placed at the
service of biblical interpretation, which rewards
them in turn. Babylon and Nineveh rise up
out of the ground, and with their great pages
of history, inscribed by their Shalmanesers,
Sennacheribs, and Nebuchadnezzars, add their
testimony to the Book of Kings and to the prophets.[1]   Egypt reveals the secret of her hiero-
glyphics, and a new column of fire comes to
illumine the Exodus[2] of the Hebrews. Punic
soil brings us a commentary of Leviticus, coun-
tersigned by the Suffetes of Carthage.[3] The
Phœnician and Syrian Pantheon is revealed
through fragments of engraved stones, and furnishes all the Astartes and Baals that fought

[1] Rawlinson, Oppert, Halévy, Schräder, Lenormant, Smith,
etc.

[2] Brugsch, Chabas, Leipsius, Mariette, Maspéro, etc.

[3] Munk. Suffetes is the Phœnician title for governor—
equivalent to the Hebrew *shophetim* (judges). — ED.

against Elohim.[1] The worn-out soil of Judea
produces a triumphal hymn of Moab, written
in the days of Elisha, which the prophet himself may have read;[2] it is the war-cry of biblical combatants reaching our ears from a distance of twenty-seven centuries, the very cry of
the "Wars of the Eternal."

Coming to the second period, it has been
ascertained, upon clearing up the chaos of Talmudic literature,[3] — the Mishna and Gemara
with their innumerable supplements, — that this
immense compilation, made without order and
without a shadow of historical thought, offers
an inexhaustible mine for history. By means
of it we may follow the development of the
Jewish mind, and up to a certain point the Oriental mind, for more than six centuries, to the
very period that saw the birth of Christianity,
and that thus became one of the decisive moments of civilization, one of the turning-points
of history. At the same time, the mass of
works produced by lay or theological science,
by Catholics and Protestants, bearing on the
origin of Christianity, have carried the Christian problem to its Jewish source, and have
demonstrated the double proposition that the

---

[1] Movers, E. Renan, Vogüé, Clermont-Ganneau, Berger, etc.

[2] The Moabite stone — at present in the Salle Judaïque of
the Louvre.

[3] Rappaport, Geiger, Derenbourg, Frankel, Jost, Graetz,
Fürst, Zunz, etc.

birth of Christianity cannot be understood without a knowledge of the Judaism of the first century, nor can Judaism be comprehended in all its phases without a knowledge of that branch of it which passes under the name of primitive Christianity.[1] The gains made through the scientific investigation of the origin of Christianity have accrued to the advantage of Jewish history as well. By the side of the Talmudical is ranged that vast apocryphal literature which is being daily enriched by new discoveries, and the character of which is so vague that one is often in doubt as to whether one has to do with the work of a Jew or of a Christian.[2]

In the third period, covering the Dispersion, the investigation of the destiny of the Jewish people branches out in many directions. In each of these branches we find the same enlargement of scope through the unexpected encounter of two worlds. The work of investigating this period was all left for our day. It involved on the one hand the recovery and the study of all the various works covering the extended domain of Jewish history during the entire Middle Ages.[3] On the other hand it necessitated

[1] See Schürer's *History of the Jewish People in the Time of Jesus Christ.*

[2] The Sibylline Oracles, the fourth book of Ezra, the Assumption of Moses, the Psalter of Solomon, Book of Enoch, etc.

[3] Zunz, Neubauer, Loeb, etc.

the detailed study of the various Mahommedan or Christian peoples with whom the Jews were thrown into contact. This work has but barely begun. The process of joining these two worlds is still going on; and as one penetrates the deeper into their history, one recognizes more and more how impossible it is to separate them, or to understand the one without the other. The historian of the Jewish people is forced to become the historian of the Arabs or of Europe; and the historian of the Arabs or of Europe finds in almost all the great changes of thought a Jewish influence, whether striking and visible or silent and latent.

In this way Jewish history accompanies universal history throughout its entire range, and is closely interwoven with it. On this account it opens to investigation a field of infinite variety, and at the same time of complete unity, giving to historical psychology an interest that no other history affords in the same degree. It furnishes the longest series of experiences yet recorded, affecting in the most diverse surroundings one and the same recognized and constant human force. Let us present rapidly some of the most important problems of this history.

II.

A nomadic tribe belonging to the Semitic race, and nomadic in its origin, after extended migrations across the plains of Mesopotamia, Syria, and Egypt, fixed its permanent abode near the Phœnicians, among the peoples of Canaan. Obscure as the material history of the Hebrews during this period is, their religious history is even more so; for, while it is possible to follow the course of their migrations by means of legends that have been preserved, no distinct trace has remained of the progress of their thought. All that is certain and generally recognized is, that primitively they were idolaters and polytheists, as were all the branches of the race to which they belonged. But it is not possible to determine the especial traits of their mythology, nor, in the various epochs of this first period, in what respects it resembled and in what it differed from the mythology of their Semitic brethren. What were their beliefs and their forms of worship before entering Egypt? What did they leave in Egypt, and what did they carry with them thence? Finally, to what extent did they borrow in Canaan from the religion of the surrounding nations with whom they were brought into contact through friendship or hatred? If the Bible is ever to give a clear answer to these questions, it will only be after Egypt has spoken her last word, when the comparative history of Semitic religions shall be definitely established upon a basis of chronological data, and when, through the labor of generations of epigraphists, the entire body of witnesses still buried at Carthage, Nineveh, Hamath, Sheba, and throughout the entire extent of the old Semitic soil, shall be made to speak.

Once established in Palestine and constituted a nation, the primitive idolatry undergoes a gradual transformation parallel to the political change. The Hebrews, as they become a nation, secure a national god, make a contract with him, set him up in opposition to the national gods of the neighboring nations. This national god, this Elohim, does not as yet differ essentially from his neighbors, either in the attributes that were accorded him, or in the manner of his worship. He does not yet involve the rejection of other gods; he is not yet the god of the world; he is but the god of Israel. When did his transformation begin? Was it at the moment when Israel became conscious of her personal existence, the time of the Exodus? Or was it when her national existence was established through the kingdom? Is the name of Moses, closely linked by Israel's historical souvenirs to the departure from Egypt and to the first organization of the nation, to be also associated with the first step in her religious transformation? Or is it only after the religious evolution was complete that the profound instinct of legend connected Moses with the beginnings of the political evolution that started Israel upon its career? However this may be, the religious evolution was a slow process, extending over centuries. The entire history of the kingdom resolves itself into a continuous struggle, often bloody, between the national god and foreign gods, which are for a long time[1] merely by-names for the national party and the foreign party. This struggle, with which the great names of ancient prophecy are connected,[2] ends in the victory of the Hebrew god about the time of the fall of the kingdom. The national god triumphs at the moment when the nation which should be the object of his care perishes. But at this very time, upon the approach of the catastrophe, the god himself undergoes a profound change. He is no longer a mere national god, in the manner of others, conceived and adored as Chemosh or Milcom might be. Had he been a mere national god, a Chemosh of Israel, a Milcom of Judah, the downfall of his people must needs be regarded as a betrayal of his trust; and the

---

[1] Until Babylon comes upon the scene.

[2] Prophets whose names only remain, the greatest of which are Samuel and Elijah.

king of Babylon, in advancing his chariots to
the very walls of Jerusalem, might properly
have echoed, without fear of contradiction, the
words of the Assyrian: "Be not deceived by
the promises of thy god! Where are the kings
of Arpad, of Hamath, of Sepharvaïm? Where
is the nation whose god has ever saved it from my
hands?" The god of Israel, exalted through
the very defeat of his people, becomes the universal god, the one god, the god of the Decalogue, the god of Isaiah and the prophets. He
remains, it is true, the god of Israel, since he
revealed himself to Israel alone and Israel alone
has divined him; but he is the god, with none
beside. He is no longer the jealous god of
the first Mosaism, who hungers for victims and
offerings, and punishes the faults of the fathers
unto the fourth generation. He is the god of
justice and of love, who looks for pure hearts
and not for full hands, who has a horror of
sacrifices and the posturings of the cult,[1] and
who no longer desires it to be said: "The
fathers have eaten sour grapes and the children's teeth are set on edge."[2] And since the
nation which sought him and found him is oppressed and bleeding, he has undoubtedly reserved a striking and magnificent reparation
for it in the future. The very people who

---

[1] Isaiah i.
[2] Ezekiel xviii. ; Jeremiah xxxi.

crushed Judah will come one day to receive the truth from her hands. Happiness and justice will reign supreme throughout the entire world in the name of the god of Israel. It is thus that during the Exile, in foreign surroundings, the historical mission of Israel, in obedience to the spirit of Isaiah, of Jeremiah, of Ezekiel, and of a chorus of prophets, begins its career. Her great dogma is found, and her great hope realized; for the one God is created and Messianism is born.

During the Exile, and upon the Return from the Exile, this new and universal element is blended with the ancient and national one, and the religion of Israel takes its definite form, — Judaism. Of its ancient national elements there remain the rites, the ceremonies, the special observances, a bizarre legacy from old Semitic idolatry, now imbued with a new meaning through the religious transformation. At first the sign of alliance of the Hebrew with his god, it became finally the sign of recognition between Jew and Jew, the bond of unity in the ruins of nationality. It is the element which isolates and at the same time preserves Israel. A new and universal element, the prophetic, provides the two ideas with which the world is to be reconstructed. Thus a religion is produced, at once the narrowest and broadest of all, — complete isolation in its cult, unlimited expansion in its idea — through the latter more strong to act, in that the former enables it resolutely to preserve its existence — an excellent condition for endurance and activity, and for converting the world to its principles, without allowing itself to be ensnared by such concessions as propagandism might find it expedient to make.

From this time the Jewish people alone, among all the surrounding nations, have a philosophy of history to guide them in their course through the world, a rational plan in the drama of the universe which is unfolded according to a fixed law, and which will culminate for the good of all. Thus, through the successive dominations of Babylonia, of Persia, Greece, Egypt, Rome, whose waves pass over Israel and bear it down without engulfing it, a religious nationality is formed that will survive the ephemeral resurrection of political nationality under the Maccabees. It was just at this time that the ancient world, grown weary of its worn-out gods and impotent systems, seeking a higher system of morality than its priests could give, and of broader hopes than its philosophers dared offer, was prepared to receive the first suggestion of faith and hope, come from what quarter it might, to fill the sad void in its conscience. The final throes of Judah, endeavoring to give birth to its Messiah and to bring in the times predicted by the prophets, give to the world the necessary impetus. Among the ephemeral Messiahs that appear and disappear upon the prophetic scene, there was one who left so profound an impression upon some of the Jews, who knew him closely, that they, instead of continuing to say, as did their brethren, "The Messiah is coming," began to say, "The Messiah is come," and, when he was dead, "The Messiah has come; he was killed; he will come again to judge the dead and the living."

This belief and this expectation had little hold upon the mass of Jews, absorbed as they were in the dream of an earthly kingdom, who knew too clearly what they desired, and what they were awaiting, to accept in exchange a mere idle hope. But these beliefs exercised a marvelous influence upon the foreign masses, to whom they carried the good tidings that evil had ceased, that a wonderful Being, all justice and mildness, had caused peace and happiness to reign. These were stirred with the desire to preach the morality of Hillel and the Haggadists, of which the priests of Jupiter had never dreamed, and which was neither included in the scheme of the pedants of the schools, nor in that of the haughty representatives of the Porch.[1]

---

[1] The School of the Stoics — so called from one of the public porticoes on the Agora of ancient Athens where the Stoic philosophers were wont to meet. — ED.

In the course of time, in proportion as reality
forced the Christians to remove the most beautiful part of their hope to a far-distant future,
the person of Jesus and the part played by him
underwent a transformation that widened the
abyss between him and Israel.   And the Christian Jews, turning to the Bible to justify their
faith, after having explained the Bible by Jesus,
ended in explaining Jesus by the Bible.   In
this way, by means of symbolical interpreta-
tions, they changed Jesus into an ideal type.
On the other hand, the Christian Gentiles
adapted the new faith to the surroundings in
which it had grown through the daily increasing addition of elements from the mythologies of Greece and Syria and the metaphysics
of the time.   From this resulted a mixed religion, a compromise between the past and the
future, which conquered the world, bringing to
it an abundance of good and much of evil, —
an abundance of good, because it raised the
moral standard of humanity; much of evil,
because it arrested its intellectual growth by
rejuvenating the mythical spirit, and by fixing
for centuries the metaphysical ideal of Europe
in accordance with the dreams of Alexandrine
decadence, and with the last combinations of
Hellenism in its dotage.   The history of Christianity is a part of Jewish history up to the time
when this mythical and metaphysical element

obtained the ascendency, — the time of the definite rupture between the two churches; the day,
in short, when Christianity ceased to be a Jewish heresy, to take its place as a new branch of
the old Aryo-Semitic mythology.

There is thus imposed on the historian a
double task, — to study Judaism both within
the Jewish people and outside of it. Each of
these tasks meets with endless ramifications.
Moreover, it is often difficult to determine the
limit of the second of these tasks; for the line
that separates the exclusively Jewish fact from
the exclusively Christian fact is fluctuating and
variable, and it is given to science alone to
reach a decision on every point of dogma and
of worship. To study Judaism from within is
a task of a more precise and definite character.
In the front of the stage we observe the innumerable vicissitudes of the political drama, from
the Exile to the definite loss of independence,
embracing the Renaissance under Cyrus and
the Achemenidians; the beginnings of expansion
beyond Palestinian confines under Alexander;
the establishment of colonies at Alexandria, in
Egypt, and in the islands of the Mediterranean;
the struggles against the Seleucidæ; the national revival under the Maccabees; the first
alliances and the first struggles with Rome; the
follies of the civil war; Herod and the Hero-

dians; Jerusalem hurling defiance at Rome, and
for four years crushing the forces of the empire
at the feet of her walls; the ruin of the Holy
City, the temple in flames, and the last agony
at Bethar. Behind the political there is the
spiritual drama, — the encounter of the Jewish
mind with the foreign mind of Chaldea, of Persia, and of Greece; its introduction of elements
taken from the religions of some, its incursions
into the philosophy of others; the formation
within Judaism of a secondary mythology, sub-
ordinated to a strict monotheism that dominates
everything, and in which are combined in variable proportions the souvenirs of the ancient
national mythology, older elements introduced
from Syria and Babylon before and during the
Exile, and the more recent Babylonian and Persian elements added after the Exile. There follows the initiation of Judaism into the Greek
philosophy and its reactions upon the latter, the
birth of Jewish Hellenism, and the Bible reconciled with Plato, leading to the division of sects
and of schools; on the one hand the aristocratic
religion of the Sadducees, on the other the
democratic and progressive religion of the
Pharisees; and thirdly, the ascetic and renun-
ciatory religion of the Essenes. The next step
involves the traditional development of fixed
law, the rabbis taking up, in their scholastic
discussions, the work of salvation where the

manufacturers of apocalypses and the thrusts of
the stiffnecked had failed. Finally, there are
the successors of the Messianists and of the
zealots, building around the sacred Book, in defiance of Roman torches, that triple impregnable
wall — the Talmud. In the sixth century of
our era is completed the immense encyclopædia
which embraces with absolute impartiality all
variety of opinions, in all the branches of
science and of belief, that were formulated during a period of six centuries in the schools of
Palestine and Babylonia. It is a work without
apparent unity, since it reproduces the infinite
contrast presented by the thousands of minds of
which it is the sum total. In turn, according
to the voice that speaks, it manifests a strange
narrowmindedness by the side of unequaled
breadth, now dull and again brilliant; open to
science and closed to it; presenting all the
timidities of thought and all its audacities; but
penetrated throughout by a spirit of faith and of
hope that brings unity into this chaos, — faith
in the one God, and hope for justice to come.
The superficial mind often saw nothing more in
this book than the babble of refined casuistry,
of a reasoning and subtle superstition. It
failed to perceive the vital force in consequence
of which Jewish thought was enabled to pass
through the intellectual night of the Middle
Ages without being extinguished. This vitality

consisted in the profound conviction that the
cult does not constitute the whole of Judaism,
that it is but the external and transitory sign,
a material and conventional symbol, recognized
by those to whom the truth had been intrusted,
but absolutely distinct from this truth itself,
which is eternal and universal, which is the all
in all, and which is destined some day to become the common property of mankind. The
pregnant thought of this book, devoted as it is
almost exclusively to the preservation of the
cult, is that the cult is transitory, and that,
when Jewish truths shall be universally recognized, Jewish rites will cease.[1] It is this fertile
idea, explicitly conveyed by the rabbis of the
Middle Ages, that assures the proscribed caste
the boon of thought at a time when all light
is extinguished, and when, from one end of
Europe to the other, the church enthrones the
Christian order in deadened intellects. Let the
Dispersion come; moral unity is established and
life assured.

This unity is so strong that the work which
consecrates it in a definite and lasting fashion
comes, not from Jerusalem, but from foreign
lands, from the schools of Babylonia.[2] It is

---

[1] Even before this time, the Jew could, in times of persecution, or in case of danger, consider himself released from all
the precepts of the law save three; namely, those prohibiting
idolatry, impurity, and homicide. Maimonides.

[2] The Talmud of Jerusalem was not widespread, and counted
for little in the development of the Middle Ages.

thence that the Talmud comes and makes its way to the Dispersed Jews, and the precepts of the *Amoraïm* of the Euphrates become the law of their brethren from the banks of the Nile to those of the Aude. Some, as the Karaïtes, wished to escape from this yoke, and turned back to the Bible as the one law. Through their failure to see that Judaism was not a fixed and immutable religion, but a progressive and ever-changing one, their revolt against the yoke of Talmudical Judaism ended only in protracted suicide. In the attempt to suppress six centuries of their past existence they were condemned to break with the future, with the result of being excluded from a part in intellectual movements. Despite the talent shown by its first adherents, and after a brief period of expansion due to its apparent liberalism, Karaïsm languishes in a condition of sterility and impotence.

We now enter the third period, that of the Dispersion, a period which, moreover, does not begin at any fixed date or hour, inasmuch as it began long before the end of the national unity. Jewish *histories* take their rise in many places before the end of Jewish *history*. Even before the advent of Christianity, these histories begin in Egypt, in Asia Minor, in Italy, at Rome, in Greece, in southern Gaul, where the dissenters from the synagogue proceeded to form the nu-

cleus of primitive churches. At a very remote period, colonies entered Arabia, converted
Arabic tribes, and founded states. Their propaganda, due rather to the exchange of ideas in
daily commerce than to a consistent plan, makes
gradual advances, and influences even those who
are not converted by it. The idolatrous Arabs
accept from its hands the Biblical and Rabbinical traditions, and recast their genealogical
legends on the basis of the narratives of Genesis. To this there is added at a later period
the preaching of the Judaic-Christian sects,
themselves repulsed by incipient orthodoxy.
Mahomet, under the influence of Jewish and
Judaic-Christian teachings, founds Islamism.
Its dogma is the Jewish dogma, degraded by
a restricted intelligence; its mythology is essentially rabbinical and Judaic-Christian.

Thus, at the beginning of the seventh century
of our era, two offshoots of Judaism occupy the
domain of human thought, — offshoots at war
with the parent stock, cursing and repudiat-
ing it, not only by the contempt with which
they pursue it, but — which is sadder and more
serious — by distorting, each in its fashion,
the principles that they received, — the Christian Occident, in retaining from its past the
mythical spirit, rendering it more dangerous
than it was at the time of the gods, because, in
carrying it over into the realm of dogma, it

forces science to silence or to blasphemy; the
Arabian Orient, by making its god the symbol of supreme will instead of supreme reason,
soon leading it gratuitously to abandon science
and thought, without Christianity's excuse of
dogma. During one or two centuries the element of reason in the Koran triumphs, and
brings about the dawn of a brilliant civilization,
saving the human mind in the Middle Ages
from total eclipse. The Jews participate in
this movement in two ways, — by their personal
action and by their influence upon the Christians. When the movement comes to an end
among the Arabs, it leads in Europe to the first
Renaissance, marked by the end of the scholastic
period, and paving the way for the second.

Literature, philosophy, science, are rejuvenated or created. Literature lays bare a new
vein by the creation of the neo-Hebraic poetry,
which borrows its models from the Arabic, and
in Spain attains a high degree of originality.
The last *Gaonim* of the schools that founded
the Talmud establish a rational theology that
drives the supernatural element out of religion,
and becomes merely the abridged expression of
demonstratable truths, with reason enthroned
as the supreme criterion. At the same time
the Cabbala opens to the imagination its great
and beautiful mystic avenues where the thought
of Spinoza often wandered in his youth. At

the court of Al-Mamoun the Jews, united with
the exiled Nestorians, cast into the current of
Arabic thought the débris of the Greek philosophy, which through this channel reënters
Europe. Finally, through the Arabic-speaking
Jews, comparative grammar makes its appearance in the Semitic world, eight centuries before Bopp.

Speaking the language of both Arabs and
Christians, the Jews became the sole interme-
diaries between the two, while their incessant
wanderings through countries, to which they
were drawn by commerce or driven by persecution, make them for three centuries the carriers
of thought between the Orient and the Occident.
The Middle Ages, fettered by dogma, with no
originality save in art and politics, are obliged
to go to the Ghetto for the science and philosophy of the Orient. The whole Arabic philosophy and a part of Aristotle make their way
into scholasticism through the medium of Latin
translations prepared by Jews on the basis of
Hebrew translations from the original Greek
or from the Arabic.

The Ghetto becomes the asylum of science as
well as of philosophy. Roger Bacon studies
under the rabbis; they have the science of medi-
cine entirely in their hands. Richard of England drives out the Jews, but when he falls sick
he sends for Maimonides. In addition, a whole

branch of literature — that of the narrative and
of the novel — issues from the Ghetto. It is
from the hand of Jewish translators that France
receives the old Indian fables that sprung up in
the days of Buddha on the banks of the Ganges,
which have attained such wonderful favor on the
banks of the Seine and throughout Europe.

Beneath the visible effect there is a silent
and invisible one, unconscious alike to those
who exercise it and to those who come under
its influence, and which justifies the subsequent
hatred of the church, brought about by religious controversy, which slowly corrodes the
foundations of Christianity. The policy of the
church in regard to the Jews had always in it
something uncertain and with an element of
trouble, unknown in its attitude towards other
religions and towards heretics. The popular
hatred of the Jew is the work of the church;
and yet it is the church which alone granted
him protection against the fury unchained by
her, for the reason that she both needed the
Jew and stood in fear of him. The church
needed him, because his book forms the basis
of Christianity; she stood in fear of him because, being the sole possessor of the secret
of that book, he could measure the faith of
those that judged him, and at times, by a
smile, by a word uttered at random, he could
condemn her, and expose her deceptions and

errors.   He is the demon that holds the key to
the sanctuary.   Hence the priest's great dream
is, not to burn the Jew, but to convert him.
Except by an accident, he is to be burned only
as a last resource.   To convert thousands of
Saracens or of idolaters is nothing, proves
nothing; but to convert a Jew, to have the
legitimacy of the new faith recognized by the
heir of the preparatory faith, — therein lies
the true triumph, the real proof, the supreme
and irrefutable testimony.   As long as a single
member of the ancient church maintains his
attitude of opposition, the new church feels ill
at ease and disturbed in its security as heir.
Hence arise all those solemn controversies provoked by the church, terminating always in an
apparent victory, — abjuration, expulsion, or
the stake, from which, however, she emerges in
a state of unconscious perturbation, for the
humble and wearisome reply of the accused
finds here and there, occasionally within the
walls of a convent, a ready ear, a restless soul
into which it falls and takes root.   The effect
is even worse upon the laity.   St. Louis, in his
terror, declares that the layman shall argue
with the Jew only at the point of the sword.[1]
Many a man, entering some squalid house of
the Ghetto to pawn his goods or to seek his
horoscope, but tarrying there to talk of the

[1] Joinville's *Chronicles*, 53.

mysteries of the universe, emerges with a disturbed soul, ripe for the stake. The Jew knows how to unveil the vulnerable points of the church, and in order to do so he has at his service, besides the knowledge of Holy Writ, the formidable sagacity characteristic of the oppressed. He ministers to the skeptic; all rebellious spirits come to him, secretly or under the open sky. He is at work in the immense workshop of blasphemy of the great Emperor Frederick, and of the princes of Suabia or of Aragon. It is he who forges all that deadly arsenal of reason and irony which was destined to become the legacy of the skeptics of the Renaissance, of the libertines of the great century. The sarcasm of Voltaire is but the last, faint echo of a word murmured six centuries before, in the shadow of the Ghetto, and earlier still in the times of Celsius and Origenes, at the very cradle of the religion of Christ.[1]

On two occasions the terrified church, recognizing its danger, perceives that the only means to ward it off is to burn the Jewish books. The first time, under Saint Louis, she succeeds, and with one stroke crushes the Jewish schools in France, and arrests the threatened birth of biblical exegesis five centuries before Richard Simon. She makes a second attempt at the beginning of the sixteenth century, but Reuch-

---

[1] Polemical writers of the first and second centuries.

lin with all Europe behind him stands up in
remonstrance.   The mighty breath of the Renaissance smothers the Dominican torch, and
the Reformation bursts forth.   Spain alone escapes the peril by a general proscription, and
haughtily enters upon her death struggle.

The Reformation was entailed with two con-
sequences for the Jews.   On the one hand, although not emancipated, they gained a measure
of peace that they had not enjoyed for centuries; the fury of extermination was directed
against other victims.   On the other hand,
the Renaissance and the Reformation bring to
the front the study of Hebrew and of Jewish
science.   The rabbis are engaged in teaching
Hebrew to the Catholic and Protestant propa-
gandists of Europe.   Luther's Bible emanates
from the commentaries of Raschi.   The Cabbala
emerges from its mystic atmosphere and takes
possession of the enthusiasts, whom it intoxi-
cates with its fumes, while fitting them for the
most audacious flights of thought, "for the Jews
alone know the true name of God."[1]   A Renaissance of the prophetic mind elevates the
soul of Europe to a height that it had never
before scaled.   The Old Testament supplants
the New among the firmest and purest minds.
The movement gives to France Coligny, D'Au-
bigné, Duplessis-Morny, and her admirable

[1] Reuchlin.

phalanx of martyrs and heroes. It gives to England the Puritans and the Republic, and establishes democratic tradition. Cromwell, in his gratitude, reopens the gates of England to the Jews.

At length the great century of free thought approaches. Voltairism, born with Celsius and the authors of the Jewish "Counter-Evangelists," had taken refuge in the Middle Ages within the walls of the Ghetto. Thence it occasionally penetrated to a few monks or story-tellers, or enjoyed a momentary triumph at some semi-pagan court. Marching abreast with the Reformation, it threads its way through the formal religion of the "great reign " and finally blazes forth in Voltaire and the philosophers. The French Revolution, in execution of the decrees of the philosophers, gives to the Jews the full and entire right of citizenship in France, and in her wake follow all the civilized countries, — Italy, England, Holland, Denmark, Servia, Switzerland, and Austria.

The French Revolution wherever it penetrates, and in France above all, opens to Judaism a new era, in a double sense, material and moral.

On one hand, by breaking down the barrier between the Jew and the Christian, it placed a bound to the history of the Jewish people.

From the 28th of September, 1791, there is
no longer a history of the Jews in France.
There is only a history of French Judaism,
as there is a history of French Calvinism or
Lutheranism, and nothing more. The marvelous rapidity with which the Jew has become a
member of the great French nationality, not
only in right and in name, but in fact, points,
moreover, to older and perhaps still deeper
causes than a sudden enthusiasm of justice on
the one side, and of gratitude on the other.
For the Jew, France is not a fatherland impro-
vised in a feverish access of generosity; it is a
country recovered by him. In fact, the barrier
raised between Jews and Christians was facti-
tious, and a late growth. The hatred of the
people was not an old popular tradition, and the
first centuries of our history show us the adherents of the two faiths living together upon a
footing of equality, and bound to one another by
sentiments of mutual toleration and esteem that
aroused the displeasure of the bishops of the
time, and against which for a long time they
felt themselves powerless.[1] It is the triumph of
feudalism which, by proclaiming the absolute
authority of the church, delivers up the Jew
to a calculating and selfish hatred, which from
the pulpit is slowly diffused among the masses.
In consequence, there exist among the ignorant

[1] Agobard.

and wretched people of the Middle Ages suppressed sentiments of hatred and repulsion, which gain in strength from a supposed religious justification, and to which the Crusades add fresh fuel. The great epic of the Middle Ages opens with the general massacre of the Deicides. To the justification of hatred by religion is added a factor which appears also to justify this hatred. The Jew, driven in turn out of political life, from all offices, from all the liberal professions, from the ownership of real estate, from everything that might attach him by visible marks to the soul and soil of his country, is forced into commerce and usury by the canons of the church, and by the financial policy of kings who wished to know where to turn when their treasury was empty. The people see in the Jew only the man of affairs, at the service of his lord and of his king, the living and detested symbol of the popular misery. As a consequence, the two great oppressed classes of the Middle Ages, the people and the Jew, are brought face to face, the one thrown as a prey to the other. And nevertheless, in the most desperate times, in the very Ghettos in which the oppressed Jew is penned up by law, contempt, and hatred, he is kept alive by the very intellectual activity that emanates from his oppressors. He aspires to break down the walls of his prison, to breathe the air of France.

The mother tongue of this pariah is not a Hebrew *patois*, it is the French of France.   And the most ancient French elegy, the most beautiful, perhaps, ever composed in that language, was written in a Ghetto, by the gleam of the stake.[1]   The Renaissance and the Reformation, by turning hatred into other channels, and by introducing a broader spirit, hastened the moral fusion.   Prejudice is already greatly weakened before the eighteenth century, when it receives its deathblow, and the Revolution, through the voices of Mirabeau and the Abbé Gregoire, has only the convictions of the Abbé Maury to combat.   Even emancipation has its precedents before 1789.   The Jews of Bordeaux and of Comte receive citizens' rights in 1776.   But the French Revolution, by establishing the general principle of religious equality, by transforming custom into irrevocable law, with an amount of firmness and decision that has made its example the rule of the civilized world, becomes the supreme and momentous era in the annals of Jewish destiny.

This era, which terminates the material history of the Jewish people, opens a new and strange phase in the history of its thought. For the first time this thought finds itself in accord, and no longer in conflict, with the general tendency of humanity.   Judaism, which

[1] *Elégies du Vatican*, Arsène Darmesteter.

from its first hour has always been at war with
the dominant religion, whether that of Baal, of
Jupiter, or of Christ, at length encounters a
state of thought which it need not combat, because it finds there the reflex of its own instincts and traditions. The Revolution is, in
fact, only the echo in the political world of a
much vaster and deeper movement, which wholly
transforms thought, and which, in the realm of
speculation, ends with the substitution of the
scientific conception of the world for the mythical, and on the practical side brings to the fore
the notion of justice and progress. In this
great downfall of mythical religion, the crash
of which fills our age, Judaism, such as the
centuries have made it, has had the least to
suffer and the least to fear, because its miracles
and rites constitute no essential and integral
part of it. As a consequence, it does not fall
with the rest. Judaism has not made the miraculous the basis of its dogma, nor installed
the supernatural as a permanent factor in the
progress of events. Its miracles from the time
of the Middle Ages are but a poetic detail, a
legendary recital, a picturesque decoration; and
its cosmogony, borrowed in haste from Babylon by the last compiler of the Bible, with the
stories of the apple and the serpent, over which
so many Christian generations have labored,
never greatly disturbed the imagination of the

rabbis, nor weighed very heavily upon the thought of the Jewish philosophers. Its rites were never "an instrument of faith," an expedient to " lull " rebellious thought into faith; they are merely cherished customs, a symbol of the family, of transitory value, and destined to disappear when there shall be but *one* family in a world converted to the *one* truth. Set aside all these miracles, all these rites, and behind them will be found the two great dogmas which, ever since the prophets, constitute the whole of Judaism: the divine unity and Messianism, — unity of law throughout the world, and the terrestrial triumph of justice in humanity. These are the two dogmas which at the present time illuminate humanity in its progress, both in the scientific and social order of things, and which are termed, in modern parlance, *unity of forces* and *belief in progress.*

For this reason, Judaism is the only religion that has never entered into conflict, and never can, with either science or social progress, and that has witnessed, and still witnesses, all their conquests without a sense of fear. These are not hostile forces that it accepts or submits to merely from a spirit of toleration or policy, in order to save the remains of its power by a compromise. They are old friendly voices, which it recognizes and salutes with joy, for it has heard them resound for centuries already, in the axioms of free thought and in the cry of the suffering heart. For this reason, the Jews, in all the countries which have entered upon the new path, have begun to take a share in all the great works of civilization, in the triple field of science, of art, and of action; and that share, far from being an insignificant one, is out of all proportion to the brief time that has elapsed since their enfranchisement.

Does this mean that Judaism should nurse dreams of ambition, and think of realizing one day that "invisible church of the future" invoked by some in prayer? This would be an illusion, whether on the part of a narrow sectarian, or on that of an enlightened individual. The truth, however, remains, that the Jewish spirit can still be a factor in this world, making for the highest science for unending progress, and that the mission of the Bible is not yet complete. The Bible is not responsible for the partial miscarriage of Christianity, due to the compromises made by its organizers, who, in their too great zeal to conquer and convert Paganism, were themselves converted by it. But everything in Christianity which comes in a direct line from Judaism lives, and will live; and it is Judaism which through Christianity has cast into the old polytheistic world, to ferment there until the end of time, the sentiment of unity, and an impatience to bring about charity and justice. The reign of the Bible, and also of the Evangelists in so far as they were inspired by the Bible, can become established only in proportion as the positive religions connected with it lose their power. Great religions outlive their altars and their priests. Hellenism, abolished, counts less skeptics to-day than in the days of Socrates and Anaxagoras. The gods of Homer died when Phidias carved them in marble, and now they are immortally enthroned in the thought and heart of Europe. The cross may crumble into dust, but there were words spoken under its shadow in Galilee, the echo of which will forever vibrate in the human conscience. And when the nation who made the Bible shall have disappeared, — the race and the cult, — though leaving no visible trace of its passage upon earth, its imprint will remain in the depth of the heart of generations, who will unconsciously, perhaps, live upon what has thus been implanted in their breasts. Humanity, as it is fashioned in the dreams of those who desire to be called freethinkers, may with the lips deny the Bible and its work; but humanity can never deny it in its heart, without the sacrifice of the best that it contains, faith in unity and hope for justice, and without a relapse into the mythology and the "might makes right" of thirty centuries ago.

THE SUPREME GOD IN THE INDO-EUROPEAN MYTHOLOGY.

COMPARATIVE MYTHOLOGY.[1]

TOWARDS the end of the last century the men of letters of Europe were astonished to hear that in Asia, on the banks of the Ganges, a more ancient and richer language had been found than that of Homer. It offered in its words and forms striking analogies with the languages of Rome and Athens. Interest once roused, systematic comparisons were made, and comparative grammar was founded. The sphere of comparisons widened and the group of Aryan languages was established.

It was thus ascertained that the languages of the Romans, of the Greeks, of the Gauls, of the Germans, of the Lithuanians, and of the Slavs in Europe, of the Hindoos and Persians in Asia, are made out of the same materials and cast in the same mould; that they are only varieties of one primitive type. The precise laws which regulated the formation of each of

[1] Cf. Max Müller: *Lectures on the Science of Language* and *Lectures on the Science of Religion;* Michel Bréal, *Mélanges de Mythologie et de Linguistique.*

these varieties were discovered, so that it is
both possible to proceed from one of these languages to the other, and to trace all of them to
the original type whence they come, to the lost
type which they reproduce.　This lost type, the
source of all the idioms of nearly the whole of
Europe and of a third of Asia, science has reconstructed.　With an almost absolute certainty, it has described the grammar, drawn up
the lexicon of that language, of which no direct
echo remains, not the fragment of an inscription
on a broken stone, — of that language of which
the life and the death are prehistoric, and
which was spoken at a period when there were
as yet neither Romans, nor Hindoos, nor
Greeks, nor Persians, nor Germans, nor Celts,
and when the ancestors of all those nations were
still wandering as one tribe, one knows not
where, one knows not when.

Closely following comparative grammar, almost at the same time rose up comparative mythology, and with the ancient words awoke the
gods that they had sung, the beliefs that they
had fostered.　It was recognized that if the
Indo-Europeans spoke essentially the same language, they also worshiped essentially the
same gods and believed in the same things.
As comparative grammar, on hearing the sister
tongues, caught up the echo of the mother,
whose voice they repeat, so comparative my-

thology, in its turn, on looking at the sister religions, has tried to see through them the original image which they reflect. As the one restore'd the words and forms of the language which lived on the lips of the Aryans at the moment of the breaking up of the Aryan unity, the other endeavored to restore the gods and beliefs which lived in their souls at the moment when, with the unity of the race, the identity of language and belief passed away. This restoration of the prehistoric gods and of the prehistoric beliefs is the final object of comparative mythology, just as the reconstruction of words and forms is the final object of comparative grammar. The object was analogous and so was the method. It is the comparative method, which, by comparing kindred divinities and kindred beliefs, finds the original divinity and the original belief which gave birth to them, and which are reproduced in them. To sketch the picture of the original mythology, it is sufficient to separate from the various derivative mythologies the essential characteristics common to them. Every characteristic common to the secondary religions will be legitimately referred to the primitive one, whenever it is essential, that is to say, neither borrowed from one of the kindred religions, nor due to an identical, but quite independent development. If, for instance, the various Indo-European mythologies agree in naming the gods *Daiva*, "the shining ones," it follows that in the primitive mythology, in the religion of the period of unity, they were known already as beings of light, and called thus.   It is a great deal easier to admit that the seven derived religions have faithfully repeated what has been handed down to them from their common source, than to imagine that once separated they have created the same conception, each one on its side, and have clothed it with the same expression.   The former hypothesis is a simple and natural induction; the second is in reality made up of seven hypotheses, and implies seven chances agreeing together, seven miracles.

Our object in the following pages is to give a sketch of one of the chapters of the Aryan mythology.   We try to show that the religion of the Indo-European unity recognized a Supreme God, and we try to find the most ancient form and the earliest origin of that conception among the Aryans, and to follow out the transformations it has undergone in the course of ages.

THE SUPREME GOD: ZEUS, JUPITER, VARUNA, AHURA MAZDA.

The Aryan Gods are not organized as a Republic; they have a king.   There is over the gods a Supreme God.

Four of the Aryan mythologies have preserved a clear and precise notion of this conception: they are those of Greece, of Italy, of ancient India, and of ancient Persia. This Supreme God is called Zeus in Greece, Jupiter in Italy, Varuna in ancient India, Ahura Mazda in ancient Persia. Let us then listen to Zeus, to Jupiter, to Varuna, and to Ahura Mazda, each in his turn.

Zeus and Jupiter.[1] About three centuries before our era a Greek poet thus addressed Zeus: —

"Oh ! Thou most glorious of immortals, whose names are many, forever Almighty, Zeus, Thou who rulest nature, directing all things according to a law, hail ! To Thee all this universe moving round the earth yields obedience, following whither thou leadest, and submits itself to Thy rule. . . . So great in Thy nature, King Supreme above all things, no work is achieved without Thee, neither on the earth, nor in the celestial regions of ether, nor on the sea, but those which the wicked accomplish in their folly."

This is the Zeus of the philosophers, of the Stoics, of Cleanthes; but he was already the Zeus of the ancient poets. Powerful, omniscient, and just is the god of Æschylus, as that of Cleanthes. He is the king of kings, the blessed of the blessed, the sovereign power among all powers, the only one who is free

[1] Maury, *Histoire des Religions de la Grèce;* Preller, *Griechische Mythologie.*

among the gods, who is the master of the might-
iest, who is subservient to no one's rule;
above whom no one sits, no one to whom from
below he looks with awe; every word of his is
absolute; he is the God of deep thoughts, whose
heart has dark and hidden ways, impenetrable
to the eye, and no scheme formed within his
mind has ever miscarried. Finally, he is the
Father of Justice, *Dike*, " the terrible virgin
who breathes out on crime anger and death; " it
is he who from hell raises vengeance with its
slow chastisement against the bold wayward
mortal. Terpander proclaims in Zeus the essence of all things, the god who rules over
everything. Archilochus sings Zeus father, as
the God who rules the heavens, who watches the
guilty and unjust actions of men, who admin-
isters chastisements to monsters, the God who
created heaven and earth. The old man of
Ascra knows that Zeus is the father of gods
and of men, that his eye sees and comprehends
all things and reaches all that he wishes. In
short, as far back as the Greek Pantheon appears in the light of history, even from Homer,
Zeus towers above the nation of gods which sur-
rounds him. He himself proclaims, and the
other gods proclaim after him, that, unrivaled
in power and strength, he is the greatest of all;
the gods, at his behest, silently bow down before him; he would hurl into the gloomy depths

of Tartarus whomsoever should dare to disobey him; he would hurl him down into the uttermost depths of the subterranean abyss; alone, against them all, he would master them. Should they let fall from the sky a golden chain on which all the gods and goddesses might be suspended, they still would be powerless, however hard they might strain to drag him from the heavens to the earth; and if it pleased him, he could draw them up even with the earth, even with the sea, and he would then fix the chain on the ridge of Olympus, and suspend on it the whole universe; so much is he above mankind, above the gods. Not only is he the most powerful, but also he is the wisest, — the μητίετης; he is all wisdom and he is likewise all justice. It is from him that the judges of the sons of the Achæans have received their laws; very good, very great, he holds learned conversations with Themis (the law), who sits at his side; prayers are his daughters, whom he avenges for all the insults of the wicked.

Thus, power, wisdom, justice, belonged from all time to Zeus, to the Zeus of Homer as well as to the Zeus of Cleanthes; to the Zeus of the poets as to him of the philosophers, in the remotest period of paganism as at the approach of the religion of Christ. A providential god rules the Pantheon of the Hellenes.

What Zeus is in Greece, Jupiter is in Italy:

the God who is above all the gods. The identity of the two deities is so striking that the
ancients themselves, forestalling comparative
mythology, recognized it from the very first.
He is the God, great and good amongst them
all, — *Jupiter*, *optimus*, *maximus*.

·*Varuna*. The most ancient of the religions
of India, which the Vedas have made known to
us, has also a Zeus, whose name is Varuna.[1]

"Truly admirable for grandeur are the works of Him
who has separated the two worlds and fixed their vast
extent : of Him who has set in motion the high and sublime firmament, who has spread out the heavens above
and the earth beneath.

"These heavens and this earth which reach so far,
flowing with milk, so beautiful in form, it is by the law
of Varuna that they remain fixed, facing each other, immortal beings with fertile seed.

"This Asura,[2] who is acquainted with all things, has
propped up these heavens, he has fixed the boundaries
of the earth. He is enthroned above all the worlds, universal king ; all the laws of the world are the laws of
Varuna.

"In the bottomless abyss the king Varuna has lifted
up the summit of the celestial tree.[3] It is the king Varuna who has traced out to the sun the broad path he is
to follow : to footless creatures he has given feet so that
they may run.

[1] See Muir, *Sanscrit Texts*, v. 58; Max Müller, *Lectures on
the Origin and Growth of Religion*, p. 284.

[2] "This Lord."

[3] The cloud often compared to a tree branching out in the
sky.

" Those stars, which illumine the night, where were
they during the day ? Infallible are the laws of Varuna:
the moon kindles itself and walks through the night.

" Varuna has traced out paths for the sun : he has
thrown forwards the fluctuating torrent of rivers. He
has dug out the wide and rapid beds where the waves of
the days, let loose, unroll themselves in their order.

" He has put strength into the horse, milk into the
cow, intellect into the heart, Agni [1] into the waters, the
sun in the sky, soma [2] into the stone.

" The wind is thy breath, O Varuna ! which roars in
the atmosphere, like the ox in the meadow. Between
this earth and the sublime heaven above, all things, O
Varuna, are of thy creation."

There is an order in nature, there is a law,
a habit, a rule, *a Rita*. This law, this *Rita*,
it is Varuna who has established it. He is the
god of the Rita, the god of Order, the guardian
of the Rita; he is the god of efficient and stable
laws; in him rest, as in a rock, the fixed immovable laws.

Organizer of the world, he is its master. He
is the first of the Asuras, "of the lords;" he is
the Asura, "the Lord;" he is the sovereign of
the whole world, the king of all beings, the
universal king, the independent king; no one
amongst the gods dares to infringe his laws;
"it is thou, Varuna, who are the king of all."

---

[1] The fire (Ignis) which is born in the waters of heaven in
the form of lightning.

[2] A sacred plant whose sap is offered to the gods. It is
pressed between two stones to extract the sacred liquor.

As he has omnipotence, he has omniscience too; he is "the Lord who knows all things," the *Asura viçva-vedas.* He is the sage who has supreme wisdom, in whom all sciences have their centre; when the poet wishes to praise the learning of a god, he compares it to that of Varuna. "He knows the place of the birds which fly in the air, he knows the ships which are sailing on the ocean, he knows the twelve months and what they will bring forth, he knows every creature that is born. He knows the path of the sublime wind in the heights, he knows who sits at the sacrifice. The God of stable laws, Varuna, has taken his place in his palace to be the universal king, the god with the wondrous intellect. Hence, following in his mind all these marvels, he looks around him at what has happened and what will happen."

As he is the universal witness, he is also the universal judge, the infallible judge whom nothing escapes; none can deceive him, and from above he sees the evil done below and strikes it; he has sevenfold bands to clasp thrice round the liar by the upper, by the middle, and by the lower part of the body. The man, smitten by misfortune, implores his pity, and feels that he has sinned, and that the hand which strikes is also the hand that punishes: —

"I ask Thee, O Varuna, because I wish to know my fault :

"I come to Thee, to question Thee who knowest all things. All the sages, with one voice, said to me, Varuna is angry with thee.

"What great crime have I committed, O Varuna, that thou shouldst want to kill thy friend, thy bard. Tell me, O Lord, O infallible one, and I will then lay my homage at thy feet.

"Free me from the bonds of my crime, do not sever the thread of the prayer that I am weaving, do not deliver me over to the deaths that, at thy dictate, O Asura, strike him who has committed a crime : send me not into the gloomy regions far from the light.

"Let me pay the penalty of my faults; but let me not suffer, O King, for the crime of others ; there are so many days that have not dawned yet ! Let them dawn for us also, O Varuna !"

Such is the supreme God of the Vedic religion, an organizing God, almighty, omniscient, and moral. The following is a Vedic hymn which sums up with singular force the essential attributes of the God : —

"He who from on high rules this world sees everything as if it were before him. That which two men, seated side by side, are plotting, is heard by king Varuna, himself the third.

"This earth belongs to the king Varuna, and this sky, these two sublime worlds with their remote limits ; the two seas [1] are the belly of Varuna, and he rests also even in this small pool of water.

"He who should leap over the sky and beyond it, would not escape the king Varuna : he has his spies, the spies of the heavens, who go through the world ; he has his thousand eyes which look on the earth.

[1] The sea of the earth and the sea of the clouds.

"The king Varuna sees everything, all that which is between the two worlds and beyond them: he reckons the winking of the eye of all creatures:

"The world is in his hand like the dice in the hand of the gamester.

"Let thy sevenfold bands, O Varuna, let thy bands of wrath which are thrice linked together, let them enfold the man with a lying tongue, let them leave free the man with a truthful tongue!"

Ahura Mazda.[1] Ancient Persia opposes to Zeus, to Jupiter, to Varuna, her Ormazd. or Ahura Mazda.[2] "It is through me," he said to his prophet, Zoroaster, "that the firmament, with its distant boundaries, hewn from the sparkling ruby, subsists without pillars to rest upon; it is through me that the earth, through me that the sun, the moon, and the stars take their radiant course through the atmosphere; it was I who formed the seeds in such a manner that, when sown in the earth, they should grow, spring up, and appear on the surface; it was I who traced their veins in every species of plants, who in all beings put the fire of life which does not consume them; it is I who in the maternal womb produce the new-born child, who form the limbs, the skin, the nails, the blood, the feet, the ears; it was I who gave the water feet to run; it was I who made the clouds, which

---

[1] See J. Darmesteter, *Ormazd et Ahriman,* §§ 18–59.

[2] Ormazd is the modern name, contracted from the ancient Ahura Mazda.

carry the water to the world," etc. This development, taken from a recent book of the Ghebers, the Bundahish, is to be found entire in the very first words of their oldest and holiest book, the Avesta: "I proclaim and worship Ahura Mazda, the *Creator*." As far as history can be traced, he was already what he is now. Near the ruins of the ancient Ecbatana, the traveler may read, on the red granite of the mountain of Alvand, these words, which were engraved by the hand of Darius, the king of kings, nearly five centuries before the birth of Christ: —

> "A powerful God is Aurâmazda !
> 'T was he who made this earth here below !
> 'T was he who made that heaven above !
> 'T was he who made man !"

This God, who made the world, rules it. He is the sovereign of the universe, the *Ahura*,[1] "the Lord." "He is a powerful god," exclaims Xerxes; "he is the greatest of all the gods." It is to his favor that Darius, inscribing upon the rock of Behistun the narrative of his nineteen victories, ascribes both his elevation and his triumphs. It is to his supreme care that he confides Persia: "This country of Persia, which Aurâmazda has given me, this beautiful country, beautiful in horses, beautiful in men, by the grace of Aurâmazda, and through me, king

---

[1] Which is the same word as the Sanskrit Asura.

Darayavus, has nothing to fear from any enemy. May Aurâmazda and the gods of the nation bring me their help! May Aurâmazda protect this country from hostile armies, from barrenness and evil! May this country never be invaded by the stranger, nor by hostile armies, nor by barrenness, nor by evil! This is the favor which I implore from Aurâmazda and the gods of the nation!"

This world which he has organized is a work of intelligence; by his wisdom it began, and by his wisdom it will end. He is the mind which knows all things, and it is to him that the sage appeals in order to penetrate the mysteries of the world.

" Reveal to me the truth, O Ahura ! What was the beginning of the good creation ?

" Who is the father, who, at the beginning of time, begat Order ?

" Who has traced for the sun and the stars the paths that they must follow ?

" Who makes the moon increase and decrease ?

"O Ahura ! I would learn those mysteries and many more !

" Who has fixed the earth and the immovable stars to establish them firmly, so that they might not fall ? Who has fixed the waters and the trees ?

" Who has directed the rapid course of the wind and of the clouds ? What skillful artist has made the light and the darkness ?

" What skillful workman has made sleep and wakefulness ? Through whom have we dawn, noon, and night ?

From whom do they learn the law which is traced out for them? Who endeared the son to his father so that he should train him? Those are the things that I wish to ask Thee, O Mazda, O beneficent Spirit, O Creator of all things!"

In his omniscience are embraced all human actions. He watches over all things, and is farseeing, and never sleeping. He is the infallible one; "it is impossible to deceive him, the Ahura, who knows all things." He sees man, and judges and chastises him, if he has not followed his law, for from him comes the law of man, as well as the law of the world; from him comes the science supreme among all other sciences, that of duty, the knowledge of those things we ought to think, say, and do, and of those things we ought neither to think, nor say, nor do. To the man who has prayed well, thought, spoken, and acted well, he opens his resplendent paradise; he opens hell to him who has not prayed and who has thought, spoken, and done evil.

THE SUPREME GOD, THE GOD OF HEAVEN.

Thus the Aryans of Greece, of Italy, of India, and of Persia agree in giving the highest place in their Pantheon to a supreme God who rules the world and who has founded order, a God sovereign, omniscient, and moral. Has this identical conception been formed in each of these cases by four independent creations, or is it a common inheritance from the Indo-European religion, and did the Aryan ancestors of the Greeks, of the Latins, of the Hindoos, and of the Persians already know a supreme God, an organizing, a sovereign, an omniscient, a moral God?

Although the latter hypothesis is more simple and more probable than the former, it cannot, however, be taken at once as certain; because an abstract and logical conception of this kind may very well have developed itself at the same time among several nations, in an identical and independent manner. To whomsoever looks upon it at any time and in any place, the world can reveal the existence of a Supreme Maker. Socrates is not the disciple of the Psalmist; yet the heavens reveal to him, as to the Hebrew poet, the glory of the Lord. But if it be found that the abstract conception is closely connected with a naturalistic and material conception, and that the latter is identical in the four religions, as it is known, on the other hand, that these four religions have a common past, the hypothesis that this abstract conception is a heritage of this past, and not a creation of the present, may rise to a certainty.

Now these Gods who organize the world rule it and watch over it. This Zeus, this Jupiter, this Varuna, this Ahura Mazda, are not the personifications of a simple abstract conception; they emerge from a former naturalism, from which they are not yet quite detached; they commenced by being gods of the heavens.

Zeus and Jupiter have never ceased to be gods of the heavens, and to be conscious of it. When the world was shared among the gods, "Zeus received the boundless sky in the ether and the clouds for his share." It is as the God of heaven that sometimes he shines luminous, calm, and pure, enthroned in the ethereal splendor, and that sometimes he becomes gloomy and gathers clouds (νεφεληγερέτης), causing the rain to fall from heaven (ὄμβριος, ὑέτιος), hurling upon the earth the eddy of fierce winds, drawing forth the hurricane from the summit of the ether, brandishing the lightning and the thunderbolt (ἐκραύνιος, ἀστραπαῖος). This is why the thunderbolt is his weapon, his attribute, "the thunderbolt with its never-tiring foot," which he hurls in the heights; why he rolls on a resounding chariot, brandishing in his hand the fiery trident, or dashing it on the wings of the eagle, or on Pegasus, the aerial steed of the lightning. This is why he is the husband of Dêmêter, "the mother Earth," whom he impregnates with his torrents of rain; this is why he sent forth, from his brow according to some, from his belly according to others, from the clouds according to the Cretan legend, Athênê, the resplendent goddess with the penetrating glance, who came forth, shaking golden weapons, with a cry which made heaven and earth resound, as she is the incarnation of the stormy light which breaks forth from the brow of heaven, from the belly of heaven, from the bosom of the cloud, filling space with its splendor and with the crash of its stormy birth. Lastly, the very name of Zeus (genitive *Dios*, formerly *Divos*) is, in conformity with the laws of Greek phonetics, the literal representative of the Sanskrit Dyaus, heaven (genitive *Divas*); and the union of Ζεὺς πατήρ with Δημήτηρ is the exact counterpart of the Vedic union of *Dyaus pitar* with *Prithivi matar*, of the Heaven-Father with Earth-Mother. The word Ζεύς is an ancient synonym of Οὐρανός, which became obsolete as a common noun; still, in a certain number of expressions, it retains something of its former meaning. Thus it is, when the Earth prays Zeus to let rain fall upon her; when the Athenian, in praying, exclaims: "O dear Zeus, rain thou on the field of the Athenians and on the plains." "Zeus has rained the whole night," says Homer: ὗε Ζεὺς πάννυχος. In all these expressions Zeus may be literally translated as a common noun, *sky*.

Jupiter, identical with Zeus in his functions, is identical with him in his material attributes.

The word Jûpiter, or better Jup-piter, is for

Jus-piter, composed of *pater* and of *Jus*, the Latin contraction of the Sanskrit *Dyaus*, of the Greek Ζεύς. Juppiter is then the exact equivalent of Ζεὺς πατήρ, and the word has preserved even more strongly than Zeus the sense of its early meaning. *Sub Jove* signifies "under the heavens:" the hunter awaits the marsian boar, heedless of the cold or snow, *sub Jove frigido*, "under the cold Jupiter, under the cold sky.". Dyaus is also in Latin, as it is in Sanskrit, the name of the brilliant sky. "Behold," exclaims old Ennius, "above thy head this luminous space which all invoke under the name of Jupiter: "

"Aspice hoc sublime candens quem invocant omnes
   Jovem."

Varuna, like his European brethren, has been, and is yet, a material god, and a material god of the same kind, a god of heaven. This is why the sun is his eye; why the sun, "the beautiful bird which flies in the firmament," is "his golden-winged messenger;"[1] why the celestial rivers flow in the hollow of his mouth, as in the hollow of a reed; why, everywhere visible, by turns full of light and of darkness, by turns he infolds himself in the night and irradiates the dawn, and by turns clothes himself in the white garments and in the black

[1] The sun is also the bird of Zeus (Æschylus, The Suppliants).

ones. Like Zeus, and from the same cause, he gathers together the clouds, he turns the sack that contains the rains, and lets it loose upside down on the two worlds; he inundates the heaven and the earth, he clothes the mountains with a watery garb, and his blood-red eyes unceasingly furrow the watery dwelling with their twinkling flashes. As Zeus is the father of Athênê, he is the father of Atharvan, "the Fire-God," of Bhrigu, "the Thunderer," that is to say, of Agni, of the lightning. Agni himself is brought forth "from his belly in the waters," like a male Athênê. Finally, like Zeus, like Jupiter, he bears in his very name the expression of what he is; and the Sanskrit Varuna is the exact phonetic representative of Οὐρανός, sky.

In fine, the sovereign god of Persia, notwithstanding the character of profound abstraction which he has acquired and which is reflected in his name Ahura Mazda, "the omniscient Lord," can himself be recognized as a god of the heavens. The ancient formulæ of the litanies still show that he is luminous and corporeal; they invoke the creator Ahura Mazda, resplendent, very great, very beautiful, corporeally beautiful; white, luminous, seen from afar; they invoke the entire body of Ahura Mazda, the body of Ahura which is the greatest of bodies; they say that the sun is his eye, and that the sky is the garment embroidered with stars with which he arrays himself. The most abstract of the Aryan gods has preserved a trait which shows him more closely tied than the others to the material world from which they have freed themselves; he is called "the most solid of the gods," because "he has for clothing the very solid stone of the sky." Like Varuna, like Zeus, the lightning is in his hands, "the molten brass which he causes to flow down on the two worlds;" like them he is the father of the god of lightning, Atar. Lastly, the most ancient historical evidence confirms the inductions of mythology, as at the very time when the Achæmenian kings proclaim the sovereignty of Aurâmazda, Herodotus wrote: "The Persians offer up sacrifices to Zeus,[1] going up on the highest summit of the mountains, as they call *Zeus the entire orb of the sky.*"

Thus the supreme gods of the four great religions of Greece, of Italy, of India, and of Persia, are at the same time, or have begun by being, gods of the skies. By the side of these four, Svarogu, the god of the ancient pagan Slavs, should no doubt equally be placed. Like Zeus, like Jupiter, like Varuna, like Ahura Mazda, he is the master of the universe, the gods are his children, and it is from him that they have received their functions; like them

[1] That is to say, "to their Supreme God."

he is the god of the heavens, he is the thunderer, and like them he is the father of the Fire, Svarojitchi, "the son of heaven."[1]

HIS ORIGIN.[2]

How did the god of the heavens become the organizing god, the supreme God, the moral God? How was the abstract conception grafted on the naturalistic conception? What is the connection between his material attribute and his abstract function? The Vedas give the solution of this problem.

As far as the eye can reach, it can never reach beyond the sky; whatever is, is under the immense vault; all that which is born and dies, is born and dies within its bounds. Now, whatever takes place in it, takes place according to an immutable law. The dawn has never failed to appear at her appointed place in the morning, never forgotten where she is to appear again, nor the moment at which she is to reanimate the world. Darkness and light know their appointed hour, and always at the desired moment "the black One has given way to the white." Linked together by the same chain in the endless path open before them, they follow their way onwards, the two immortals, directed by a God, absorbing each other's tints. The

---

[1] G. Klek, *Einleitung in die Slavische Literatur-Geschichte.*

[2] See *Ormazd et Ahriman*, §§ 62 *sq.*

two fertile sisters do not clash with one another; they never stop, dissimilar in form, but alike in spirit. Thus run the days with their suns, the nights with their stars, season following season. The sky has always in regular course ushered in by turn the day and the night. The moon has always lit up at the fixed hour. The stars have always known where they should go during the day. The rivers have always flowed into the one ocean without making it full.

This universal order is either the motion of the heavens, or it is the action of the God of heaven, according as we think of the body or the soul, and view in the heavens the thing or the God. Thus, in the Rig-Veda, to say "everything is *in* Varuna," — that is, "in the heavens" — and to say "everything is *through* Varuna" — that is, "through the heaven-God" — are one and the same thing; and in these formulæ of the Veda, so clear in their uncertainty, theism is ever found side by side with unconscious pantheism, of which it is only an expression. "The three heavens and the three earths rest in Varuna," says a poet, and immediately afterwards, giving personality to his God: "It is the skillful king Varuna who makes this golden disc shine in heaven." The wind which whistles in the atmosphere is his breath, and all that exists from one world to the other was created by him. "From the king Varuna come this earth below, and yonder heaven, too, these two worlds with remote limits; the two seas are the belly of Varuna, and he rests also even in the small pool of water."

This pantheistic theism, which makes no clear distinction between the God of heaven and the universe over which he rules, or which is comprised in him, penetrates Jupiter as well as Varuna. The Latin poets offer the equivalent of the vacillating formulæ of Vedism. "The mortals," says Lucretius, explaining the origin of the idea of God, — "the mortals saw the regular motions of the heavens and the various seasons of the year succeed each other in a fixed order, without being able to discover the causes. They had, therefore, no other alternative than to attribute all to the gods, who made everything go according to their will, and it was in the sky that they placed the seat and domain of the gods, because it is there that may be seen revolve the night and the noon, the day and the gloomy planets of the night; the nocturnal lights wandering in the sky, and the flying flames, the clouds, the sun, the rain, the snow, the winds, the thunderbolts, the hail, the sudden convulsions, and the great threatening rumblings." [1]

---

[1] " Præterea, cœli rationes ordine certo
　Et varia annorum cernebant tempora vorti ;
　Nec poterant quibus id fieret cognoscere causis.
　Ergo perfugium sibi habebant omnia Diveis

This view of the heavens as the universal centre of the movements of Nature might just as well have led to pantheism as to theism. The line of the poet, "Juppiter est quodcunque vides, quocunque moveris" — "Jupiter is everything that thou seest, everywhere that thou movest," — does not refer only to the Jupiter of the metaphysicians of the Porch; it also expresses one of the aspects of the Jupiter of primitive mythology. It was not by a deviation from his earlier nature that Zeus was confounded with Pan; he was Pan by birth; and if the epopee and the drama show us only a personal Zeus, it is because by their very nature they could and should see him only under this aspect, and had nothing to obtain from the impersonal Zeus, although in this form he was as old as in the other. And the Orphic theologian is not quite unfaithful to the earlier tradition of religion, when he sings of the universal Zeus: —

"Zeus was the first, Zeus is the last, Zeus the thunderer; Zeus is the head, Zeus is the middle ; it is by Zeus that all things are made ;

> Tradere, et ollorum nutu facere omnia flecti.
> In cœloque Deum sedes et templa locarunt,
> Per cœlum volvi quia nox et luna videtur,
> Luna, dies, et nox et noctis signa severa,
> Noctivagæque faces cœli, flammæque volantes,
> Nubila, sol, imbres, nix, ventei, fulmina, grando,
> Et rapidei fremitus, et murmura magna minarum."
> — v. 1182.

Zeus is the male, Zeus is the immortal female;

Zeus is the base of both the earth and the starry sky ;

Zeus is the breath of the winds, Zeus is the jet of the unconquerable flame ;

Zeus is the root of the sea, Zeus is the sun and the moon. . . .

The whole of this universe is stretched out within the great body of Zeus."

In the same manner, although Persia has in general preserved the personality of her Supreme god, yet she suffers him, especially in the sects, to become confounded with the Infinity of matter through which he first revealed himself to the mind of his worshipers. After having invoked the heavens as the body of Ahura Mazda, the most beautiful of bodies, she placed above Ahura himself, and before him, the luminous space, where he manifests himself, what the theologians called "the Infinite light," and then by a new and higher abstraction declared *Space*[1] to have been at the beginning of the world. Between this wholly metaphysical principle and the naturalistic principle of the primitive religion, there is only the distance of two abstractions: Space is only the bare form of the luminous Infinite, and the luminous Infinite, again, is an abstraction from the Infinite and luminous sky, which was identical with Ahura.

[1] In other systems, having regard to the eternity of the God and no longer to his immensity, boundless Time became the first principle (Zarvan Akarana).

Thus, according as the heavens were considered as the seat or as the cause of things, the god of the heavens became the matter of the world or the demiurge of the world. From the period of Aryan unity, he was without doubt the one and the other in turn; but it is probable that the theistic conception was more clearly defined than the other, as is the case in the derived mythologies; it has, besides, deeper roots in the human heart and human nature, which in every movement and in every phenomenon sees a Living Cause, a Personality.

This god of the heavens, having organized the world, is all wisdom; he is the skilled artisan who has regulated the motion of the worlds. His wisdom is infinite, for of all those mysteries which man tries in vain to fathom he has the key, he is the author. But it is not only as the Creator of the world that he is omniscient; he knows all things, because, being all light, he sees all things. In the naturalistic psychology of the Aryans, to see and to know, light and knowledge, eye and thought, are synonymous terms. With the Hindoos, Varuna is omniscient because he is the Infinite light; because the sun is his eye; because from the height of his palace, with its pillars of red brass, his white looks command the world; because under the golden mantle that covers him, his thousands, his myriads of spies, active and untiring agents, sunbeams during the day, stars during the night, search out for him all that which exists from one world to the other, with eyes that never sleep, never blink. And in the same way, if Zeus is the all-seeing, the πανόπτης, it is because his eye is the sun, this universal witness, the infallible spy of both gods and men (θεῶν σκοπὸν ἠδὲ καὶ ἀνδρῶν.). The light knows the truth, it is all truth; truth is the great virtue which the god of heaven claims; and lying is the great crime which he punishes. In Homer, the Greek, taking an oath, raises his eyes towards the expanse of heaven and calls Zeus and the sun to witness; in Persia, the god of heaven resembles in body the light, and in soul the truth; Aryan morality came down from heaven in a ray of light.

HIS DESTINY.

Thus, the Indo-European religion knew a supreme God, and this God was the God of the heavens. He has organized the world and rules it, because, as he is the heaven, all is in him, and all passes within him, according to his law; he is omniscient and moral, because, being luminous, he sees all things and all hearts.

This god was named by the various names of the sky, — Dyaus, Varana, Svar, — which, according to the requirements of the thought, described either the object or the person, the heavens or the God. Later on, each language made a choice, and fixed the proper name of the God on one of these words; by which its ancient value as a common noun was lost or rendered doubtful; thus, in Greek *Dyaus* became the name of the heaven-god (Zeus), and Varana (Οὐρανός) was the name of the heavens, as a thing; in Sanskrit *Dyaus* or *Svar* was the material heavens; the heaven-god was Varana (later changed into Varuna); the Slavs attached to the word Svar, by means of a derivative, Svarogu, the idea of the celestial god; the Romans made the same choice as the Greeks with their *Jup-piter,* and set aside the other names of the heavens; lastly, Persia described the god by one of his abstract epithets, the Lord, Ahura, and obliterated the external traces of his former naturalistic character.

This god, who reigned at the time of the breaking up of the religion of Aryan unity, was carried away, with the various religions which sprang up from it, to the various regions where chance brought the Aryan migrations. Of the five religions over which he ruled, three remained faithful to him to the last, and only forsook him at the moment when they themselves perished; — they are those of the Greeks, of the Romans, and of the Slavs, with whom Zeus, Juppiter, and Svarogu preserved the titles and attributes of the supreme god of the Aryans, as long as the national religion lasted. They succumbed to Christ; "Heaven-father" gave way to the "Father who is in Heaven."

India, on the contrary, very soon forgot that god for whose origin and formation, however, she accounts much better than any other Aryan religion does; and it was not a foreign god who dethroned him, — a god from without, — but a native god, a god of his own family, Indra, the hero of the tempest.

In fact, the supreme god of the Aryans was not a god of unity; the Asura, the Lord, was not the Lord in the same sense as Adonai. There were by the side of him, within himself, a number of gods, acting of their own accord, and often of independent origin. The wind, the rain, the thunder; the fire under its three forms — the sun in the heavens, the lightning in the cloud, the terrestrial fire on the altar; the prayer under its two forms — the human prayer, which ascends from the altar to heaven, and the heavenly prayer, which resounds in the din of the storm, on the lips of a divine priest, and descends from the heights with the torrents of libations poured from the cup of heaven, all the forces of nature, both concrete and abstract, appealing at once to the eye and to the imagination of man, were instantly deified. If the god of the heavens, greater in time and space, always present and everywhere present, easily rose to the supreme rank, carried there by his double Infinity, yet others, with a less continuous, but more dramatic action, revealing themselves by sudden, unexpected events, maintained their ancient independence, and religious development might lead to their usurping the power of the king of the heavens. Already during the middle of the Vedic period, Indra, the noisy god of the storm, ascends the summit of the Pantheon, and eclipses his majestic rival by the din of his resounding splendor.

He is the favorite hero of the Vedic Rishis; they do not tire of telling how he strikes with his bolt the serpent of the cloud, which enfolds the light and the waters; how he shatters the cavern of Cambara, how he delivers the captive Auroras and cows, who will shed torrents of light and milk on the earth. It is he who makes the sun come out again; it is he who makes the world, annihilated during the night, reappear; it is he who recreates it, he who creates it. In a whole series of hymns he ascends to the side of Varuna, and shares the empire with him; at last he mounts above him, and becomes the Universal King:—

"He, who, as soon as he was born, a god of thought, has surpassed the gods by the power of his intellect, he whose trembling made the two worlds quake by the power of his strength, — O man, it is Indra!

"He, who has firmly established the tottering earth

and arrested the quivering mountains ; he, who has fixed the extent of the wide-stretching atmosphere, and who has propped up the sky, — O man, it is Indra !

"He, who after slaying the serpent, unpenned the seven rivers ; who brought forth the cows from their hiding-place in the cavern ; he, who by the clashing of the two stones has engendered Agni, — O man, it is Indra !

"He, who made all these great things ; he, who struck down the demon race, driving it to concealment ; he, who, like a fortunate gamester who wins at play, carries off the wealth of the impious, — O man, it is Indra !

"He, who gives life to both rich and poor, and to the priest, his singer, who implores him ; the god with beautiful lips ; the protecting god who brings the stones together to press out the soma, — O man, it is Indra !

"He, who has in his hands the herds of horses and cows, the cities and the chariots of war ; he, who has created the Sun and the dawn ; he, who rules the waters, — O man, it is Indra !

"He, who is invoked by the two contending armies, by the enemies facing each other, either triumphant or beaten ; he, whom, when they meet in the struggle on the same chariot, during the onslaught, they invoke against each other, — O man, it is Indra !

"He, who discovered Çambara in the mountains where he had been hidden forty years ; he, who killed the serpent in his full strength, who struck him dead on the body of Dânu,[1] — O man, it is Indra !

"Heaven and earth bow down before him ; when he shakes, the mountains tremble ; the drinker of soma, look at him ! bearing the bolt in his arm, the bolt in his hand, — O man, it is Indra ! "

But the usurper does not enjoy his triumph

---

[1] His mother.

long; in the heat of his victory he is already stung to the heart, mortally wounded by a new and mystic power which is growing at his side, the power of prayer, of sacrifice, of worship, of *Brahma*, whose reign begins to dawn towards the end of the Vedic period, and which is still in existence.

What Indra did in India during an historical period, Perkun and Odin did in a prehistorical period, the one among the Lithuanians, the other among the Germans. Perkun and Odin are the Indras of these two nations, and have each dethroned the god of the heavens. Perkun was the god of the thunder with the Lithuanian pagans, and one can recognize in him a twin brother of the Hindoo *Parjanya*, one of the forms of the god of the storm in Vedic mythology. This king of the Lithuanian Pantheon is a king of recent date; what proves it is that the Slavs, so closely related to the Lithuanians in their beliefs, as well as in their language, and who also knew the god Perkun, have still as their supreme god the supreme god of the ancient Aryan religion, the god of the heavens, Svarogu.

The same revolution took place in Germany, but in a more remote period. The god of the heavens has vanished; he is replaced by the god of the stormy atmosphere, Odin, or Wuotan, the Vâta of India, the warrior god who is heard in the din of the tempest, leading his disheveled bands of warriors, or letting loose on a celestial quarry the howling packs of the wild chase.

Thus did the Greeks, the Romans, and the Slavs allow their god to be vanquished by a foreign god; the Germans, the Lithuanians, and the Hindoos themselves forsook him for an inferior creation. Only in one single nation he finds worshipers faithful to the last. They are not numerous, but they have not allowed their belief to be encroached upon either by time or by man. We mean the few thousands of Ghebers or Parsis, who, during the great political and religious shipwreck of Persia, fleeing before the victorious sword of the Prophet, kept from Islam the treasure of their old belief, and who to this day, in the year 1879 of the Christian era, in the fire temples in Bombay, offer up sacrifices to the very same god who was sung by the unknown ancestors of the Aryan race at a time which eludes the grasp of history.

www.ingramcontent.com/pod-product-compliance
Lightning Source LLC
Chambersburg PA
CBHW060512030726

47498CB00004B/916